IF THE SHOE FITS

IF THE SHOE FITS

DAWN WHITE

Dawn Elaine-Gilbert White

Published by
Dawn Elaine-Gilbert White
P. O. Box 35
Rock Island, TN 38581

Printed and bound in the United States

ISBN 978-0-578-79796-0

CONTENTS

ACKNOWLEDGEMENTS

I want to thank my writing partner, friend, and mentor, Diane Tilton-Mauer. Without her careful editing and insight into the characters of Carol, Adele, and Tessa, this multi-generational book would not have been possible,

I also want to thank my loving and supportive family who know that when I'm writing, I'm lost in another world. Thanks for allowing me to visit that world when I need to.

To my friend and former neighbor, Shannon, who went on a road trip with me back in 2007 to workshop the complete draft, thanks for being an early fan. And to my family and friends who helped me review over three hundred cover designs, thanks for your perseverance!

Finally, thank you to all of the women out there who love shoes as much as I do.

CHAPTER 1

Madeline

Madeline hated courthouses. When her friend Sharon had gone through her divorce, Madeline had been by her side. Every time Sharon had a court appearance Madeline was there, waiting around. Waiting while Sharon conferred with her lawyer. Waiting through the other cases on the roster. Waiting through the inevitable delays and long lunch breaks. She had grown to detest the inefficiency of the whole process as well as the stale smell of the courthouse. And she had a hundred items on her To Do list for today. Of course she'd never told Sharon how she felt. Sharon had enough to deal with. After Sharon's divorce was finalized, Madeline had hoped she would never have to set foot in a courthouse again. But now Sharon was fighting to retain custody of her teenage daughter and needed her best friend more than ever.

Standing in the foyer, Madeline kept glancing at the glass doors. One of theses times when they opened it would be Sharon walking through. Madeline closed her eyes and took a deep breath.

When she opened them a security guard who looked like

her grandpa was staring at her and smiling. She was suddenly aware that she had been swaying from side to side.

"Old habits die hard," she said to him. And made the motion of rocking a baby in her arms. He winked at her. Even though her youngest was three and no longer an infant in her arms, Madeline still couldn't break the habit of sway-rocking. New mothers learn early on never to stand still.

The glass doors opened again, and suddenly, there she was. New pumps, check. Gray suit, check. This outfit was definitely the right choice. It said I'm confident, well-put-together, I deserve to keep my daughter. Madeline smiled and waved, and then waited for Sharon to go through the metal detector, past the nice security guard, and join her on the other side.

"Thanks so much for coming." Sharon gripped her in a tight squeeze. "I'm sure he'll bring The Evil-Know-It-All."

Madeline chuckled at the nickname Sharon had given her ex-husband's new wife. As she returned Sharon's hug, she gave her an extra couple of pats on the back before pulling away. "You look great."

Sharon straightened her jacket. "Thanks for reminding me to leave my cell phone in the car."

"Before you got here I saw the guard send a woman outside with hers."

"Good thing I have you to keep me straight."

"How are you feeling?" Madeline said.

"Okay, I guess. I just left another voice mail for Tessa. She hasn't been answering her cell this morning."

Madeline sensed an imminent meltdown. She looked around. "Which way to your courtroom?"

She followed Sharon as they wound their way through the maze of white hallways to a set of mahogany doors. The warm, earthy doors seemed out of place in this cold, impersonal building.

"I'm sorry you can't come in with me," Sharon said.

"That's all right. I'll be fine out here. Is your attorney already in there?" She'd been hoping to meet Sharon's new attorney. Size him up.

"Marcus? Probably." Sharon stared at the doors. She didn't seem to be in a hurry to go in. "We might be in there for awhile, you know."

"Don't worry, I brought a book. I'm yours all day. Except for picking up the kids this afternoon and taking them to Tessa. Then Jack's ready to take over this evening if you still need me."

"What a guy," Sharon said. "Thank him for me."

"You know he doesn't mind having the kids. Now, if I were to ask him to miss the Reds-Cardinals game tonight—"

"Look, here they come," Sharon said under her breath. A couple had just rounded the corner and was headed down the long hallway toward them. Sharon's ex-husband, Wes, and his new bride, if you could call her that. Sharon was right. The woman had to be in her fifties.

"Wait a minute," she whispered to Sharon. "I know her. I work with her."

"I thought I mentioned she worked at your college."

"I don't think so. Crap, she's in my department, too," she said, just in time to watch Wes Trent and Carol Wheaton blow past them and storm through the courtroom doors.

When the doors had closed behind them, Madeline turned

back to Sharon. "She's a full-time English professor. Been there at least a decade. Since before I started teaching there."

Sharon perked up. "Know any dirt on her?"

"No. I mean, we've passed each other going in and out of the faculty lounge, the restroom, at the copy machine. We've never spoken or anything. She's not very friendly—"

"I don't know why I never thought of this before, but I have a perfect idea," Sharon said, lowering her voice and leaning in. "You can spy on her for me."

She could see the wheels turning in Sharon's head, plotting how Madeline could sneak around campus, darting in and out of dark corners, wearing night goggles and those soft shoes cat burglars wear that don't make a sound.

Great, she thought. Why does The-Evil-Know-It-All have to be from my world?

CHAPTER 2

Stephanie

Stephanie Powell didn't bother stopping by her office that morning. She left her apartment at 8:00 a.m., plenty of time to arrive at court by nine, but now she was in this insane traffic jam heading north. She turned her Barenaked Ladies CD louder and took a sip from her travel mug of coffee. As always, she kept her lips pursed wide so as not to smudge her lipstick.

Good thing she'd taken time to bring coffee from home. She definitely wouldn't have time to stop for a latte if she was going to arrive before Wes Trent, a new client who, along with his wife, was suing his ex-wife for custody of their fourteen-year-old daughter. This situation she was handling for Wes was exactly why she went into family law, and why she also knew she'd never get married.

Why should she? There was nothing a husband could provide for her that she couldn't get on her own. She'd made sure of that. Throughout her childhood she'd observed up close how marriage doesn't work. Both her parents were married and divorced multiple times after divorcing each other when she was five. It seemed fitting that she practice family law. Because she knew families would always fight, she knew she'd always have enough clients to keep her financially independent.

Traffic still wasn't moving. Stephanie glanced out her window just in time to catch the suit—salesman? executive?—in the Mercedes next to her checking her out. He was grinning like an idiot. She tossed him a half-smile, then went back to looking straight ahead while she took another sip of coffee. She was sure he was still watching. He was probably drooling from watching her lipsticked mouth wrapped around the mug. Guys always got off on that kind of thing. They were all the same, so easy to figure out. Come to think of it, though, if it weren't for her own sex drive, she wasn't sure what she'd ever need a guy for anyway. Besides, she already had a male to keep her warm in bed at night, her two-year old boxer, Riley.

Too bad she'd had to close Riley out of her bedroom this morning before she left. He'd prefer to lounge on her bed while she was gone, but she still didn't trust him with the designer shoes lying on the floor of her closet. He'd just have to make do with lying on the couch in the living room until this afternoon. Which reminded her, she'd better call Marisa right now. Her older sister lived in the suburbs just west of her and didn't mind helping out with Riley when Stephanie's career got in the way of responsible dog ownership.

She slid her cell phone out of her black leather briefcase that sat on the passenger's seat and hit speed dial #1. No answer. She hit speed dial #2. The secretary at Paul's firm patched her through to him.

"Do you know where your wife is? She's not answering her cell."

"Hey, Kiddo. No. I'm not sure what all she's gotten into today. Why, do you need something?"

"Yes, well, maybe. I forgot to mention to her that I have court today and I don't know how long it's going to run."

"And you need someone to let Riley out. I'm on it. As soon as I track her down I'll let her know."

"You're the best, Paul." She had to admit it—Marisa was married to a great guy.

She set her phone down quickly because traffic was starting to move. But then, wouldn't you know it, it rang again. Probably Wes Trent. She looked down to check Caller ID. It wasn't her client, it was Justin. Her impulse was to answer it, but then she decided to let it go to voice mail. When she looked up, she was about to hit the stopped car in front of her. She barely slammed on her brakes in time. "Just perfect!" she said.

When was Justin going to get the hint anyway? She hadn't even slept with the guy yet and he was already starting to bore her. Marisa would probably chastise her for being mean. Not only did her sister like Justin, she always hoped each guy Stephanie dated would be the one. Marisa's optimism had paid off in her own life, though. She'd been with Paul since grade school.

Stephanie glanced over at the suit in the Mercedes. He was still staring at her. This time she flipped her head away as if she were annoyed. There was a fine line between showing interest by checking a girl out and turning into a psycho stalker. "Get a life," she muttered under her breath. She drummed a beat to the music on her steering wheel. He did have a nice smile, though. It reminded her of Paul's smile. Paul had that good ole boy smile from ear to ear that just made you trust him instantly. She couldn't remember a time when she didn't know that smile.

Because they'd grown up in a small town, Paul had been in Marisa's classes from first grade all the way through graduation. So he was already in the picture when Stephanie came along. Paul was just Marisa's friend at first. Then when they were thirteen and Mom and Dad divorced, Paul stuck by her when others in their class had shied away.

He'd also been there for Stephanie in those days. She closed her eyes and saw herself getting off the bus from elementary school to walk into her mom's empty house. Just when she imagined that the shadow passing across the window was someone trying to get in, Paul and Marisa showed up.

"How you doing, Kiddo?" he said to her. Then he flopped down on the couch beside Marisa to watch TV. Stephanie tried to squeeze in between them. Marisa rolled her eyes, but Paul said it was okay, he didn't mind. He always let her crash their twosome. Those were the good days.

On the other days, when Stephanie and Marisa spent time at their dad's, Marisa walked to Paul's house after school. On those long afternoons, Stephanie had to hang out with her step-mom, who alternately ignored and glared at her as if she were an interloper. That was worse than being alone.

Stephanie opened her eyes to see if traffic was moving yet. Still at a standstill. She didn't even bother to look over at the suit.

At least Carol Wheaton didn't seem to be that kind of stepmother to Wes Trent's daughter Tessa. She'd never met

Tessa, but she knew what Tessa must feel like all alone in the afternoons, especially as an only child.

Stephanie laid her head back against the headrest and closed her eyes again. She might as well have been an only child. By the time she was in third grade, Paul and Marisa had moved their friendship into a romance. Marisa moved in with Paul's parents that year. She almost never saw either one of them after that. How she'd missed them. Maybe things would have turned out differently if she'd met Justin back then. He was similar to Paul. Stable. Dependable. Mature beyond his years. But she didn't need all that now.

She shrugged off the chill that swept over her and opened her eyes. Still not moving. She checked her mouth in the rearview mirror. In spite of her best efforts, most of her lipstick was now residing on her travel mug. She reapplied, then smiled at herself in the mirror. Good, nothing on her teeth. The shade was called Bronze, which was subtle, yet perfectly accented her reddish-blond hair, lashes, and eyebrows. She pushed the fast-forward button on her CD player to "One Week," the Barenaked Ladies song she and Max had danced to when she took him to their concert.

She blinked at herself in the mirror. Her sixteen-year-old nephew had her coloring and not his parents'. In fact, he looked more like he was related to her than to them. "My friends think you're the bomb," he'd said to her after watching her sing those quick-paced, tongue-twisting lyrics. It was fun being an aunt now that they could really hang out together. They even enjoyed quite a bit of each other's music, although Max's taste was louder than hers.

Finally the car in front of her started to move. She checked the clock on her dashboard then floored it. She could still make it.

She always tried to beat her clients there on court day. In the two years she'd been practicing family law, she'd learned that clients tend to get out of control from the start if they walk into the courtroom and don't see a confident face waiting for them. She also preferred to arrive first because she'd rather her clients didn't see her in this old, beat-up Escort. She had her office looking chic and her wardrobe up to Vogue standards. Next she'd worry about getting the car to go with them, maybe a Beamer.

The suit in the Mercedes didn't seem to have been bothered by her mode of transportation. But that was different. He wasn't a client. He was just a guy. And guys would still want a woman no matter what she drove.

She whipped into an empty parking space in the back. Soon she was running up the courthouse steps in her high heels, which she was really good at.

While passing through the metal detectors, she noticed there was no anxious Wes or Carol in sight. Good.

As she hurried down the hallway her heels echoed sharp staccatos—how she loved that commanding sound.

When she got closer to the courtroom doors, she saw that Wes's ex-wife, Sharon Connor, was standing in front of the doors talking to an attractive woman. Sharon glanced at Stephanie and then turned away, but the woman with her smiled at her as she passed. The woman reminded Stephanie of Marisa. They were about the same age and both had warm, engaging smiles, only this woman was far more stylish. Although it wasn't her personal taste, she admired the woman's bold fashion choice—bright pants and flowery slingbacks. Now why couldn't Marisa dress more like that? If she were married and a mom like Marisa, and probably this woman, she'd want to look this well-put together. Casual and comfortable, yet hip and fun.

Stephanie walked through the doors and almost ran into Wes and Carol. He'd made it there first after all. But what was Carol doing in the courtroom? She'd already explained to her, more than once, that the hearing was restricted to biological parents only. To top it off, Carol was clutching a stack of papers to her chest. Her own set of notes and documentation, no doubt. Carol rubbed her wrong sometimes. Why couldn't she just trust Stephanie to do her job instead of hovering? Stephanie forced a smile.

Before any of them could speak, the bailiff—a new guy who looked like a body builder—leapt to Carol's side. With his arm under her elbow, he spun her around and walked her right out the doors. Wes stood there helpless. Stephanie could tell from the look on his face that he knew even better than she did just how pissed Carol must be right now.

Stephanie raised her eyebrows and shrugged, as if to say, I tried to warn her.

Marcus McDermott, Sharon's attorney, was standing off to the side of the doors smirking. Obviously he'd been the one to instruct the bailiff to remove Carol from the courtroom. He probably had no idea he'd just done Stephanie a huge favor.

He nodded at her. She smiled at him, flipped her long hair over her shoulder, then straightened her pencil skirt. Her fitted, black wool crepe Dolce and Gabbana suit had been a good choice. She looked good. And the leopard print lining on the inside of the jacket provided just the right amount of flash on her turned-back cuff.

She put her arm under Wes's elbow and led him toward a bench in the back, then slid in beside him. Marcus sat in the back on the other side of the aisle, but he wasn't taking his eyes off of her.

She and Marcus had gone up against each other once before and she'd won. It had driven him crazy. In typical male fashion he'd offered to buy her a drink afterwards to congratulate her, but she'd declined. He was cute, but she preferred to keep her romantic liaisons confined to men she didn't have to see at work the next day. It was less messy that way. Then when it was time to end it, she could just avoid their phone calls.

CHAPTER 3

Madeline

Madeline turned as the courtroom doors burst open. A flustered Ms. Wheaton stumbled out with a burly bailiff in close pursuit. He stopped, blocking the doorway.

Ms. Wheaton turned to face him. "This is ridiculous. I am, for all practical purposes, his secretary. I need to be in there to keep his papers organized."

"Sorry, Ma'am. Judge said only biological parents right now."

"That would be me," Sharon said. A look of triumph spread across her face as she sidestepped Ms. Wheaton and walked towards the doors.

Carol shoved the stack of papers at the bailiff. "See that my husband gets these," was all she had time to say before Sharon shut the heavy doors behind her with a definitive thud.

Ms. Wheaton didn't move. She glared at the doors, her empty hand clenched into a fist, as if she were posing so a theme-park artist could sketch a caricature of her.

Madeline slid into one of the molded plastic chairs in the makeshift waiting room just outside the wooden doors. She could tell the bailiff enjoyed dealing with Carol Wheaton's type. Probably because he knew, at least at the courthouse, he'd always win. But her amusement at Ms. Wheaton's defeat didn't last long. There was only one other chair in the waiting area. And sure enough, a few seconds later, the woman darted into the chair next to her. With her head turned away, she folded her arms and let out a forceful huff. Now they were only inches apart. Thankfully Ms. Wheaton's gaze stayed on those doors.

So they'd pretend not to see each other. Fine, Madeline thought. She could play this game. It was better than pretending to enjoy small talk. With her hands in her lap and her legs crossed, she passed the time by bouncing her foot, in its new slingback, in the air. A silent tapping. She never could sit still. She stared at her shoe, admiring the orange and fuchsia floral-fabric kitten heels she'd just bought at J. Crew, her favorite store. Even her two small children knew a little of her secret indulgence. "Mommy loves this store," they'd divulge with wide-eyed disbelief to the salespeople each time she dragged them away from the mall's central play area to go in there.

She stared at the ceiling. She stared at the white plaster wall in front of her. She glanced at her watch: 9:15 a.m. They'd been sitting there for only fifteen minutes? If time was going to pass this slowly, Sharon would owe her big time.

She looked at the back of Ms. Wheaton's dark head. Although only a few inches of space separated them, the woman gave off no fragrance whatsoever. No trace of perfume, soap, hair spray. Not even sweat. Was she even human?

One thing was clear. Both of them were working hard to ignore each other. Madeline was going for relaxed, casual. Sunk back in her chair, long legs jutting out, still crossed, top foot still bouncing. She could have been waiting for a bus. Ms. Wheaton seemed to be going for the opposite effect. She was on high alert, staring at the closed courtroom doors, leaning as far away from Madeline as possible, perched like a hunter whose aim was steadied, waiting for the deer to get in her sights.

The woman could have been a mentor to her. She wouldn't dare tell Sharon this, but over the years her students had spoken highly of Ms. Wheaton. Some even compared their teaching styles and suggested that they were two of the best teachers on campus. In fact, she'd been looking forward to officially meeting Ms. Wheaton some day. But not like this.

The silence in the hallway was maddening. Why wasn't anyone coming or going from that room? How bizarre was it that her best friend and her colleague had both been married to the same man?

She willed herself not to get claustrophobic. It was a small, enclosed space, after all. No windows. If it weren't for her friendship with Sharon, she'd be outta here.

Ms. Wheaton must have sensed she was being watched because at that moment she spun around. Their eyes locked for an instant.

Madeline held her wrist up and looked at her watch, as if that's where she'd been intending to look all along. Ten o'clock now. An hour had passed and Ms. Wheaton still had that wild look in her eyes, hadn't calmed down at all. Was her head going to start spinning out of control like in that famous scene from The Exorcist? Madeline went back to staring at her shoe. She wanted to pull out the book she'd brought in her purse, but she knew she wouldn't be able to concentrate.

So this was The Evil-Know-It-All she'd been hearing about. Just six months after her divorce was final, Sharon got slammed with the news that Wes had remarried. Madeline had just put the kids to bed when her doorbell rang at eight o'clock.

"The prick went and married the whore," Sharon said, sweeping through the door. "What have you got to drink?" Obviously she already had a head start. Madeline searched her kitchen until she found an old bottle of whiskey on the top shelf in the back and began pouring it generously. By nine o'clock she'd called a few other girlfriends from the neighborhood to come over for an emergency "Anti-Bridal Shower."

By ten o'clock she'd plopped a veil on Sharon's head that she borrowed from Olivia's dress-up clothes. She put on a DVD of one of her favorite 80's movies, *She-Devil*, the ultimate ex-wife's revenge comedy, starring a young, glamorous homewrecking Meryl Streep and a scorned, overweight Roseanne Barr. Yes, the movie was full of exaggeration and cliché, down to the disgusting hairy mole on the first wife's face, but it was just the kind of farce they needed for a good laugh.

As the party was ending, Madeline became anxious about sending a drunk driver out on the roads, so Jack agreed to drive Sharon home. The other women lived close enough that they had walked.

The next day Sharon called her from work. "Thanks for last night. What would I do without you? Who needs a man when you've got girlfriends?"

She knew she'd done well. But soon Sharon was at her door again. This time it was about Tessa. Wes and The-Evil-

Know-It-All were suing Sharon for custody. "Here we go again," Jack had whispered to her on her way to the kitchen to look for tequila.

She startled when the courtroom doors opened. When she looked up, she was hoping to see Sharon, but it was a couple in their forties. They paused in the open doorway. Weeping softly, the woman hid her face with her hands while the man cradled her in his arms. Hopefully Sharon wouldn't be crying when she finally came out of those doors. A good-looking young guy in a dark suit appeared behind the couple. Probably an attorney. He backed his way into the courtroom, slowly pulling the doors with him. The couple walked away clutching each other. Before the guy disappeared behind the doors, he looked Madeline's way and smiled. "How you doing out here?"

"Fine," she said. Did he know who she was? Could he be Sharon's attorney, Marcus? If he was, Sharon hadn't mentioned her attorney looked like a Calvin Klein model. Hopefully he knew what he was doing. Maybe she should've recommended her divorce attorney to Sharon, a man with gray hair and twenty years' experience under his belt.

When the only thing left to look at was closed doors, Ms. Wheaton shifted in her seat. She hadn't acknowledged the commotion in the doorway other than to crane her neck to peer inside the courtroom. This loss of control had to be killing her.

Madeline pretended to stretch and glanced at her again. No words had passed between them the whole time they'd been sitting there. Had the woman recognized her from campus? Maybe it was best if she hadn't. Madeline didn't need an enemy at the college.

From the corner of her eye she noticed that Ms. Wheaton was staring at, of all things, her shoes. Suddenly the woman shifted sideways in her seat to face her. When she looked up, Ms. Wheaton looked her dead in the eyes.

"I hope you don't wear shoes like that to teach in," she said. Her deep voice shook.

The mystery was solved. Ms. Wheaton did recognize her. She scanned the woman's outfit—black polyester pantsuit, clunky black shoes with thick, black socks, and a low ponytail bound by a white scrunchie. She was slim and had a nice bone structure, but with the severe hairstyle and not a trace of make-up on her pinched face, Madeline had to look hard to see the possibility of attractiveness.

She would ignore the insult. Instead, she said, "I thought I recognized you. We teach in the same department."

"I would never wear shoes like that," Ms. Wheaton said again. "Students are so easily distracted these days. I always try to dress professionally."

Was this matter so insurmountable that she couldn't move on until it was addressed? The nerve. She glanced at Ms. Wheaton's scrunchie again, trying to place that in her repertoire of professional attire, then she nodded toward her slingback. "Actually, I find that a fun pair of shoes can be a conversation starter with students."

Ms. Wheaton snorted and flipped her head away.

Had this woman really just called her unprofessional? She pictured herself hoisting her leg and flailing her rebellious feet over the podium to distract her students from learning. She thought of all the times students had said, "I love your shoes," before or after class when she stood around chatting with them.

She looked down at this particular pair again. They were no rival of Carrie Bradshaw's Manolo Blahniks, but she understood how Carrie felt in that much-played Sex and the City clip. Carrie pauses on the street to window shop and seeing a pair of frilly pink Manolos, the latest design, sighs and says, "Hello, Lover."

Madeline glanced down at the rest of her own outfit. Bare ankles showing above her colorful slingbacks was the one part of her outfit that could be considered remotely daring. Certainly not the ivory cardigan or the green chinos—those were casual, maybe, but definitely not daring. The shoes? Well, they just added flair. What was the harm in a touch of flair? In fact, she'd bought the shoes with the same motivation that kept her from buying a minivan to tote her children around in. Yes, she was a wife and mother and housekeeper and part-time English teacher living in Columbus, the biggest small town in the Midwest, but she was also still a girl who liked fun shoes.

She reached for her purse and smeared clear gloss across her puckered lips. Who cares what Carol Wheaton thinks? She could be herself and would still be taken seriously by the people who mattered. And neither her shoes, nor her eye shadow, nor her lip-gloss made her weak or ineffectual in the classroom. She smiled at the white plaster wall. Too bad it wasn't a mirror so she could smile at herself right now.

Why would a woman fifteen to twenty years her senior spend her energy de-feminizing herself while plotting to steal another woman's husband and child? According to Sharon, The Evil-Know-It-All had already raised her own children. Why was she now using her time and energy to fight other women? Didn't she realize there were enough fun shoes to go around? In some alternate world where competition over men doesn't exist, she and Sharon could have been friends with Carol Wheaton. She wanted to tell Ms. Wheaton she might actually enjoy trying on a pair of colorful, pointy-toed shoes for size.

But she didn't say what she was thinking. As usual, she'd remain dignified and keep a pleasant smile on her face. Of course she'd share this with Jack later, and they'd laugh about it. But for now, she'd just stare at the wall. Then her shoe. Then her watch.

CHAPTER 4

Adele

When the phone rang, Adele was getting ready for work, trying to decide between the taupe pumps and a pair of pewter ballet flats, rotating slowly in front of the three-way mirror as she considered her outfit. Black linen trousers and a sleeveless white turtleneck. Nubby gray-and-taupe tweed blazer. Silver earrings that brought out the platinum-gray of her hair. The trousers dragged a little in the ballet flats, but she felt more relaxed in flat shoes, and if she felt relaxed, her clients would pick up on that and relax, too.

On the other hand, the pumps, with their sporty saddle stitching, gave her outfit a polished but informal look that made her feel friendly yet authoritative. And maybe the flats were a little too youthful for a woman in her sixties. Sixty on the nose, in fact. Could she really be that old? For that matter, was sixty old? Some people seemed to think so, but she certainly didn't feel her age, just a little stiffness in her joints.

The phone rang again. From downstairs, her husband called, "Are you going to get that, Dell? I'm on my way out."

She sighed. Why was Roger still home? Didn't he have an appointment across town, at the building site? Ever since he'd downsized his architectural firm and started working from home, his work hours had gotten more and more irregular. And why did he so seldom pick up the phone these days?

"I've got it," she shouted as the phone rang again.

With one ballet flat on her left foot and the other still in her hand, she hurried to the bedside phone. She pushed her new glasses up and squinted through the lowest portion of her progressive lenses. Caller ID came into focus—Carol Wheaton.

She'd told Carol to call her at home this morning if she needed to—Carol and her husband were asking for custody of her husband's teenaged daughter, and the hearing was today. Given Carol's difficulty channeling her anger, Adele had half-expected a call, but she'd hoped her client would be able to manage on her own, using the relaxation and visualization techniques they'd been practicing in the office. Apparently not.

"Dr. Adele Martin," she said into the cordless, pitching her voice low and keeping her rate slow.

"Finally," Carol said through a crackle of static.

"Did you have trouble reaching me? I may have missed an earlier call." She didn't say "...because I was in the shower and my husband refuses to answer the phone." To say too much to a client would blur boundaries.

Carol was breathing hard into the phone, as if trying to contain her rage.

Adele let the seconds tick by, waiting.

Finally Carol spoke. "It took me forever to get through to you. Are you aware they no longer allow cell phones in the courthouse?"

"No. What was it you called about?"

"Of course not. You mentioned at our last session that I should call if I felt I was, to use your term, 'losing it.'"

"And are you?"

"No. But I'm on the verge. Fuming, actually."

She set the ballet flat on the cherry writing table next to the bed and pulled out the desk chair. "What happened?"

"First of all, I was thrown out of the courtroom by that goon of a bailiff, barred from my husband's side, where I was needed. But, ironically, that's not what set me off. There were only two seats in the waiting area, if you can believe it. I had to sit next to another professor from the college, an adjunct no less." Carol described their interaction. "And I'm still furious, though I hardly know the woman."

Adele eased herself down into the chair—this was going to take a while. "Does your anger seem out of proportion to what occurred?"

"Yes and no," Carol said.

Adele strained to see the numerals in her new glasses, which had slipped down on her nose again, just enough to misalign her lenses. She was now looking through the distance portion at the nearby clock, which blurred. A minute went by, then another.

Carol let out an exasperated sigh. "Obviously it's out of proportion. That's why I called. Sorry. I suppose that sounded harsh."

"It did. Why don't you try again? Take a breath. Visualize your anger floating above you and away, like a dark cloud dissolving into mist."

While Carol audibly inhaled and exhaled, Adele slipped

the ballet flat on her right foot and flexed her toes. Though maybe a little too youthful, the flat shoes felt more comfortable on her arthritic feet than high-heeled pumps, and of course ballet flats were a classic design. Hadn't Audrey Hepburn worn them in Sabrina? She and Roger had started to watch that film the other night on cable, but after twenty minutes he'd gone to his home office to "doodle at the drawing board," after first labeling Sabrina "one of those 'chick flicks'" that didn't hold his attention.

She shook her head and reminded herself that she had a client on the phone. Or did she? Had the call dropped out?

"All right," Carol said through the static. "You win. My anger seems out of proportion to what happened."

She could only imagine what it had cost Carol to say that. "Great," she said. "That sounded exactly right."

"Thanks." Carol's voice had a bitter edge, but underneath that a hint of real pride—the healthy kind that could spur healing.

"What do you think set you off?"

"Well, I suppose it was the shoes. It's totally ridiculous, I know, but Madeline Greenfield's silly shoes annoyed me from the moment I sat down beside her."

"Don't assume your reaction is ridiculous. Let's go a little deeper. When you see a pair of shoes like that, what do they bring to mind?"

Carol was tapping something. The toe of her shoe, on concrete? A cigarette on a lighter? Adele hoped not—Carol had quit smoking months ago, afraid the habit would jeopardize the custody case, but now she was off the patch and under stress.

The tapping stopped. "A witch," Carol said. "Like the witch in The Wizard of Oz. The wicked witch. Because of the pointed toes, you see."

"Anything else?"

"The flowery fabric. Pink and orange, no less. And linen, which stains so easily. Totally impractical. Could they be any more frivolous? And yet this young woman fancies herself a good teacher, a role model for youth. Oh, she's popular enough with the undergrads, but I can't tell you how many times I've worked with one of her former students, only to discover dozens of purposeless fragments littering their prose—"

When Carol finally wound down, Adele said, "You see this woman as both witch-like and frivolous."

"I know what you're thinking. That's contradictory. A paradox. But that's what popped to mind."

"How might those two qualities go together?"

"How should I know?" Carol paused. "Sorry. I suppose I don't really know."

"Imagine the shoes are a symbol in a story. The author says they represent both witchcraft and frivolity. How can that be?"

She could almost see Carol's thumb and forefinger go to her lower lip and pull it out as she pondered this. Meanwhile, she glanced at the taupe pumps on the floor of the walk-in closet, their squared toes gleaming in the morning sun, stacked heels in shadow.

"The flowers are camouflage," Carol said. "It's a witch's trick. She wants people to think she's silly and frivolous, but she's a powerful, evil force in the universe. She uses the flowers to disarm her enemies, to make them think she's weak and inconsequential."

"You see this young woman as a powerful, evil force in the universe. A threat. Is that right?"

Carol exhaled hard into the phone. "No, of course not. Madeline's a lightweight. That's why I told her I'd never wear such ridiculous shoes to teach in."

"But?"

"You simply don't give up, do you?"

She laughed, glad that Carol was loosening up a little, sounding less tense. "No," she said. "That's part of my job."

"Don't remind me. I'm probably on the clock right now."

No wonder Carol had a hard time in relationships—she always assumed the worst about people, about women in particular. They were making progress, though. At least Carol hadn't launched into a diatribe about the high cost of therapy this time.

"Go on," Adele said.

"Well, I suppose I see Madeline Greenfield as a symbol of what's wrong with young women these days," Carol said. "She won't get anywhere in academia if she doesn't dress more professionally. Like so many of her ilk, she came of age after the feminist movement peaked. She's blissfully unaware that women like me paved the way for her generation. But you know how I feel about that, Dr. Martin."

Did she ever. During every session, Carol made bitter comments about the decline of feminism, most of them true. Younger women today didn't seem aware of what those in her generation had gone through. Still, that wasn't what Carol was angry about at the core. She was about to pull Carol back to exploring the true source of her anger when Carol cut in again.

"These ambitious girly-girls take it for granted they can work outside the home and raise well-adjusted children and have electric sex with their husbands six times a week. Today they can aspire to any career that interests them, yet these...these immature ingrates don't recognize the sacrifices women of my generation made for them. I gave up watching my twin boys take their first steps so I could make full professor. Do you think Madeline Greenfield gives a damn about that? Do the Madelines of the world ever express gratitude for the privilege of, say, working part-time, which wasn't even an option when my two were toddlers? Madeline Greenfield didn't even thank me for suggesting she eliminate the too-cute shoes from her professional wardrobe. Professor Greenfield thinks she can win respect in academia wearing flowery shoes and pants the color of Gatorade. Well, there's more to female success than that. She'll discover that in a decade or two, when her breasts start to sag and her chin doubles. The power she has over men now—the men who do the promoting and the salary-raising—will plummet in the years ahead, and then where will she be? Thrown on the professional discard pile, and no amount of flowery shoes can change that, ever." Carol was panting now, out of breath from her rant.

She gave Carol a few seconds to recover but not enough time to reboot. "You say you missed seeing your twins' first steps," she said softly. "Do you find it hard to say no at times?"

"Definitely not. I learned to assert myself years ago. I don't say no when I mean yes. Or, rather...what I meant was—"

“I think I know what you meant to say, but that isn’t what you said.”

“Oh, please. You can’t possibly think that was deliberate. That’s just Freudian nonsense. I thought you were smarter than that.”

“Carol, did you hear what you just said? Your tone?”

Carol let out a low, muffled groan. “I didn’t mean...I’m sorry. I just... this whole custody dispute is excruciating. I spent so much time putting Wes’s papers in order, so he’d be prepared to give exactly the right testimony, as we rehearsed. I even laid out his clothes this morning, took barely a minute picking out my own.” She sounded close to tears, her voice breaking at the end. “And what happens? That moronic bailiff ushered me out of the courtroom as if I were a sack of rotting potatoes that offended his nose. You should have seen the way he looked me up and down. And, on top of that humiliation, there sits Ms. Madeline Greenfield, looking like the cat that ate the canary in her girly shoes, showing her solidarity with Wes’s ex-wife, who, as you know, has no business mothering Tessa as she does. Totally irresponsible.”

“I know you’re hurting,” she said, “but go ahead and feel that hurt, just for now.”

At first Carol was quiet, then let out a long sigh that suggested relief.

Adele was tempted to end the call then, but she paused so Carol could feel the full impact of what had just happened. Hard to tell if this small shift in awareness would carry over into a permanent change, but at least Carol was starting to internalize and act on what they’d practiced so often in the office. With some long-held angry energy discharged, maybe she'd begin to heal, to transform herself into a softer, more loving woman. More self-loving as well.

"Call me later if you need to," she said. "I'll be in session most of the day but I'll check my voicemail at intervals."

To her surprise, Carol thanked her and ended the call, her tone much less tense now, softer, lower in pitch. That was encouraging.

After replacing the cordless, Adele tried on the squared-toed pumps and checked out her reflections in the mirrors that covered the door to the walk-in closet and the two slanted panels on either side. The three-way mirror had been Roger's idea. When he'd designed their house as his wedding present to her, he'd added that detail as a surprise. Now, nearly twenty years later, it was still one of her favorite features.

"Hmm," she said to her mirror images. The shoes felt tight this morning, and the weight of her foot tilted forward at that angle made her toes ache. Still, the pumps were just right with her outfit, and she'd be sitting most of the day.

She slipped her appointment book into her briefcase, along with an alligator clutch purse, and hurried down the staircase. At the bottom of the stairs she pivoted, about to walk through the great room, when the doors to Roger's office caught her eye. He'd left them open again.

With a sigh, she reversed course. She didn't want their cats, Isis and Osiris, to disturb his things. That would provoke an outpouring of grumbles from Roger, who'd return later today to find his drafting set all over the floor or the crumpled drawings from his wastebasket batted into the dining room.

She reached for the knobs to pull the doors shut, head

down, eyes on her Anne Kleins. Yes, she'd made the right choice, even if they pinched her feet.

Then, a shock. As she lifted her chin, Roger came into focus in the distance portion of her lenses. He was perched on his tall stool, poring over some plans unrolled on his drawing board, his long legs folded up like pocketknives, the few strands of silver in his otherwise black hair highlighted by the overhead halogens. He was dressed in a blue oxford cloth shirt, pleated khaki pants, and a pair of light hiking boots, his usual worksite get-up, yet here he sat. Had the appointment slipped his mind?

"Roger?" she said, but not too loudly—she didn't want to startle him.

He didn't look up, only mumbled a distracted, "Uh-huh?"

In a sharper tone, she said, "I thought you had an appointment this morning, on the other side of town. In Hilliard, isn't it?"

This time he looked up. Without another word, he rolled up the plans, stuck them in the basket next to his drawing board and hurried off, leaving her feeling as chilled as if a winter wind had just blown through the house.

CHAPTER 5

Tessa

Alone on the front porch, Tessa took her house key out of her new Louis Vuitton bag—the white one with the multicolored logos, a super-special gift from her mom—and slid her skinny red duplicate key into the lock on the front door. The bolt clunked into place. Even so, she made herself rattle the big brass door handle anyway, just in case.

Her mom had left her a hugely long voicemail on her cell phone to remind her to do that, as if she was some kind of idiot. As if she hadn't tested the stupid door handle on every single late-arrival day, when she had to lock up the house on her own. And she'd set the electronic alarm. And brought her inhaler with her, along with all her track stuff.

"Wish me luck," Mom had said at the end of her message, and Tessa had wanted to say, "Wish me luck, Mom."

Okay, maybe she did have a bad attitude toward her mom, and sometimes even her dad. At times she so wanted to tell her mother exactly how she felt, even if it hurt her mom's feelings. Neither of her parents got how this whole custody thing was affecting her. All they seemed to care about was who won in court.

The only person who truly understood what she was going through was Emily Trockler, her best friend since sixth grade. Em's parents had been divorced for over ten years, and Em had been the soccer ball in their custody battles most of that time.

Where was Em, anyway? Tessa slipped the key into her purse and pulled out her cell phone to check the time.

"Crap," she said under her breath. Two more voice mails. From Mom, probably.

She ignored the prompt to check her messages and looked instead at the time. They had a little more than twenty minutes until the second bell rang. If Em didn't get to her house soon, Tessa would have to walk to school by herself, which she definitely didn't feel like doing today.

She set her pink backpack on the porch floor. With her thumb, she pressed down hard on the 3 key, Em's speed-dial number.

As soon as Em picked up, she said, "Where are you? It's way late."

"I'm almost there," Em said.

"Well, hurry. I want to get to school a little early, okay?"

"So you can stand around in front of Tommy Leonetti's locker and get him to notice you?"

"I'm hanging up now, Emily." She snapped the phone shut, but not in a mean way. She and Em fake-hung up on each other all the time.

She slid her phone into the Vuitton bag and hoisted her backpack to her left shoulder, where it dangled at a crazy angle. It was supposed to be bad for her back to carry so much weight by just one shoulder, but she didn't care if the freaking bag gave her scoliosis. She would not look like a total dork bending low under a backpack. That would be social suicide at Patterson Middle School.

She trotted down the three steps that led to their front walk and started to jog. She was supposed to run two relays today after school, and her track coach always said she should use every opportunity to build stamina and endurance. Considering how bad she'd been running lately, she figured she ought to do what Coach Stanley said for a change.

The backpack kept shifting, though. She had to stop in front of the Reed's house to put it on both shoulders—just for now. As soon as she met up with Em, she'd slip it off one shoulder again, in case they ran run into somebody from Patterson during the last few blocks of their walk.

Once she got the backpack balanced on both shoulders, she picked up her pace, detouring around the Martin's sidewalk, which was wet from the built-in sprinkler system that automatically watered their lawn for a half-hour every morning, usually when she was passing by. She wondered if the Martins, this old couple who had no kids and hardly ever came out of their house, did that on purpose, because they didn't like teenagers. Or maybe they were just oblivious, to use one of the vocabulary words that Mr. Schilling made them learn last year in English. Adults could be like that—totally unaware of what bothered kids. Maybe the Martins were like that—not anti-kid, just oblivious.

She jogged back up on the sidewalk and rounded the curve that led to Gleason Road. Em was walking toward her, waving.

Tessa stopped, folded her arms, and looked Em up and

down, but she sure didn't like what she saw. They'd agreed last night to wear the same basic outfit today—loose khaki cargo shorts, tight scoop-neck t-shirts to cover their even tighter, against-the-school-dress-code tank tops, and all-white Nike Shox with low socks that didn't show. But Em, who was sort of fashion-impaired, had worn a pair of brown leather sandals with thick platform soles.

Tessa frowned, peeled off one backpack strap, and pointed to Em's sandals.

"I had to take the dog out before school," Em said in her high, don't-blame-me voice. "I stepped in his poop, okay?"

Tessa wrinkled her nose, but really she was envious—she wasn't allowed to have a dog because of her asthma. Her mom worried that the dander would set off an attack of wheezing, though it never had.

"It was so gross," Em said. "His poop was really soft and it got in between the little treads and smelled so nasty—" Em looked up at her. "I really didn't have any choice, Tessa."

Tessa pretended to think that over for a second. "I guess I'll let it pass this time. But next time the Fashion Police are definitely going to issue you a ticket. I mean, platforms with cargo shorts?"

"What?"

"That's, like, so weird."

"No, it's not," Em said. "I saw it in Seventeen. In an ad."

"Geez, Em, don't copy your style from ads. They're just trying to get you to buy stuff." She'd heard this from her mother so many times she couldn't count, but it was true. Ads were fashion dead-ends.

Em frowned. "I guess. Although—"

"No althoughs. Come on, who's your number one personal stylist?"

"You are."

"Okay, then." She gave Em a quick, one-armed hug, and Em hugged back, but just barely. Slowly—probably to be a pain—Em adjusted her backpack and her purse, only a Dooney and Bourke, but the cute one, with the little logos in the same colors as the Vuitton bag but on a black background.

When Em was finally done, she clomped to the light pole and pressed the button to cross Gleason.

Tessa winced. "God, Em, you sound like a freaking horse in those things. Plus they're brown. Your bag's mostly black."

"What's with you today?" Em said, hands on hips now. "It's the custody hearing, isn't it? You're worried about it."

"Not really," she said, nudging Em onward as soon as the light changed. "I mean, I'm sort of upset about it, but I wouldn't say I'm worried or anything."

"You want to talk about it?"

"Not really."

"Will you please stop saying 'not really'?"

"Not really," Tessa said, thinking maybe a joke would get Em off her back.

"Okay," Em said when they got to the other side of Gleason. "I get it."

"Great." Tessa picked up the pace. If they kept on at Em's short-legged rate they'd be late for first period and draw a detention.

Em stretched out her gait to keep up. "Although—"

"Although what?"

"Although my counselor says it's important to talk about

stuff that's bothering you. She says you need to deal with small problems so they don't turn into big ones."

Tessa snorted. "I'd hardly call this a small problem. I mean, I could end up at my mom's practically twenty-four-seven, which would so suck. Like, no midweek visitation. Just one weekend a month with Dad."

"Get out. Can they even do that?"

"If they both agree to it. That's what Mom's asking for."

Em shook her head as a school bus chugged by. "Your dad will never agree to that," she shouted over the roar of the bus engine.

"I'm not so sure. My dad's been acting really strange ever since he married Carol. He pays even less attention to me than he did when he and Mom were married, and he's all over Carol, in front of me, even, which is totally disgusting."

"He's just adjusting to his new marriage," Em said. "My mom did the same thing. He'll be over that in a few months."

"Yeah, and then he'll let freaking Carol raise me, like he did with Mom. That's why I don't want to end up living with Daddy and Carol. Going there for visitation is fine, but living there? Carol's already starting to put pressure on Dad. Now he's making all these rules, like I have to be in bed by eleven, with the lights out?"

Emily frowned. "What's so bad about that? I have to be in bed by ten."

"With the lights out?"

"Well, no—"

"And that's just the tip of the iceberg. Carol's trying to get me to go to this big-deal drama camp this summer—she actually got them to reserve me a place. I mean, it sounds awesome, but she and Daddy didn't even ask me first. They just signed me up for it. Well, Carol did."

"You mean it's already paid for? A done deal?"

"Yes! And it cost a ton. Seriously, Em, Dad and Carol have spent a gazillion dollars on me, so I don't want to make them feel like I'm ungrateful, only—"

"Only you'd really rather live with your mom."

"That's just it. I really wouldn't. Mom's changed so much since the divorce. She used to be so much fun. Well, she's still fun, but now she works hard at doing nothing but girl stuff. And she's not a girl, you know? She's my mother. It's so weird. Plus she says all this crappy stuff about my dad and Carol. She tries to make it sound nice, but it's not. And when she doesn't think I can hear her, she'll call Carol 'the Evil Know-It-All.' She really starts running her mouth when she's talking to her friend Madeline."

"That so sucks," Emily said.

"That's what I think. But will Mom listen?" Her ponytail bounced against her back as they walked down Gleason. Normally she liked that sensation. She'd picture how she looked to the people driving by, the pale blond streaks in her straight brown hair glowing in the sun. But right now, the bouncing annoyed her. Right now, everything annoyed her.

"Your mom's still hurting," Em said. "My dad went through that. My counselor says the parent that leaves usually goes through most of their grieving before they go. The one that gets left takes longer to over the breakup. Sometimes way longer. Your mom's still trying to get it together, okay? You just have to let her move through that, Tessa. Give her some time."

"I guess," Tessa said. For a midget, Em could be pretty bossy at times. But good-bossy. She wished her mom would be good-bossy once in a while. Now, her stepmom—that was a totally different story. Carol had no problem telling people what to do. Sometimes Tessa wished she could combine what she liked best about Carol and what she loved about her mom and get rid of the bad stuff in both. Like the way her Mom kept calling her all the time. That was so annoying.

"I wish my mom would give me some time," she said to Em. "She called me twice this morning and then left three voicemails."

"What did she want?"

"Oh, you know, the usual. Did I have my inhaler? Did I lock up? You know how she is."

"That's it? Five calls for that?"

Tessa ran her tongue over her teeth, enjoying the smooth feel of no more braces. "I haven't checked all the voicemails yet."

"Don't you think you should? I mean, maybe they're about something important. Plus, you'll have to turn your phone off when you get to school."

Tessa's stomach started to knot up, the way it did before tests. "Maybe you're right."

Tessa pulled the phone out of her purse, and played the voice mails. The first was something long and boring about her and Em maybe babysitting for Madeline Greenfield's kids later today, which she already knew about. The second message was shorter, in her mom's fake-cheery voice. "Hey, sweetie, just wanted to remind you, don't plan on going to your dad's after the meet tonight. I'm going to pick you up, not Dad, and we'll go out to eat and celebrate." Celebrate? It was all she could do to keep from throwing the phone down on the sidewalk.

"Great," she said, snapping her phone shut.

Em's eyebrows twisted up. "What?"

"She wants to celebrate her victory over Dad with me tonight after the meet."

"Ouch."

"I know! It's so...mean. Plus I don't want to give up Wednesday nights with my dad, even if I have to do study table."

"Your stepmom's idea?"

She nodded. "And now Dad's all over me, too, making me study at the kitchen table, where they can both, get this, monitor my progress."

"Your grades did come up last nine weeks."

"True. But having to sit there and get tutored makes me feel like such an idiot. I mean, I'll be sitting there and Daddy will come by and say, 'You forgot to factor in the exponent,' and I'll feel so dumb."

"I know," Emily said. "I hate that. I like the help, but sometimes parents have a way of making you feel like you're in first grade or something."

"Carol doesn't do that. She'll point out my mistakes, but she acts as if I'm one of her college students. Which isn't that bad. At least she doesn't talk down to me. She acts like she thinks I'm really smart but maybe a little lazy?"

Em gave her a look that said, Well, are you?

"Shut up," Tessa said, breaking into a smile. Sometimes she wished she could just get an apartment with Em instead of living with either parent. Why couldn't adults work things out the way kids did? Did adults get more immature as they aged? Or did divorce sort of turn adults into temporary morons, as Em always said?

"Come on, Midge," she said. "Let's move it. If you're going to win your sprint today, you'd better lengthen that stride."

CHAPTER 6

Sharon

Sharon Connor sat beside her attorney on a bench in the back of the courtroom, while Wes and his attorney waited across the aisle on the other side. Sharon couldn't help but stare at them. Of course Wes had picked a young, pretty female attorney. He'd always been comfortable with his ability to manipulate women. Damn, he looked good. She hated how he always looked the same, impeccably polished and groomed, no matter what the circumstances. At least The Evil-Know-It-All wasn't in there to make it more difficult for her to keep it together.

"Don't let him rattle you," Marcus said, touching her arm.

"I just want to get this over with." She watched yet another couple slide out of their bench and head up to the front. "How much longer do you think we'll have to wait?"

"We could be in for a long day. All of these people were probably told to be here at nine o'clock, just like you."

"Don't you think there's something wrong with a system that is designed to make people wait?" she said. Marcus just blinked.

Of course he didn't understand how she felt. All of this

waiting around meant something entirely different to him. He was getting paid for his time no matter how long it took. It may have been an inconvenience, a nuisance even, but it didn't strip him of all of his power. The woman behind the bench didn't hold his fate in her hands, dangling it there to increase his vulnerability with each passing hour.

"Now remember," Marcus said, "when it's our turn, don't say anything. Let me do the talking."

"Okay," she said. Why fight it? She was utterly powerless. She tried to take a deep breath, but it caught in her chest before she could finish it.

Had they prepared enough? Today meant everything. Without Tessa, without seeing her daughter on a daily basis, nothing else mattered to her. Her anxiety wasn't helped by the fact that this attorney was new. And a man. She preferred to work with females. Her office was made up of females. Her gynecologist was female. The attorney she'd had during her divorce had been female. But she was wrapped up in a big case right now, so she recommended this young guy from her firm to handle the custody battle. She'd been leery, but Margie had insisted that he was bright, motivated, and on top of things.

"I saw your friend out there," Marcus said, keeping his voice low.

"Madeline's a real trooper."

"How did you two meet?"

"My magazine published an article she wrote—How to Lose the Baby Weight in Three Months."

"How many kids does she have?"

It was obvious he was just trying to distract her, but she was still grateful.

"Two. Noah and Olivia," she said. "My Tessa babysits for them."

"That's good that your families are close. Could end up helping us in court if we ever need character witnesses. I assume Madeline would be willing to testify on your behalf?"

"Definitely. We're at each other's houses all the time. Our subdivisions are only ten minutes apart. We exercise together, have coffee together, my kid is close to her kids. She was there during the last few hellish years of my marriage and she stood by my side during the divorce—"

"Which magazine did you say you worked for?"

"Women's Fitness"

"Oh, yeah? That's great."

Did he just look at her stomach? She pulled her jacket closed to cover her waistband. She'd lost about fifteen pounds during the divorce when she'd been too upset to eat, but most of it was back now. With her large frame, she could pack on the pounds without realizing it. And her love of rich foods and red wine meant that she had to work out every chance she got. Lucky for Tessa she hadn't gotten her mother's build, but that didn't mean she couldn't have a weight problem some day if she didn't watch it.

And Madeline, well, she seemed to be able to eat whatever she wanted, exercise or not, and still maintain that cute little curvy figure. Madeline was so comfortable with her body. She said she actually preferred a few extra pounds because she'd once heard that a little fullness in a woman's face would help hide the fine lines that develop with age. And of course Jack would think she was the hottest thing on earth no matter how much weight she gained or how many lines appeared on her face.

She did have to hand it to Madeline and Jack, though. They were one of those couples that gives you hope that true love really is out there and can be maintained past the first year of sex-crazed bliss everyone gets to enjoy.

"Poor Madeline, having to wait out there with The Ev— Wes's new wife," she said.

"That's got to be awkward," Marcus said.

"Madeline can handle it, though. She's pretty savvy when it comes to reading a situation."

Like the day Sharon had learned of the motion for change of custody. A week later, she still couldn't figure out what had happened. She'd said to Madeline, "Why would he try to take Tessa away from me? He knows a girl needs her mother."

Madeline said, "I think this new woman he's with has taken over every aspect of his life. I mean, think about it. Everything he's done since he met her has been bonkers. Leaving his wife of twelve years within the year, getting married four months after his divorce to you was final. And the advice he's been giving you lately about how to handle Tessa. I just don't think it's coming from him. It sounds like she's running the show."

"But why would he want another woman who's going to run the show?" she said. "That's what he complained about with me. That I had been raising Tessa like a single mom ever since she was born. That I neither wanted, nor needed, his input."

Cradling her cup of coffee and sitting on Sharon's new chaise lounge from Ethan Allen, one of her divorce presents to herself, Madeline curled her legs up under her. "But this one's got him fooled. You said she's a few years older than Wes, and a decade or so older than you. He thinks she's wise. She's got a Ph.D. She's one of those women who's smart enough to figure out how to make him think everything's his idea. And she thinks she's smart enough to know what's best for everyone, including Tessa."

When Sharon had looked at the motion again, she realized it wasn't in Wes's handwriting. It had to be The-Evil-Know-It-All's. Madeline had been right. But it was easy for Madeline to stay calm and rational. She had her fabulous engineer husband by her side sharing all of her burdens.

How many times had she witnessed Jack wrap his supportive arms around Madeline and say, "Take a deep breath, Babe. We'll figure this out together." Even over something as mundane as one of the kids having a tiff with a friend from playgroup. If Wes had propped her up that way over the years when she needed it, maybe things would be very different right now.

Marcus crossed his leg, leaving it spread wide, the way men usually do. "I like what you're wearing," he said. "Image matters."

"Thanks, I tried," she said. She felt a little bit like she was playing dress-up, especially with her shoes.

She and Madeline had gone shoe shopping together just a few days before. Madeline had first spotted the Cole Haan gray pumps with a bow on the toe on display at Macy's.

"Those would be perfect with your gray suit," Madeline had said. "You want to look like a professional, but motherly, too. So keep it feminine."

She'd bought them without trying on any other pair. She had to wear closed toe shoes anyway because of the black nail on her left foot's big toe. The day the custody motion came in the mail from Wes's attorney, she was so rattled when she was trying to make dinner that she'd dropped a can of baked beans on her toe. She couldn't believe how bad it hurt, or how much blood there was. Besides having to live with the ugly blackness for months, she'd probably lose the nail as well. Her feet had always been a point of pride, the one part of her body that had absolutely no flaws. Even Wes used to comment on how she could be a foot model, but now he'd taken that away from her along with everything else.

She leaned forward and tuned into what was going on at the front of the courtroom. Judge Francis was asking a rather beaten-down looking man if he was ever planning on holding down a job for longer than six months. Good. A female judge who's tough on men.

"Does she usually side with mothers?" she said.

"It could go either way with her. I've seen her come down hard on mothers and fathers, depending on who irritates her the most."

"How do I keep from irritating her?"

"Don't insult the other parent. Don't interrupt anyone. Calmly answer any questions she may ask you. Keep Tessa's best interest as your focus."

"That's exactly what Madeline told me. Don't make it about your ex or the new wife. Focus on your motherhood."

"She's right. Has she been through a divorce?"

"Yes. She met him while she was still in college. The marriage only lasted a year. They didn't have any kids together."

Sharon and Madeline had spent a lot of time dissecting that relationship in the early days of their friendship. It was a textbook example of what happens when love at first sight meets opposites attract. Reese was never going to be an adult. He spent their whole marriage in their garage practicing with his band. Madeline was already working on her master's degree. She was just too smart to end up as somebody's groupie.

"Divorces aren't usually as messy when kids aren't involved," Marcus said.

"Yeah. No kids, no reason to keep in touch." Sharon sighed. "Now she's married to an engineer who's perfect for her and terrific with their kids."

Marcus was looking over her head now. Obviously he'd lost interest.

Yes, Madeline would never have to worry about her motherhood being threatened by anyone. She would never truly know how Sharon felt.

"What's our strategy again?" she said.

"We'll focus on the fact that Tessa has always lived with you. That's her comfort zone. To change her living situation now would only add volatility to her life. And as everyone knows, the teenage years are already volatile enough."

"Right, right." She bit her bottom lip.

She was indeed Tessa's comfort zone. In fact, she had spent Tessa's whole life making her comfortable. That's what parents are for, isn't it? As a matter of fact, she thought Madeline and Jack could be a little too hard on their kids at times. They expected so much from them for their ages. She'd always been a big believer that childhood only comes around once. They have the rest of their lives to be adults.

She'd definitely allowed Tessa to just be a kid. She couldn't imagine The-Evil-Know-It-All sitting beside Tessa on the Millennium at Cedar Point, screaming together with their hands thrown in the air. She and Wes had taken Tessa to that amusement park every year since Tessa was tall enough to ride the rides. She knew how to have fun, all right. In fact, that was one of the reasons Wes had been attracted to her in the first place. He had watched her sing her sexiest version of "Makin' Whoopee" at that karaoke bar after she'd had too much to drink with some friends. He'd complimented her on her performance and offered to buy her another dirty martini. They'd been inseparable after that night.

When had Wes stopped wanting to have fun? Sure, things had gotten more and more tense between them over the years. But it was a long-term marriage. Didn't all couples eventually learn that some of the traits that originally drew them to each other became the exact source of frustration later? Wasn't there a "flipside" lesson here? A taking the good with the bad approach?

When they first met, she'd been so impressed that he could sell any house to anyone. He had such a way with people. But then, in the last few years, she'd wanted to throw his cell phone against the wall every time it rang. They might be driving to dinner, or sitting in the bleachers watching Tessa's track meet, or hosting a dinner party, but he would always answer that thing. Her skin crawled when she had to listen to him schmooze yet another client in the exact same way she'd heard a thousand times before, and she'd tell him so. Maybe she could have kept some of her opinions to herself, but how could he possibly have gone from a woman like her to a woman like The-Evil-Know-It-All? Where she was tall, athletic, and full of life, the other woman was tiny, pinched, and bookish.

She looked over at Wes. She wanted to slap that mole right off of his chin.

How could he put her in this situation? And The Evil-Know-It-All? That was even worse. Who did she think she was? She was a mother, too. She should know that you don't mess with another woman's child. It was hard enough for her to push away images of Wes and the petite college professor going at it in the sack, while she was still married to him no less. But it was even harder to overcome the idea of The-Evil-Know-It-All mothering Tessa. Hadn't she been the one to mother Tessa for twelve years before the other woman came along? That woman hadn't been around for the childhood illnesses, the elementary school plays, the first crush. And besides all that, Tessa had come out of her body, for god's sake. Didn't that warrant some special consideration for her? She glanced across the aisle at Wes to shoot him a dirty look, but he was whispering something to his leggy attorney.

Marcus must have sensed she was working herself up again because he reached over and gently squeezed her forearm. When she looked at him, he smiled and winked. Until then, she hadn't noticed how translucent his blue eyes were. Or how his thick mop of black hair starkly contrasted them. Blushing, she turned away.

Just how young was he anyway? Plenty of women her age dated younger men. Why the hell shouldn't she?

CHAPTER 7

Carol

Standing on the courthouse steps, Carol snapped her cell phone shut and took a deep breath. The day was as clear as her mind now, the sky deep blue and cloudless overhead, with no breeze to speak of. She felt better after talking to Dr. Martin, though she'd been told that the goal of therapy wasn't to feel better so much as to get better, and sometimes that involved feeling one's pain.

Right now, though, she was determined to enjoy the buoyant feeling that resulted from getting rid of all this unproductive anger. Dr. Martin had a gift for cutting through the crap, as her stepdaughter might say. Tessa might have used a more vulgar term, but in this case, the teenager's choice would have been apropos—her own thought processes had become tinged with anger since her first husband's sudden death nearly three years ago. Light years ago, it seemed. Still, dark thoughts intruded in times of stress, resulting in embarrassing outbursts. It was time she started letting her anger go, once and for all. She'd let it float away, as Dr. Martin had said, like clouds dissolving into mist.

She wouldn't have minded a few soft, white clouds to

shield her from the sun, though—her face was starting to flush, a sure sign of a hot flash coming on. After unbuttoning her jacket, she tossed her phone into the roomy black vinyl bag that doubled as her briefcase and purse.

Why other women carried two bags was beyond her—besides the expense and time involved in purchasing two items, there was the inconvenience of having to manage two when one would do just as well. She slipped out of her jacket and felt immediate relief. Ever since Dr. Kennedy had taken her off hormone replacement therapy, she'd had one annoying hot flash after another. This one was especially bad. The white cotton shirt she'd thrown on this morning was already drenched under the arms.

She should have tucked another shirt into her bag, but she'd been in such a rush this morning, trying to get Wes to line up his ducks in a row before the hearing. He'd scowled and dragged his feet like a child forced to wash behind his ears. That wasn't like Wes. Usually he was more attentive to the details that mattered to the "two most important girls" in his life. Girl wasn't a word she'd ever have chosen to describe her adult self, but Wes said he loved bringing out the passionate teenager she'd never had a chance to be, the smart, sexy girl who looked great in the slinky silk camisoles he bought her. And of course Wes adored Tessa. But today, though he faced the possibility that the judge might rule in favor of Sharon, Wes seemed strangely unmotivated to fight for custody of his only daughter.

She shrugged and, draping her limp jacket over her arm, turned to go back into the much cooler courthouse, then hesitated. A sudden craving for a cigarette was starting to outweigh her desire for air conditioning. She'd quit smoking in January, after she and Wes had decided to marry. She'd compared the costs of quitting a thirty-five-year-old habit to endangering the asthmatic Tessa and got a prescription for the patch. Now, four months later, the patch was gone, but the cravings had returned.

Fierce cravings, in fact. Cravings that a wad of Nicorette would not quell. Furthermore, the nicotine-laced gum made her feel like a cow chewing its cud. That might be all right in the privacy of her home or office, but she refused to stuff a lump of the vile-tasting stuff between her teeth and return chomping to the waiting area, where Madeline Greenfield, she of the sharp eyes and stolen glances, would likely form a negative opinion of her friend Sharon's arch-rival.

Carol's hand reached deep inside her black bag, into the zippered compartment where she'd hidden a few emergency Marlboros in a plastic tampon holder. She hadn't bothered to slit the bag's lining, as she'd done as a teenager. Wes, unlike her mother, wasn't the type to go through her things. Even if he happened to come upon the tampon holder while looking in her bag for a misplaced set of keys, Wes would never question why she was still carrying tampons, though she hadn't had a period in months.

Without removing the tampon holder from her bag, she took out one cigarette. Just one. She'd hold it between her fingers for a moment, as she had done so often in the past. The cigarette felt lighter than she'd expected. The tobacco inside the thin tissue rustled when her fingers compressed it, dry and stale after months in her bag. She ought to throw away this nasty bit of temptation and go back into the courthouse.

She looked at the cigarette between her fingers, so slim and white, so light. Like a thin, cylindrical cloud. A memory of nicotine-induced well-being rushed back to her, beckoning like a seductive man in a silk suit—like her Wes. She could never say no to Wes. Only once had she done so, after she'd learned he was married. Even then she'd taken him back, but not till he'd divorced Sharon and begged forgiveness.

"Why not," she said to the cigarette. Hadn't she conquered her anger just moments ago? She could smoke one cigarette and never touch another. She had the power. She was in control.

She trotted down the courthouse steps, out of the sunshine and out of sight of any snooping eyes that might spy her indiscretion. Madeline Greenfield's, for instance. The cigarette was indeed stale, but she smoked it down to the filter, in the cool of the shaded side of the courthouse, where she milled around with the other smokers who'd been exiled from the building by harsh stares and harsher statutes.

After locking the banned cell phone in Wes's Mercedes and inserting a Tic-Tac between her lips, she made her way up the courthouse steps, glad she'd worn her sturdy, thick-soled slip-ons. She proceeded through the foyer, past Madeline Greenfield, who was now engrossed in a paperback—something as frothy as Madeline herself, no doubt.

She hurried down the corridor toward the restroom so she could wash thoroughly before sitting down next to Madeline. If only she'd slipped a bottle of spray cologne into her bag before she'd elbowed Wes out the door this morning. Well, perhaps she'd find some scented liquid soap in the women's restroom. That would do the trick.

Her rubber soles squeaked as they struck the hard floor, and twice she nearly tripped. She reminded herself to pick up her feet, that these weren't her usual professional shoes. Ordinarily she wore smooth-soled Liz Claiborne pumps with one-inch heels, enclosed toes and heels, no frippery whatsoever—no bows or flowers or buckles to send the wrong message to the dean. Today, though, she'd grabbed the first pair of black shoes in her closet, her "dyke shoes," as a brash young male colleague had tactlessly called them. The unisex shoes, as she preferred to think of them, were reserved for days when she had a lot of walking to do, at a conference in New York City, say, when she was away from Wes, who liked seeing her in "something more feminine."

She pushed open the swinging door and was delighted to discover that, except for a pair of shadowed feet beneath one of the two stall doors, the restroom was empty. She was craving another cigarette, even though the first had made her lightheaded and slightly nauseous. When this woman left, perhaps she'd slip into a stall and indulge in another puff or two.

She had to be careful, though. Those feet might belong to Sharon, who'd be sure to tattle to her attorney, who'd then raise a ruckus in the courtroom. Or they might belong to Stephanie Powell, Wes's attorney, whom she'd so confidently assured of her victory over tobacco. She couldn't risk another humiliation today, especially one caused by a twenty-nine-year old.

Why Wes had chosen Stephanie as his attorney mystified her. She'd told him the young woman was too inexperienced, but Wes had waved away her concerns. "She's the best in town," he'd said. "A real custody shark." Carol thought Stephanie looked more like an Ionic column—nearly six feet tall, with no curves to speak of, at least none visible beneath her impeccably tailored power suits and impossibly high-heeled pumps.

Unfortunately she hadn't noticed Stephanie's shoes this morning. She'd been too busy gaping at the woman's coloring to notice her feet. She'd seen Stephanie before, of course, but today, in the bright light that came in through the courthouse windows, her lashes had looked almost transparent, and her pale, reddish-blond mane had glowed like a golden waterfall catching the sun's last rays—a simple and beautiful coiffure, but far too dramatic for a woman wanting to influence a judge, especially a female judge.

Rather than risk being caught smoking, Carol went straight to the sink nearest the door, determined to wash away the evidence of tobacco smoke.

A toilet flushed. The stall door opened. No six-foot alabaster Amazon appeared. No plump, overdressed ex-wife. Only a slim, tanned woman of about forty, wearing a sleeveless lavender dress that strained across her thighs. Her hair had been plaited into hundreds of tiny braids ending in multicolored beads that clacked together, like ice-glazed branches in a strong wind.

The woman with the braids bustled to the sink next to Carol's and began humming as she turned on the water, smiling, as though they were old friends.

"Nice day," the woman said, smiling even more broadly. The gap between her upper incisors made her look not much older than Tessa.

"Lovely," Carol said as a shiver shook her body. Not only did she have to endure annoying hot flashes but follow-up chills as well.

"You okay?" The woman's glossy forehead rose along with her thin eyebrows. "You look real pale. You're not gonna faint on me, are you?"

Carol shook her head as she pulled her jacket back on. "I'm fine."

"You sure? Cause I'm a nurse, and I know light-headed when I see it."

"I just had a cigarette," she said, surprised at her own candor. "The first one since last winter."

"And it went straight to your brain, didn't it?" The woman shook her head, which made the beads clack louder.

Carol nodded again, ready to end the girl talk.

"If you don't mind me saying so," the woman went on, "you look a little green. You want a Tums? I got a roll in here." She held up a pink patent-leather purse.

"No, I'm fine." Carol gripped the sink. "I just need to splash some cold water on my face."

"Well, you don't look fine." The woman squirted a puddle of pink liquid soap into her damp hands. "You're supposed to wash hands for twenty seconds, enough time to sing Happy Birthday, but who's gonna do that while they're washing hands in a public restroom?" The woman laughed and shook her head and turned back to Carol. Would she never give up? She was worse than Dr. Martin. "You here for domestic court?"

"A custody case." Carol pressed hard on the soap dispenser and then turned on the water, which gushed out so fast it quickly filled the small porcelain sink, though there was no stopper.

"Grandchild?"

"Certainly not." She stepped back from the miniature Niagara Falls, which was soaking her jacket. "My stepdaughter. My husband is asking for custody."

"Uh-huh," the woman said, rinsing her hands. "What about the mother?"

Carol struggled to get control of the gushing water. "She's had difficulty managing Tessa. The girl is fourteen."

"Fourteen, huh? You wait a year, see if Dad still wants custody." The woman reached for a paper towel. "Fifteen's the worst, if you ask me. But you didn't ask me. My kids are always telling me to keep my opinions to myself, but I never do." *Clack, clack, clackety clack.*

Carol washed her hands and face and turned off the spitting tap. Liquid soap stung her eyes. By the time she'd groped to the paper towel dispenser, the woman with the braids was gone. For an instant, she wondered if she'd imagined her.

Frowning, she went back to the sink where the woman had stood—it was still wet. Someone had used it moments ago. She was being ridiculous, imagining things. She needed to freshen up her appearance and get back to that wretched waiting area, in case Wes needed her.

She looked into the water-spattered mirror over the sink. The woman with the braids was right—she did look pale and sickly. Worse, wisps of hair had pulled out of the elastic band and were now springing up around her face, creating a dark, wiry halo. Her hair stylist had suggested she tame the gray by adding chestnut highlights or perhaps covering the coarse gray strands with dark ash-brown dye, but she'd laughed aloud at that. "Tie myself down to monthly hair-coloring? Have you lost your mind?" Perhaps that had been a little too blunt, but, really, the woman had no clue about a tenured professor's priorities.

She sighed and groped in her black bag for a hairbrush. She was nearly as angry now as she'd been when she'd called Dr. Martin, and she looked like a crazy lady, with her hair askew and her jacket damp from the self-imposed Niagara.

After easing the satin-covered elastic band onto her wrist, she brushed out her hair, parted it in the middle, pulled it back, and nudged the band onto the smoothed column of hair that ended just below the collar of her damp jacket.

She took a final look in the mirror, blinked, and looked again. It was as if she was seeing her mother's face. The same high cheekbones and hazel-green eyes. But her mother's hair had been blond, blond that came out of a bottle.

For an instant, she thought she smelled Chanel No 5, her mother's scent, chosen because it was "Marilyn's perfume." Her mother had adored Marilyn Monroe but despaired over her only daughter, with her slat-like build and stubborn lack of interest in fashion. "If I like it, you have to reject it," her mother had said. More than once.

She blinked away the vision and turned sideways, to be sure she'd caught every stray strand. "Don't skin your hair back like that," her mother's voice said. "You don't have the face for a severe style, not without makeup. Now if you'd let me—"

But she hadn't let her mother put makeup on her or do her nails, not after the incident in the kitchen, when her mother had grown so enraged at her adolescent defiance that she'd kicked her daughter in the ribs with her pointed pumps while Carol lay curled in a ball on the floor.

She felt her anger rising, her face flushing, her muscles tightening. Her legs started to buckle. She grabbed for the edge of the sink to steady herself. Her mouth was filing with saliva, and she could feel the strong black coffee she'd downed on her way to the courthouse pressing its way upward. She dashed into the stall that the woman with the clacking braids had vacated, hung her head over the toilet and retched.

CHAPTER 8

Tessa

Tessa was hoping to make a fast dash out of fourth period so she could sit with Em during lunch, but Mrs. Sinclair took her aside after social studies and jumped her case for not paying attention in class.

"Look, I'm sorry," Tessa said, "but besides the track meet after school—and I absolutely have to win all my events, because I've had two bad meets in a row—my mother and father are in court today, arguing over who gets custody of me from now on. So that may have me a little distracted." That last part came out kind of sarcastic, but Mrs. G didn't seem to notice.

"Oh, my goodness," Mrs. Sinclair said. "That certainly explains why you've been tuning out." She excused Tessa to go to lunch, but by then everybody else had already thundered into the cafeteria, including Em.

But at least good old Em had waited for her at the back of the lunch line. When Tessa tapped her on the back, Em startled and then squealed. "Tesseract! Where have you been? I thought maybe you heard from your mom and freaked out."

Tesseract was her nickname from sixth grade, when they'd all had to read A Wrinkle in Time. Nobody but Em was allowed to call Tessa Tesseract, and only then when there were no cute boys around.

"Chill," she said and stepped in line behind Em. "It's all good. Sinclair just ripped me a new one for zoning out in class again."

Em rolled her eyes. "Like you could help it today."

"I know. She's so lame." She pointed to a table a few feet away. "And watch it with the Tesseract, okay? Tommy might hear."

"Has he asked you out yet?"

"Shut up," she said, to get Em to change the subject. And Em did shut up for a second or two but not much more.

"So—" Em unscrewed the little tube of lip gloss that dangled from her Dooney and Bourke. "You in a better mood now?"

Tessa pretended to survey the whiteboard menu, although she really wasn't hungry. "I'm fine. Seriously."

"Right." Em re-screwed her gloss tube. "Like you were so fine this morning."

"I am. Truly."

"Uh-huh." Em took a tray from the stack near the steam table and stood on tiptoe, straining to see what was in the stainless steel rectangles. Tessa got it now—Em, who was only five feet, had worn the platform sandals to look taller, not because she had doggy doo on her Nikes or had seen the look in Seventeen. Plus, she'd used one of those self-tanners—there were yellowish-brown streaks up and down her legs. The streaks hadn't been all that noticeable this morning, but they looked like crap in the glare of the fluorescents.

"What's with the tan?" Tessa said.

Em's eyes got big. "Does it look that bad?"

"It's...no, but it's kind of splotchy. Why don't you go to the tanning booth instead? It's so much more even."

"You know why. My mother thinks tanning causes skin cancer."

So did Carol, but Tessa's mom had overruled that idea, and her dad hadn't said word one about it. Now she and Mom went to the tanning booth weekly. "Why don't you just go with your pale skin, then? Like Nicole Kidman?"

"Nicole Kidman has long legs," Em said. "Like yours. Mine are too freaking short and muscular."

Tessa shook her head. Em was obviously just trying to imitate her. "Emulate" was the word Carol had used, along with some quote about imitation being the sincerest form of flattery. And, really, Tessa was sort of flattered, but Em just didn't have the height to pull off a whole supermodel look—she was sort of cute in a compact, cheerleadery way, and as Tessa had told her a gazillion times, she ought to play up her cuteness and not go for the drama. But would Em listen? She was as bad as Mom sometimes.

"Crap," Em said, "they're all out of pocket sandwiches."

"Whatever." Tessa shrugged. "I'm not all that hungry."

"You have to eat something. We have the meet after school."

"Maybe some yogurt."

"And some chicken nuggets. You need the protein."

"I'm not that hungry."

Em put the nuggets on her tray. "If your mom was here, she'd make you eat."

"Well, you're not my mom. And, no, she wouldn't make me eat. She'd say, imagine how those'll look on your thighs."

"I doubt it. Like, last week? When she took us to Wendy's after practice? She let you order Biggie fries and a Frosty and didn't say a word."

"We'd just run track for an hour. My mom knew I'd already burned off a ton of calories."

"Maybe. But I think she's going through her let-Tessa-do-whatever-she-wants phase."

"Huh?" Tessa took two containers of honey-mustard to go with the nuggets.

"She's slacking with you right now because she's afraid to lose you like she lost your dad. But that won't last. If she gets more time with you, she'll start coming down on you again." Em picked up a dish of green beans, put it back.

"You think you know everything, don't you?"

"Not really."

"Yes, you do. You're worse than Carol about that. You're so freaking smug. Like you're the world's greatest authority on divorce."

"I know a lot more than you do, Tessa. Admit it."

She kept her mouth shut while they crossed over to the cold table, trying not to show how pissed off she was. She knew Em was right, but she wanted to argue anyway.

"Okay," Tessa said, "let me ask you this. Who's stricter? Your mom and stepdad, or your dad?"

"Are you kidding?" Em took a salad and a packet of low-fat ranch dressing. "My mother. Both my dads are, like, total pushovers. Well, not pushovers, but a lot easier to budge. My mom's a concrete wall."

"So why don't you live with your dad, then?"

"Because," Em said, "they hardly ever place teenage girls with their dads."

"But they do sometimes, don't they?"

"I guess. I mean, the mom would have to be really whacked out or something, or not want the daughter to live with her...you're not thinking of asking to go live with your dad, are you?"

"Not really."

"Well, don't. And whatever you do, don't say you'd rather live with your mom, either. That'll screw up the whole process."

Tessa nodded as she took a yogurt container. "Really," she said, "I have no clue about how all this legal stuff works. I just—"

"You just want this all to be over, and for them to decide on something that works for you. So—" Em took a tall bottle of water and handed Tessa a half-pint milk carton. "Never let them make you tell who you want to live with. Make the court decide. But load the deck. Make more positive comments about the parent you'd rather spend more time with. That way you'll get to spend plenty of time with both and you won't have to pick. I did that with my guardian ad litem and he totally got it."

Tessa set the milk on her tray. All of a sudden she felt queasy. What if her mom loaded the deck? Or her father? And who did she want to spend more time with? She loved both her parents. How could they ask her to make this impossible choice? Would they?

"Tessa?" Em nudged her. "You're supposed to pay Mrs. Fiedler now."

"Huh? Oh, right." She handed today's parent-volunteer a five and waited for her change, glad it wasn't her mom sitting there. If her mom didn't work full-time, Tessa was pretty sure she'd be at her school all day in addition to hanging out with her and Em at home or at the mall or even at the movies. It was so humiliating.

Her mom had better not try that when she brought Tommy home—well, if she brought him home. Maybe next week she'd bring him home right after school, before her mom got home from work, or while her mom was resting in her room. Her mom did a lot of resting these days.

"Where do you want to sit?" Emily was looking desperate, struggling to balance her lunch plus the bottle of water on her warped tray.

"Over there." Tessa pointed to the table opposite the one where Tommy Leonetti sat with his buddies. "Let me sit on the end, okay? At an angle. Like we did last week."

"So you can flirt with Tommy, right?"

"Shut up," Tessa said. "It's totally harmless."

She positioned her tray so that Tommy couldn't help but see her. She dipped a chicken nugget into the honey-mustard and then licked it off the nugget and then off her fingers, giving him a sidelong glance while she ate. Then she looked quickly away and pulled her straw out of her milk.

"Em," she whispered.

"Oh, right." Em, who sat with her back to Tommy, was supposed to drop a napkin or a fork at the signal—when Tessa took her straw out of her milk—to see if he was looking at her, and if so, how.

"He's elbowing Kyle Brooks," Em whispered after the fork-drop. "And now Kyle's looking at you, too. Well, they're looking and eating French fries, which they're dipping in ketchup."

"How?"

"How are they dipping, you mean?"

She nodded. "Yeah. Slow and sexy or just ordinary?"

Em rolled her eyes. "I don't know. Ordinary, I guess."

Tessa took another chicken nugget, dipped it in the honey-mustard, licked off the thick yellow goo and pushed back from the table to show off the contours of her new push-up bra, which was softly padded to make her look fuller. She repeated the dipping movements again, but this time, while she was bringing the nugget to her mouth in slow-mo, a drop of honey-mustard fell on her new shoe. She pulled her foot back really fast, so no one would see how clumsy she'd been, and bit into the nugget, acting as if it tasted as good as the filet mignon her mom had splurged on for last night's dinner.

"My god, Tessa," Em said. "Bring it down a notch."

She laughed and pulled her straw out to signal another drop. Em sighed and dropped her napkin. After bending to pick it up, Em looked toward Tommy's table but turned back to Tessa, eyes wide, like she'd just flunked all her nine-week tests.

"What?" Tessa said.

"Duck," Em called out, but by then it was too late. Kyle and Tommy were already flinging plastic spoonfuls of ketchup at them, mostly at Tessa. One landed on the shoulder of her hot pink t-shirt. The other fell on the laces of her all-white Nike Shox. Before she could stop herself, she let out a long, loud scream.

"Chill out," Em said, grabbing a napkin. "Mr. Schilling's on his way over."

"Forget Schilling," she said. "Look at my shirt! And my freaking shoes!"

CHAPTER 9

Carol

After she'd emptied her stomach, Carol continued to retch until she was spitting nothing but bile into the toilet. She stepped back from the toilet, thinking she had nothing more to vomit up, and hit her shoulder on the hook that stuck out from the stall door. That brought out a loud spew of profanity, which was rare. Ordinarily she kept a close watch on her speech. Today, though, she needed the release.

Her stomach contracted again, but she forced herself to stand upright, determined not to vomit again. She took a deep breath and then another, trying to will the nausea away. Her eyes were watering, and the stall reeked of vomit. Thank God no one had walked in while she was puking her guts out, as Tessa would say. Poor Tessa had a nervous stomach, too, sometimes vomiting in the mornings, before high-stakes tests.

If Tessa would only begin to prepare a few days before a major exam, she'd have no reason to feel those "butterflies." Carol had told her so, in fact, but that had gone nowhere. Then Wes got into the act. After sitting his daughter down at their kitchen table, he told her that she was to do her homework where he could see her, not in her room, where the computer and telephone were constant temptations. Wes had sounded again like the firm but caring father-figure he'd been to her boys after her Lyle's untimely death—exactly what she felt Tessa needed.

Sure enough, after a few weeks of this regimen, Tessa began to relax before tests, and once she relaxed, her performance improved. "Success breeds success," she'd told Tessa. "Now you're on your way to making honor roll." And success had bred more success. Not once in the last month had Tessa thrown up before an exam. Her grades were improving as well. She hadn't made honor roll this past nine weeks, but her name had appeared on the lesser merit roll for the first time in a full year.

Thinking about Tessa allowed her to focus on something other than her own nausea, a technique Dr. Martin had recommended, along with deep breathing. "If possible, when you feel anxious or annoyed, think of someone you care about, someone you might help out of a similar spot. That allows you to let go of your feelings of helplessness."

Did Dr. Martin see her has a helpless victim? Certainly she'd been victimized in her past—by her own mother, in fact. The bile rose in her throat again, and in spite of her determination not to vomit, she retched again, this time missing the toilet and throwing up down the front of her shirt.

She no longer looked even remotely presentable, and she had to remedy that, and as soon as possible. The hearing might be over any minute now, and though she felt almost certain she and Wes would win custody of Tessa, there was always the off-chance that Stephanie Powell might bungle it, or that Wes would fail to display the requisite passion. The judge—herself a woman and a mother, according to Carol's careful research— might think he was less than committed, and in fact, Wes had seemed lukewarm about Tessa's coming to live with them from the start. He kept saying that they were newlyweds who needed time to adjust to each other, just as Tessa needed time to adjust to them. And that was true, of course. But Tessa was starting high school in the fall. The girl needed a firm hand now, before she ruined her chances at getting into a top college by spending all her free time tanning and getting bikini waxes with her mother.

She took a quick survey of her appearance. Her jacket and trousers were still clean though somewhat rumpled, but the white shirtfront was soaked through with a yellowish stream of vomit. What to do? She took another series of deep breaths, this time focusing even harder on helping Wes and Tessa. She visualized herself at Tessa's Yale graduation, giving the keynote speech.

At last the nausea passed. She looked down at her bag, which she'd set beside the toilet. It bore damp speckles of bile mixed with what looked like thin snot. So did her shoes. Sighing, she pulled off a length of tissue-thin toilet paper and wiped off her shoes and bag, thankful the bag was made of vinyl. Her stomach acid might have permanently etched leather.

She tossed the vomit-soaked wad of paper into the toilet and unrolled another, but no amount of dabbing would save the shirt. Carefully she removed her jacket, which she hung on the hook. Perhaps she could rinse out the shirtfront in the sink and dry the wet spot with the hand-dryer. But she'd seen no hand-dryer, only stiff, brown paper towels. In any case, the shirt was made of heavy oxford cloth. It would take a long time to dry, and even if it did, residual vomit-stink would remain. She had to get rid of the shirt.

She could stash it in the trash can and perhaps retrieve it later—it was a perfectly good shirt, after all, if a little worn at the cuffs. Or she could wash it out with soap and...what? What would she put it in, dripping wet? And what in heaven's name would she do for another shirt? Dash out in her underwear and pantsuit and buy another?

Fortunately, under her shirt was the camisole Wes had bought her for her birthday, delicate white silk topped with a girlish row of black eyelet lace, through which a white satin ribbon had been woven, ending in a tiny bow secured with an even tinier cluster of pearls. Acceptable as underwear, certainly, but as an alternative to a sensible shirt or tailored blouse?

Stephanie Powell sometimes wore camisoles under her power suits. When Carol had commented to Wes on that, in private, after a consultation in Stephanie's office, he'd said he liked the look. "I think it softens her edges a little, makes her seem tough but not hard-edged. Perfect for a family-practice lawyer." And of course Tessa and her friends often wore camisoles under jackets, layering the frivolous with the sensible. Furthermore, this camisole—except for the row of black lace—was simple and modest. Its one-inch straps and high bodice completely covered her bra and any hint of cleavage. In fact, with her jacket buttoned, the camisole would look to the casual observer as if she were wearing a sleeveless blouse with a bit of lace trim.

If only the camisole weren't lacy. That communicated

weakness, a willingness to give in, as women had for millennia. For an instant she thought of ripping off the offending row of lace, but the fragile silk would never withstand that. She'd look like one of the homeless in her shredded top and damp jacket. And her hair had come undone again. She should have spent more time on her appearance this morning—more time on herself, if fact. Wasn't that what Dr. Martin was always preaching, in between telling her to focus on helping others? What did the woman want her to do—become a selfish narcissist, focused only on her appearance and on "having a little fun now and again," or a selfless, caring woman who looked out for the welfare of others?

Quickly, with rough motions, she began unbuttoning the shirt. When she got it off, she'd dump it in the trash can, along with the annoying satin-covered elastic band that simply would not hold her slick hair in place. Better to let her hair graze her shoulders than to look unkempt. After all, Stephanie Powell wore her hair long and sleek, and she, apparently, was doing all right.

Perhaps she'd been a little too hasty in her judgment of Stephanie. It might be that one touch of the feminine might disarm others in a positive way. A peek of lace could, for instance, cause an opponent in court—Sharon's equally young male attorney, for instance—to underestimate a female attorney.

Inhaling deeply, she stripped off the shirt and, exhaling slowly, grabbed her jacket from the hook.

CHAPTER 10

Madeline

Madeline set her book in her lap. Her stomach was starting to rumble and groan. At least Carol Wheaton wasn't sitting beside her right now to hear it. She'd stomped down the hallway about an hour ago, then after a bit had stomped back by and headed down the alcove across from the chairs toward the restrooms.

Madeline was stretching when a tall woman with Jamaican braids and beach-ready flip-flops walked out of the courtroom doors and in the direction of the restrooms. She liked the way the woman's hair swung behind her, the beads clicking against each other. It sounded like a musical duet as the beads harmonized with the slap of her flip flops. She'd almost had her hair braided like that once, when she and Jack went to Aruba without the kids for the week, but she'd decided against it. Jack hadn't seemed enthused. He enjoyed looping his fingers around her silky curls when they made love, and he was such a creature of habit.

She brought the book up to her face and inhaled. During the reprieve from Carol's intense presence, Madeline had been able to pull her book out of her purse and lose herself in it.

Holding the closed paperback with both hands, she kneaded the ends back and forth like dough. She relished the whole experience of falling in love with a book. Completing her ritual, she fanned the pages with her thumb. She was halfway through now.

A friend from playgroup had recommended it to her. "Don't let the title fool you," Sadie told her. It's really smart, not fluff." Madeline had been skeptical at first, but since it was a loaner, she'd decided to give it a shot. And she was glad she had. She loved the idea of all these different women in the book coming together - neighbors, friends, fellow book club members. The book traced all the significant events in their lives. And they were always there for each other. Madeline believed in the solidarity of women. She never ceased to be amazed at how women's friendships possessed a mystical quality that men just didn't seem to get.

Like the time Sharon had stayed with Jack and her when Wes first moved out. Tessa was at her dad's for a long weekend, and Sharon was just too raw to stay in that big house alone. After she and Sharon had spent a few days together, Madeline started her period early. She knew from taking out the guest bathroom trash that Sharon was already on her period, so when her own cycle started five days early, on the tail of Sharon's, she marched into the guest room holding a tampon in front of her like a torch. "You made me start early, you stinker!"

Sharon hesitated for only a second. "You look like the damn Statue of Liberty standing there!"

They laughed so hard Madeline fell to the floor and

Sharon wet herself. It was the first time Sharon had laughed, or even smiled, in weeks.

Jack walked by the open door of the guest room to see what the commotion was, and when he saw them there doubled over, he smirked and shook his head. Later she told him about the cycles-in-sync part. His reaction was the usual raised eyebrows. He didn't fully get her connection with Sharon, but he wasn't threatened by it either.

Just this morning he'd offered to go in late to work so he could drop Noah off at kindergarten and Olivia at drop-in day care. "Just concentrate on Sharon," he'd said. She wanted to jump his bones every time he was kind to her friends, even when he really didn't know them that well or didn't particularly care for their personality quirks. Like Sharon.

Jack thought Sharon was a little flighty. And needy. Especially since the divorce. But he knew Madeline would never give up on her, and he respected her loyalty. No different than his loyalty to Pete Rose when the Cincinnati Reds' all-time hits leader was accused of betting on baseball. Jack was crushed when he saw the shocked face of his favorite player from childhood splattered all over the TV and The Columbus Dispatch. But he would go to his grave believing Pete Rose should still be elected to the Baseball Hall of Fame. Jack understood that her friends were friends for life. And he trusted her intuition about people.

Right now her intuition was telling her she needed to find something to eat. She checked her watch - 11:30 a.m. What could be taking so long? She didn't want to leave in search of a vending machine in case Sharon came out and found her gone. She re-crossed her legs and silent-tapped her slingback in the air again. What to do, what to do. Maybe she'd read for a bit longer. Just as she opened her book, her stomach growled again.

At least she'd be able to get something to eat by two o'clock. If Sharon was still stuck in the courtroom by then, she'd have to leave to pick up Noah and Olivia and take them to Tessa's track meet so she and her friend Emily could watch them until Madeline was through with court or Jack was through with work. It was a perfect plan. Tessa adored Noah and Olivia, and they loved watching her compete. Fortunately, Madeline had remembered to throw their noisemakers and pom poms into the back of her car on her way to court this morning.

She glanced up from her book when she heard the clicking braids and slapping flip-flops again. "Good book?" the woman said, stopping in front of her.

"It's terrific." Madeline held the cover up for her to read.

"Angry Housewives Eating Bon-Bons." The woman let out a deep, throaty chuckle. "Have to put that one on my list. Now I'm divorced, I got a lot more time to do what I want to do. My ex never let me read. He wanted all my attention on him. So, these women really angry?"

"No, well, at times. When it's appropriate, I guess. The title really doesn't do the book justice."

"Isn't that the truth for us all?" she said. There was that laugh again.

"Right, you can't judge a book." Madeline didn't bother to finish the cliché.

"You sure can't," the woman said, lips pursed, shaking her head from side to side. "You have a good day, now."

"You, too," Madeline said. She watched the courtroom doors close.

She liked that woman. So open. And that laugh. It had reverberated all the way through Madeline's bones. She admired the fact that the woman wore flip-flops to court. She was just going to be who she was, not putting on a show for anybody. Although Madeline appreciated the que sera sera attitude, she could never pull it off. She was far too strategic and goal-oriented. Even now she wanted to get back to her book while she had time to read. There were three other novels sitting on her nightstand that she promised herself she'd finish by the end of the month.

But before she could get back into what the housewives were doing, she heard a rhythmic thumping coming toward her from the restroom alcove. Without looking up, she knew what was making that sound—Carol Wheaton's thick-soled clunkers.

When she saw the woman herself, Madeline almost dropped her book. Ms. Wheaton's tight ponytail was gone. Her hair was soft and loose. Her white buttoned-down shirt had been replaced by a silk cami. Madeline flashed to one of her favorite Cheers episodes. Lilith, the repressed psychiatrist with dark, tightly-pulled back hair, decides she wants to attract her colleague Frasier. Rebecca, the girlie girl, helps transform her into a sex kitten by pulling out her bobby pins and pulling off her suit jacket to expose the feminine layer underneath.

Ms. Wheaton, head held high, floated past Madeline down the long hallway toward the metal detectors. Was that vomit she smelled?

CHAPTER 11

Adele

Adele limped across her office and opened the top drawer of her desk.

"Lauren," she said to her client, who sat in the saffron yellow chair opposite, "I'm going to refer you to a doctor I've worked with for years." She pulled a business card from the drawer. "I think it's a good idea for you to have a checkup as soon as possible. If you need anti-depressant medication, she'll discuss it with you." She limped back to her client, wincing in her too-tight Anne Kleins, and handed Lauren the card. "Here's Dr. Prescott's phone number and address. When you call, be sure to tell her receptionist I referred you."

Lauren looked at the card and nodded, still a little teary from their session. Then she looked up. "I was wondering," she said in a quavering voice, "if we could we make next week's appointment for later? I thought I could do mornings, but that doesn't work for me, with the kids and all. I mean, it was nice of you to work me in at the last minute, but—" She shrugged.

Adele felt like sighing. Why hadn't she just said no to Lauren's request in the first place? Usually she didn't take clients on Wednesdays before one, but she'd made an exception for Lauren, against her better judgment, and, as it turned out, the time slot hadn't worked for Lauren, either. "Why don't you call me after you've talked to Dr. Prescott," she said. "We'll make another appointment then."

"Do I really need to see someone else?"

"I'm a clinical psychologist, Lauren. I can't prescribe medication."

"Oh. Right. I forgot." Lauren picked up her faded denim bag and slung it over her shoulder as if it weighed a thousand pounds. "Talk to you later, then."

She ushered Lauren to the empty waiting room and shut the door softly behind her, careful not to slam it, then retraced her painful steps. As soon as she heard Lauren pull the outer door shut, she sank into the Aeron desk chair that Roger had bought her.

Roger. What was wrong with him lately? His behavior this morning had been peculiar, to say the least. Jumping up like that, without a word. Forgetting his appointment. Altogether atypical. She tilted back in the chair and tried to recall how long he'd been so scattered. A month? Longer?

She shook her head, about to get back to work, but when she looked up, she was startled by the glow of silvery white hair reflected in the glass front of the cabinet opposite her desk. Was that her hair? For an instant, she thought she'd been looking at an old woman. She blinked and looked again. The woman she now saw reflected there was distinguished. Mature. Experienced. Her wavy platinum bob was, in a sense, her badge of honor, symbolizing all she'd gone through in life. It told clients she was well-qualified to guide them on their inner journeys.

But her clients weren't the only ones who sized her up by hair color. Just last month, a twentyish department store clerk had offered her the senior citizen discount without first checking her ID, a discount she didn't yet qualify for. Maybe her badge of honor was turning into something not so desirable.

But now was not the time to dwell on that. She ought to be taking notes on Lauren's session, while they were still fresh in her mind. She opened the file folder on her desk, happy to shift her focus from the troubling thoughts that were sprouting up like weeds.

After jotting down Lauren's case notes and filing them, she pushed back from her desk and swiveled around to gaze at the fish tank bubbling in the center of the bookcase wall. Good thing she had a two-hour break between clients today. Now she could slip out of her torturous shoes, meditate for twenty minutes to restore her focus, and then feed the fish. After that, she'd think about grabbing a bite of lunch.

But she really ought to find time to visit her mother today. It was too late for lunch at the nursing home, but she might have time to grab a bite from a drive-through, followed by a quick visit to Mom before her next appointment.

No, that wouldn't work. If traffic was bad, she'd never make it back on time. Who did she have at three? If it was Beth Ann Macgregor, she might get away with it—Beth Ann rarely made it to a session on time.

She slipped out of her pumps and flexed her toes against the soft pile of the Persian rug. When her toes stopped aching, she tilted forward in her desk chair and opened the appointment book.

Stuck on top of today's date was a square yellow Post-It note. She didn't recall seeing that first thing this morning, when she'd checked her book. Usually she didn't use Post Its—she'd once missed an appointment with a client because of a sticky note that hadn't stuck. No, the handwriting wasn't hers. It was Roger's, precise and linear, with no slant whatsoever. "Meet me at one-thirty," the note read. "Late lunch. Pablito's." It was their favorite restaurant, the place where he'd proposed.

Adele felt her throat tighten. She swallowed, fighting down her first thought: What if he forgets he put this here? He'd become so absent-minded lately. It was really starting to worry her.

She took a deep breath, and then another, as she advised clients to do. When she felt calm again, she phoned Roger on his cell. No answer. She called him at home. It rang once, twice, three times. After the fifth ring, the call went to their machine.

"Hello, love," she said after the tone. "I got your note about Pablito's. How sweet. I'll be there at one-thirty." She paused, then added, "It's Adele, Roger. Your wife."

After she'd hung up, she shook her head. Why had she said that? Certainly Roger had been acting odd lately, but surely he'd recognize her voice put their lunch date into his BlackBerry. She was jumping to conclusions, getting irrational. She needed a break, a chance to refresh before seeing Beth Ann and the rest of her clientele today. She could always visit her mother tomorrow—Mom was hazy about time distinctions these days.

She swiveled around in her chair and eyed her pumps. There had to be an alternative between two-inch heels and girlish ballet flats. Maybe she had time to stop by Macy's to buy a pair of lower-heeled pumps before meeting Roger. Her feet couldn't stand one more hour in the Anne Kleins. She pictured herself hobbling like an old crone into Pablito's while Roger, a few years older but still slim and spry, carried on a lively conversation with Pilar, their favorite waitress.

She frowned as a new thought hit her. Could Roger be thinking of leaving her? At sixty-six, Roger was no satyr, but maybe he had more interest in sex than she did these days, and his still-dark hair and tall, slim physique gave him the appearance of a younger man. She still enjoyed their lovemaking, of course, but she didn't initiate as often as she once had, said no more often. And they didn't seem to spend as much time together as they once had. Had he found a younger woman with a more vibrant libido?

"It can't be," she said aloud. Roger wasn't consumed by sexual urges anymore. He wasn't asking her to lunch today to tell her he was leaving her. He'd changed at midlife. He'd actually wanted to settle down after decades of bachelorhood—of "playing the field," as he'd called it. No, this couldn't be about splitting up.

He'd seen his doctor. That was it. He'd been told he was exhibiting early symptoms of dementia, like her mother. He'd asked her to meet him at Pablito's, their special place, to soften the blow. That's why he'd been so forgetful and distracted lately. He'd been keeping the diagnosis a secret until he'd found the strength to tell her.

She reminded herself that she didn't really know what Roger was about to say. Her anxiety was taking over—her heart was fluttering and her chest had tightened, the same symptoms Carol Wheaton had complained of when she first came in for treatment. If only she had someone to calm her as she'd calmed Carol this morning. Usually that calming influence was Roger, but today he was the cause of her anxiety.

She needed to get out of the office and do something productive, to get her mind off her troubles, as she'd often advised Carol to do. She needed a change of scene. Maybe she would buy a new pair of shoes before meeting her husband, a comfortable pair, as comfortable as her relationship with Roger had once been and would be again soon. It had to be.

CHAPTER 12

Stephanie

Stephanie glanced at her watch. It was almost noon and nothing had happened with her case yet. She turned to Wes. He'd started out looking self-assured, but for awhile now he'd been sitting slumped forward with his elbows resting on his thighs, his head down, staring at the floor. They'd finished the whispered review of their strategy long ago. What more was there to say?

She'd love to go over other case files from her briefcase to make use of the time, but it was impossible to focus on anything besides keeping Wes calm. The more distracted she was, the more demanding he seemed to get. What was taking Judge Francis so long today? Why was the docket so completely overbooked? She reached for the Buchanan file in the front of her briefcase.

Wes looked up at her and smoothed his hair back on either side with both palms, as if sculpting his hair would settle his soul. "I mean, Carol . . . I . . . we just want what's best for Tessa," he said, a little too loudly.

She let the file slide back into her briefcase.

"Sharon hasn't been herself lately, you know?" he said. "And Tessa's at that age. She needs to get back on track."

"Right," she said in her most soothing tone. "And you and Carol are in a better position to provide her a stable environment right now."

"Yes. I mean, we wouldn't even be here right now if Sharon would have just listened to reason. Now she's gone off the deep end, trying to punish me. It's only going to hurt Tessa. What is she thinking?" He nodded towards Sharon. "Just look at her."

Sharon was sitting there staring straight ahead with her arms crossed and her chin firmly planted in the air.

"I hate that smug look of hers," he said.

"She's obviously hurt and overreacting. The judge will see that," Stephanie said. "It only makes our case stronger."

"I sincerely hope so. You, uh, don't think Sharon's going to bring up . . . the affair, do you?"

"Very possible. In fact, I'm sure Marcus will throw that in for the shock value. Don't worry. I'll handle it."

A woman with long braids who'd been waiting a couple of rows ahead of them all morning was being called up. Good, she and Wes should be next. She'd had enough of babysitting this middle-aged player.

"Are you Monique Charles?" Judge Francis said to the woman.

"That's me," the woman said, her beads rattling as she nodded her head.

"Do you have representation?"

"No, ma'am."

"Is Mr. Charles here?" Judge Francis looked around the room, waiting for someone to respond. No one did.

"Well, let's get to it then," she said. "I see here that you have filed a motion to reverse custody of your fifteen-year-old daughter back to you?"

"Yes, ma'am."

"And it would appear that Mr. Charles doesn't disagree, or he would be here."

"I reckon so. I didn't think she'd last long with him. Knew it would only be a matter of time before she came back. You know teenagers, Your Honor. Grass is always greener, and the like."

Stephanie looked at Wes, then over at Sharon. They were both riveted.

"Since this motion is undisputed," Judge Francis said, "I'm going to grant the request. Do you have a problem with Mr. Charles retaining standard visitation rights?"

"No, Your Honor, but I doubt he'll use it. He's, what you'd call disillusioned with raising a teenage daughter right now." The woman let out a hearty chuckle. Stephanie strained to get a better look at her. Were those flip flops she was wearing? She smiled and shook her head.

Judge Francis removed her glasses. "And what is he disillusioned about?"

"I believe it had something to do with Larry coming home with a hot date and finding Charlene entertaining her own guest," the woman said. "He kicked her out right then and there."

"And I suppose you're going to keep a better eye on the company she keeps?"

"You better believe it."

"All right then. Motion granted." Judge Francis reached for her gavel. "The court is in recess until two o'clock."

When they stood, Stephanie was taller than Wes in her Prada heels. As a teenager she'd hated being taller than all the boys, but now she actually enjoyed it. Wes turned to speak to her and had to look up.

"Two o'clock? We've got to hang around for two more hours?" He was coming unglued.

"Listen, take Carol out for a nice lunch, and then meet me back here at a quarter to two." She rested her hand on her hip. "And try not to worry. Now, I've got to go check my messages."

Wes was watching Sharon head out the door with Marcus. Was he even listening to her?

"I'm sure Carol is dying for an update," she said, hoping he'd move so she could get out.

"Yeah, okay." He side-stepped his way down the bench.

Those rows of benches always reminded Stephanie of pews in a church. Marisa and Paul had taken her to church those few years she lived with them. It was a comforting feeling for her, sitting in a pew, except when she had to sit for this long. Like when it had been a long-winded preacher that just wouldn't wrap up his message. But she sometimes enjoyed this vantage point in the courtroom, being a part of the congregation and watching the sermon in the front. The plaintiffs and defendants were like the sinners who had come forward for judgment, or forgiveness. Like with this Monique woman. Now that her husband had made an ass of himself, she was vindicated, back in the fold.

Just as Wes started to move into the aisle, Monique came barreling by.

"Excuse me, if I can just squeeze by," she said. "Got to get to work, and I'm running real late."

Wes stepped back and bowed his head.

"Thank you so much," she said.

What a funny response from Wes. Bowing. Not looking her in the eyes. Did this woman intimidate him? She must represent Sharon to him. He's thinking, what if Tessa doesn't make it with him and wants to go back with her mom, or what if he wants her to go back, like Larry had. Clients never could make up their minds about what they wanted. But that's what kept her in business, helping kids of divorce play musical families, and round and round they go.

When she followed Wes out of the courtroom doors, no one was in the waiting area. They stood for a moment and watched Monique until she turned the corner at the end of the hallway. She'd been humming softly. For some reason, the sight of her made Stephanie sad.

"I guess I'd better find Carol," Wes said. He looked lost.

"Maybe she's in the bathroom. Do you want me to look for you?"

"No, that's all right. I'll just wait here for a moment."

"Suit yourself. See you soon." She zipped her briefcase on the walk down the hall.

When she stepped outside into the sunshine, Carol was heading up the steps towards her. Had she changed her hair?

"Nothing's happened yet," Stephanie said. "Wes is waiting for you outside the courtroom doors. I'm meeting him back here a little before two."

"Thank you, Counselor," Carol said as she brushed by.

Obviously she was still fired up. Stephanie forgot to check as they passed, but she imagined Carol had put on her combat boots.

She made her way to the back of the parking lot, where her Escort was discreetly parked, and searched for her keys in the side pocket of her briefcase. She really needed keyless entry. After she opened her driver's side door, she threw her briefcase across the console into the passenger's seat then sat down. Bottom first, then, picking up her feet, knees together, she twisted her legs in. She was expert at maneuvering in a pencil skirt.

She picked up her cell phone and sat there while she listened to her messages.

"Steph, it's me. Paul said you needed help with Riley, so I'm going over there around noon to let him outside. Call me when you can."

Stephanie hit speed dial #1. Pick up, pick up.

"Marisa? Have you gone by my apartment yet?"

"I'm just pulling out of your parking lot."

"How's the baby?"

"Full of it, as usual. Your sixty pound baby needs more exercise, Steph."

"I know, I know. Listen, do you want to meet me for lunch? We're on recess. And there's something I wanted to ask you."

"Sure, but can it be a working lunch?" Marisa said. "I'm headed over to Polaris Mall."

"That works. I'm already up that way."

"Meet me in Macy's shoe department."

Stephanie turned her ignition and threw her car into gear. "See you there in a few."

CHAPTER 13

Sharon

Sharon leapt toward the courtroom doors ahead of Wes. She didn't feel like seeing him or talking to him. She didn't even feel like goading Carol on. She just wanted to get Madeline and get out of there.

She opened the heavy wooden doors and walked into the waiting area, holding the door for Marcus who was following close behind.

Madeline was sitting there by herself reading a book. "You're done?" she said with her book still in mid-air.

"Actually we haven't even started," she said. "Lunch break. Let's get outa here."

"Great, I'm starving." Madeline reached for the purse under her chair.

Marcus patted Sharon's back. "I've got to run to the office. I'll meet you back here in a couple of hours."

"See you then." She motioned for Madeline to follow her. They didn't speak again until they were safely tucked into Madeline's white SUV.

"Thanks for hurrying," she said. "I was hoping to avoid

an unpleasant encounter with Wes and The Evil-Know-It-All. I'm not sure what I might say right now."

"I still can't believe The Evil-Know-It-All is Carol Wheaton from my college. I'm sure you've mentioned that she was a teacher, but with all the schools around here— and I never would have put her with Wes." Madeline accelerated out of the parking lot.

"I'm glad it's not just me who thinks they make a weird-looking couple."

"She doesn't even seem like the type to be the other woman," Madeline said. "She seems like the type that men would cheat on. Sorry, no offense."

"None taken. Affairs are complicated. Someone once told me, it ain't about pretty."

"How wise, and yet, how illiterate," Madeline said. "Where do you want to go for lunch?"

"Anywhere that's out of this town. I don't want to run into anybody I know." She rested her forehead in one hand.

"How about Panera Bread?" Madeline said. "By the mall. I could go for a Portobello Panini, and we won't have to bother with a waitress interrupting our conversation."

"Sounds good." She rubbed her temples. "This damn headache. I need my pills."

"You're not still taking those muscle relaxers are you?" Madeline said. "The ones your doctor prescribed to help you sleep?"

"I've just been getting these bad headaches lately, and nothing else seems to work on them."

"You probably want to be sharp for court, though."

"You're right," she said.

"It's probably tension headaches. You have been under a lot of stress lately. How is work going anyway?"

"I haven't sold any ad space for the summer issue yet, and the deadline is coming up soon. If I don't get focused back on work, I'll probably get fired. Which is exactly what Wes and The Evil-Know-It-All are hoping. I fall apart, they get Tessa."

"You're good at what you do, Share. You'll get back on track."

"Maybe."

"Do you remember the day we met?"

"At the coffee machine. At my office."

"Remember how you said Hazelnut was your favorite creamer, too? I told you I was there to sign the contract for my article, you asked me what I'd written about, then we started talking about our favorite exercise routines—pretty soon we'd bonded over working mother issues."

"And you gave me your cell number, and I called you the next week, and the rest is history. Any particular reason you're taking me down memory lane?"

"You were stressed out then, too. Your marriage was falling apart. But when I met you, I was so impressed with you. You were funny, friendly, charming. We clicked right away. You're stronger than you think, Share."

"Thanks. I just don't know what I'm supposed to do any more."

"You'll figure it out."

She stared out the window at the blurry landscape passing by. "You know," she said, "there was a woman in the courtroom this morning who went up right at the end. She looked like she'd just come back from the Caribbean. Name was Monique, I think."

"I saw her when she went to the bathroom," Madeline said. "She asked me about my book. What a stitch, in those flip flops."

"Well, she was getting custody of her teenage daughter back from her ex-husband. Her daughter had wanted to go with him, I guess, but then things didn't work out like she thought, so she wanted to come back to her mother. And the father wasn't even fighting it. And this Monique woman looked like she had known all along that that's what would happen."

"She did seem to have a calmness about her, which isn't typical for court." Madeline turned off the Parkway into the shopping complex where the Panera Bread was located. "Don't worry be happy, man," she said in her best Jamaican accent. "W, W, B, M, D. What Would Bob Marley Do?"

Despite the attempt at humor, Sharon didn't laugh. "What if I gave everybody what they wanted? Do you think they would get tired of being together all the time and Tessa would come back to me?"

"Are you saying you think Tessa wants to live with them full time?"

"I'm not sure," she said.

Madeline turned off the ignition. "We'd better get in there. In case the lunch crowd is thick."

Sharon looked at the overhead menu. She didn't have a favorite meal at this place. The names all sounded so weird. What the hell was asiago anyway? At least they were at the back of the line. She'd have plenty of time to make up her mind. “Tessa really hasn’t said much on the subject of where she prefers to live,” she said. “She starts busying herself with something else when I try to talk about it. In fact, she’s been pulling away from me lately.”

“But what do you think she wants?” Madeline said.

Sharon fiddled with her top button. “I think she wants us all to leave her alone.”

“I think all kids of divorce want their parents to not fight.”

“That would be fine with me, if I just didn’t want to pinch his nose every time I looked at his stupid face. And The Evil-Know-It-All, don’t even get me started about what I’d like to do to her.”

The man in line behind them touched Madeline’s shoulder. “Is that your purse ringing?”

“Oh, yes, I think so, sorry.” She scrambled to find her phone in her oversized bag and checked the Caller ID. “It’s Jack.”

“Hi, Honey,” Madeline said into the phone.

Sharon tried to tune out the conversation. Tried to tune out the lilt in Madeline’s voice as she talked to the man who adored her. Tried to ignore the light dancing in her eyes as she giggled at everything he said. Dammit.

She noticed two businessmen in a corner booth looking her way. Were they checking her out? Or were they eyeing Madeline? No, Madeline was turned the other way talking to Mr. Wonderful, oblivious to her surroundings. It had to be her they were trying to make eye contact with. Plus, she was the blond. And tan. Men always noticed tan blonds before pale brunettes, right? But Madeline did have the flowing goddess hair and the boobs.

Sharon adjusted the lapel on her suit jacket, then straightened her skirt. She casually looked around again, sneaking a peak at their ring fingers as her gaze swept past them. Damn. Double damn. Both had on wedding rings. She'd never dated a married man before. And since Wes had left, there hadn't been many men at all. Oh, she'd been on a few dates. Some were set up by friends. Some she met through work. A couple were writers at the magazine. But she always found excuses to end the evening early. She'd rather spend time with Tessa anyway. Being with Tessa made her feel young, vibrant. Hanging out with middle-aged divorcees just made her feel old. Or maybe she was gay and just didn't know it yet. Those married men probably weren't even looking at her anyway. Thank God Madeline was off the phone. Just in time to order.

They stood back to wait for their salads to come up. Just more damn waiting in a day full of waiting. Finally, their order was up. Trays in hand, they found a seat in the back.

"What did Jack have to say?"

"He just wanted to see how my day was going. Then we were talking about how funny Noah is. Before I left the house this morning Noah said, Mommy, how can I marry another woman when I grow up when I already love you with all my heart? Isn't that just adorable? And then when Jack was packing his lunch Noah said, Daddy, did you pack me a fruit cottontail? Fruit cottontail instead of fruit cocktail. I could just eat him up."

"I miss that age," Sharon said. "When Tessa was in kindergarten she used to say, 'My heart is beeping so fast,' instead of 'beating.' And one time she said, out of the blue, 'Mom, if someone said do I want a million dollars or you, I'd pick you.'" She swallowed hard. "How is it that kids can make you feel like the most important thing when they're little, then one day, you're nothing to them?" Her voice was starting to shake.

Madeline put down her fork. "You are not nothing to Tessa."

"Wes used to think I was great, too, and now I'm nothing to him. Why shouldn't it be the same with Tessa?" A lone tear was trying to make its way out of the corner of her eye.

Madeline put her hand over Sharon's. "Husbands aren't the same as kids."

"But what about your husband? He loves you as much as he loves his kids. Why didn't my husband love me?"

"Share, you know he did. As for why he stopped, I don't know. He might not even really know. We've all got our own stuff going on, personal stuff that rubs up against the people who are closest to us. And sometimes we just rub each other raw. Don't forget, I'm divorced, too. Reese doesn't love me anymore, probably barely remembers me. Jack and I are just lucky. We're lucky that our own personal issues happen to fit well together."

"Marcus said it's luck, too. So I guess I'm just unlucky."

"Well, you were unlucky with Wes. That doesn't mean you'll always be unlucky with men."

"But I'm pushing forty, and I've got a teenage daughter to worry about. How in the world can I date and try to build a life with somebody when my daughter is getting ready to date? She's going to need me more than ever." She pushed her salad aside. She couldn't stand the thought of eating another bite.

"You're right, Share, your daughter does need you. But she also needs her mother to be a happy woman, and you haven't been happy in awhile. She needs her mother to have her own life, a life that doesn't just revolve around her kid."

Silent tears were falling, but she nodded in agreement.

"If Tessa sees that she's important to you, but that your life can go on without her being around all the time, she's going to feel better about leaving you to go to Wes's, and better about growing up and having her own life some day. And that also means she's going to enjoy her time with you more when you are together."

"How can you possibly understand these things when Noah and Olivia are only five and three?" She wiped her eyes with her napkin.

"Maybe it's easier for me to understand because they are only five and three. Maybe you'll have to explain it to me when they're sixteen and fourteen."

She leaned over and hugged Madeline.

When they were back in the SUV, Madeline held up her watch and said, "We've got a little time and I'm almost on empty. Do you mind if I gas up?"

There was a gas station across the street. "Sure. Maybe I can find some of those really strong mints to take back into court with me."

"Altoids?"

"Yeah. I'm doing an awful lot of close whispering with my attorney in there. I hope I haven't already unleashed any dragon breath on him," she said as she stepped out of the car to wait with Madeline while she pumped the gas.

“That reminds me,” Madeline said, “does model-boy know what he’s doing in there?”

“He seems to. He’s given me a lot of the same advice you’ve given me.”

“Then I like him already. Doesn’t hurt that he’s easy on the eyes.”

“Down, girl. You’ve got Jack. Leave some for the rest of us, okay?”

“Ha ha,” Madeline said. “Go get your Altoids.”

In spite of her headache, Sharon smiled. Madeline could always make her smile.

She moved her way up and down the candy aisle until she found the distinctive tin box, then she got in line at the checkout counter. There was an older woman in line ahead of her meticulously counting out her change to buy a bottle of water. She saw through the glass windows that Madeline had finished pumping the gas and was back in the car waiting. Geez, could this woman move any slower?

Sharon studied the woman from top to bottom. Stylish haircut, but it didn’t look right with gray hair. Actually, not gray. It was a steely white. So bright she’d never be able to cover that color, even if she wanted to. Nice tailored jacket. Could do without the pleats on the pants. Her pumps were cute, though, for old lady shoes. The stitching was a nice touch. But the woman’s feet were swollen, bulging like dough over the sides of her shoes. Poor thing. Even at her age, women will still suffer for style.

As the man behind the counter rechecked the coins and dropped them into the correct compartment, the woman stared off to the side, her gaze was fixed. What was that expression on her face? Was it concern? Fear? Sharon regretted being so impatient. Maybe this woman was having just as bad a day as she was.

CHAPTER 14

Stephanie

Stephanie stopped in the center of the mall and looked around. Where was Macy's anyway? She wasn't a mall shopper. Overwrought mothers pushing strollers owned this domain. She spotted a map. After she got her bearings, she stepped into an elevator to go to the first floor. She was relegated to the back as three women with toddlers and strollers barged in at the last minute.

A little boy wearing a pirate hat was watching her. In her designer suit and heels she must stand out in this place, even to a child. He moved in very close, looking right up into her eyes, although she towered over him. Why did children have no sense of personal space? And why did mothers allow their children to wear ridiculous get-ups out in public?

"Have you seen Pirates of the Crampion?" he said to her.

She couldn't help but smile at his mispronunciation of Caribbean and wondered if his mother had been complaining about having cramps.

"No, I haven't," she said. "But I think my nephew has."

The boy's mother stopped pushing a bottle into the

mouth of the baby in the stroller. “Matthew, leave the lady alone, okay, Lovey?”

The mother looked like she hadn’t slept in days. Stephanie was glad she didn’t know what that was like.

“How old is your nephew?” the little boy said.

“He’s sixteen.”

“I’m going to be sixteen next year,” he said.

He couldn’t have been more than three or four. “Cool,” she said.

The glass doors opened and when it was her turn to exit, the mother pushed her stroller with one hand, and reached for Matthew’s hand with the other. “Come on, Lovey.”

She followed them out of the elevator. Matthew turned to wave to her as his mother dragged him in the opposite direction. He reminded her a little of Max at that age. She waved back. Cute kid. From a distance.

When Marisa and Paul married after high school and moved into their first apartment together, she talked them into letting her come live with them. She’d just turned twelve. Everything was working fine until a few months later when Marisa announced she was pregnant. Stephanie had groaned. “Why can’t anything in my life stay the same for one minute?”

She found Macy’s entrance. Fortunately the shoe department was in the front. She scanned the green leather chairs for any sign of Marisa. Near the clearance rack she spotted her sister sitting beside an older woman. They were both trying on shoes. Marissa, clad in one of her loose mom dresses, was leaned over lacing up a boot.

Stephanie propped herself against the column next to

Marisa's chair. "What on earth do you have on your feet, Rissa?"

Marissa looked up. "Hey there, Baby Sister. They're on sale - end of the season clearance."

"I can see why they didn't sell the first time."

"Don't you look sharp, Miss High Powered Attorney."

Stephanie model-walked forward, turned dramatically, and model-walked back to the column. Holding her arms out she said, "Do you like it? It's Dolce & Gabbana."

"Like I would know anything about that. Geez, Steph, how much does a suit like that cost?"

"Somewhere in the market of last month's rent. But don't you think it was worth it? I'm sure it impressed my new client, Rissa."

"Let me guess, he's male."

"Now that you mention it, yes. Why do you ask?"

"Do you really think a man knows that suit costs over a thousand dollars?" Marisa said. "And even if he did, do you think he would be impressed by that kind of frivolity?"

Stephanie motioned with her eyes towards the older lady beside Marisa. A little sister gesture that Marisa would recognize immediately—shut up, you're embarrassing me. The lady was sitting on the edge of the chair with her legs extended straight, feet pointed. She was admiring a pair of flats she had on, but she had to be hearing their entire conversation. She was just too classy to let on.

She probably agreed with Marisa about Stephanie's extravagance, though. Look at the practical shoes she was considering buying. But she was, after all, an old woman. Stephanie was in her prime. She was entitled, wasn't she? At least the flats the woman was trying on were snakeskin, and nothing like the taupe orthopedic shoes her grandmother used to wear. Good for her.

Marisa held her boot-clad foot in the air. “So you don’t like them?”

“If they were thigh-high boots with the laces going all the way up,” she said, “then yes. But short little ankle boots, laced all the way up the front, and the turned-down cuff?”

“But they’re comfortable, and they remind me of a pair I used to love.”

“Exactly! Maybe you should join the cast of Flashdance for a reunion.”

“Hey, don’t mess with my favorite movie.”

“Remember how you used to make Paul watch it over and over with you? What was it, 1983? ‘84? How many guys, who aren’t gay, would be caught dead watching that movie?”

“Well, he did get to see some boobs out of the deal, and when you’re fifteen that’s no small thing.”

“Maybe Auntie Steph needs to introduce Max to that movie. Let him see what his mother is really all about.”

“You do and you die.”

“It’s an aunt’s prerogative. He’s not a baby, after all. He’s a year older than Paul was when you two started dating.”

“You would have to remind me of that, wouldn’t you?”

“Of course,” Stephanie said. “Besides, he’s just now getting to the fun age. I wouldn’t mind having a kid of my own if I could just adopt a teenager like Max.”

“You just think having a teenager is fun because you’ve never had to raise one. Well, I’ve raised two.”

“Are you saying I wasn’t fun to raise, Sister Dear?”

"No, I'm just saying it's never easy. When your kids are little, the work is mostly physical. Then they get older and the work is mostly mental," Marisa said. "In the beginning you've got to clean up after them all the time and do everything for them, and just when they're starting to get more independent and you think you're going to get a break, you realize you have to use all of your brain power to stay one step ahead of them or they will screw everything up for themselves and ruin their future." By the end Marisa's voice was starting to shake.

The older woman packed her old shoes into their box, and stood up. "You can have my chair," she said to Stephanie.

"Thanks." She sat down as the woman walked to the register to make her purchase.

"Rissa, is something going on with Max?"

"Actually, yes. I'm just so angry." Marisa turned to face her, but she didn't look angry. She just looked sad. Her long, mousy brown hair was pulled back in a single, thick braid. She usually hated it when Marisa didn't bother to style her hair, which was pretty often, but today it made her big sister look young, vulnerable.

"What's going on?" Stephanie said.

"Well, you know how Max has always loved baseball more than life itself?"

"Of course."

"Well, he's been kicked off the team."

"What? What happened? But he's so good. That team couldn't make it without him."

Marisa lowered her voice. "He was caught drinking on Monday. At school. He swears this is the first time he's ever done anything like this, but they have a zero tolerance policy.

One drink, and no extra-curricular activities for the rest of the school year, which includes baseball."

"Marisa, I'm so sorry," she said. "What was he doing bringing alcohol to school?"

"He didn't have anything at school. Apparently he and some friends of his left campus at lunchtime and walked across the street to one of the guy's houses. They drank there then walked back to school. A teacher noticed the smell on his breath and sent him to the principal's office."

"What did the principal do?"

"Called the police. They gave him a breathalyzer. They actually handcuffed him and took him to the police station, Steph. Under the influence while under the legal drinking age was his crime. Then they called us from there to come pick him up."

"This happened two days ago? Why didn't you tell me before?"

"It's embarrassing, Steph. Not so easy to talk about."

"Schools don't mess around any more do they?"

"That's just it. I wondered if you could give me some legal advice. I don't think the principal should have questioned Max or called the police until they called me in. Don't I have some parental rights while he's still a minor?"

"That's really not my specialty," she said. "I don't know all the ins and outs of what a school can legally get away with, but I do know from hearing other attorneys' stories that school law falls under a different category than criminal law."

"What do you mean?" Marisa chewed her fingernail.

"Well, for instance, a citizen being charged with a crime has to be read their Miranda rights by the police. However, a school official has the legal right to question students in the school environment based on their charge to maintain order and discipline in the interest of safety. For instance, 'Where did you see Jimmy put that bomb?' It would be ludicrous to expect the principal to call that kid's parents first before asking that question. Also, can you imagine if every first grader through twelfth grader enacted a right to remain silent every time a teacher or administrator asked them whether they had cheated on a paper?"

"I know what you're saying, Steph, I really do. But that principal has just ruined the rest of Max's sophomore year. Baseball could help keep him out of trouble. Don't you think this is overkill for a first offense? My god, he's got a criminal record now!" Marisa struggled to keep her voice low.

"At least the year's almost over. And that juvenile record will be expunged in a few years. It won't follow Max around forever."

"You act like this isn't a big deal," Marisa said.

"I'm not saying it's not a big deal. I just don't think it's the end of the world."

A shopper paused at the table of shoes in front of where she and Marisa were sitting. Stephanie gave her a dirty look. She moved on.

"What happened to sneaking a drink with your friends while you're in high school and adults looking the other way, allowing you to experiment a little?" Marisa said. "They never would have brought the axe down this hard when I was in school."

"Times are different. With all the lawsuits these days, schools can't afford to look the other way, not even for a minute." She had to look away from the painfully raw fingertip at Marisa's mouth before she could continue. "Can you imagine if Max had gotten into his car after drinking at lunch and actually killed somebody on the road while he was impaired? The school could have been sued for negligence, and Max would be looking at an involuntary manslaughter charge instead of an underage drinking charge."

"I know you're right," Marisa said. "It's just not what I expected to happen to us. I mean, I've always tried to be there for Max. I barely had any parental supervision, and I never got arrested!"

"He's a good kid, Rissa, you know that. You have nothing to feel guilty about."

Marisa snorted. "What kind of mother would I be without the guilt?" She had a point, although motherhood had never looked more unattractive.

"You guys will get past this," Stephanie said. "How is Paul handling it?"

"Neither one of us knows what to say to Max now. He's crushed about baseball. And he's been suspended from school for ten days. How is he going to catch back up? He's got finals coming up."

"Do you want me to talk to him?" She wound her long hair up into a bun then let it drop.

"Sure. Why not?" Marisa said. "He'll be easy to reach. He's home until a week from Monday. And we've taken away his driving privileges for the rest of the month."

She patted her big sister's arm.

"Hey, didn't you want to ask me about something?" Marisa said.

"Oh yeah. It's this case I've got. There's a fourteen-year-old girl caught in the middle of a custody dispute between her parents. I keep thinking about us at that age. Why do you think Mom and Dad never fought over us?"

"I guess they were just too wrapped up in their own mixed-up lives."

"Which do you think is better, being wanted too much, or not at all?"

"Paul and I wanted you, Steph."

"Thank goodness," she said. "Or I'd really be screwed up!"

"Have you seen Justin lately?"

"No. He wants a wife and kids, the whole shebang—I can smell it a mile away."

"And what's wrong with that?"

"Rissa, you know me. It's just not my thing. And there's already enough unwanted kids out there. Come on, can you see me changing a diaper?"

"What about Max?"

"That's different. I didn't have a choice."

Marisa slumped in the chair, rested her head on the soft back and looked at the ceiling. She didn't have to remind Marisa that Max had been a high-maintenance baby. That he cried all the time when she was trying to study in the next room, or when she had a friend over. That Marisa expected her to babysit at times when she'd rather go out. Tessa Trent was lucky she didn't have a newborn nephew screwing up her middle-school years. After dealing with her parents' divorce and remarriages, Stephanie had decided she'd never get married, and after seeing up close how much trouble a baby was, she knew she'd never have one of those either. And in sixteen years she hadn't changed her mind, except for enjoying her role as aunt more now.

"You know I've always loved Max," she said, "but I'm glad he's not a little kid anymore."

Marisa went pale. "I know, but—"

"Can I get you another size?" A sales clerk, who she'd seen tentatively trying to come over, finally dared to step up.

"No thanks," Marisa said. "These aren't going to work for me." She turned to Stephanie. "I suppose you'd have me try on a pair of heels like yours?"

"You wouldn't like them. I'm used to being uncomfortable," she said. "Hey, are you feeling all right?"

"I'm fine. Really."

"I think you should get those boots you have on."

"But you made fun of them."

"I was wrong," she said. "They do look good on you."

CHAPTER 15

Adele

Adele pulled into Pablito's parking lot a few minutes early. She unscrewed the cap on the bottle of water she'd bought at the gas station, popped three pills into her mouth, and took a sip. The water was warm now and tasted of plastic. She swallowed anyway and screwed the lid back on. It had been a mistake to leave the water in her hot car while she shopped for shoes.

The trip to Macy's had been a mistake, too. Halfway to the shoe department, her feet had ached so badly she'd considered walking barefoot back to the car and driving home for her ballet flats. Instead, she'd forced herself to walk through the pain. Now her feet, even in the new snakeskin flats, were killing her. But that wasn't what was bothering her. Not really. What troubled her most was the pair of sisters she'd sat beside while trying on shoes at Macy's. Their conversation had kicked up all sorts of disturbing feelings she'd thought she'd worked through years ago.

After finding a pair of lower-heeled shoes she liked, she'd sat down in the closest chair, next to a woman trying on a short, cuffed boot. A moment later, while slipping off her torturous Anne Kleins, she'd been about to ask the woman next to her if she had the time, but at that moment the other shopper's six-foot "baby sister" showed up. The tall one didn't look like anyone's baby sister. Didn't act like one, either. She was obviously an Athena-type, a she-warrior who didn't need a man in her life. Certainly Athena's profession, "high-powered attorney," fit the archetype. And what a contrast to her slightly dowdy older sister, clearly a Demeter type, a woman for whom caring for others was paramount.

Still, their easy banter suggested they were only teasing each other, just getting warmed up, and sure enough, a minute later they lapsed into an even more intimate conversation. She knew she ought to leave at that point, to avoid eavesdropping, but her curiosity got the better of her. The older sister, as it turned out, had raised Athena from an early age but now seemed momentarily disenchanted with raising a teenage son. Still, the woman would probably get past her disenchantment. From her practice, Adele knew that good mothers usually did. And this woman seemed like one of the good ones, clearly invested in motherhood.

While she sat in her slick leather chair, pretending to admire the brushed gold buckles on the snakeskin flats, Adele couldn't help imagining what the older woman, "Rissa," had given up for her baby sister. Part of her youth, for one thing. And her time. How much time kids took from a mother's day—she'd learned that much from watching her Aunt Helen juggling farm chores and homemaking, riding herd on her three cousins and even on Uncle Walt, teaching Sunday school, baking bread. Yet, like this Rissa, Aunt Helen had taken Adele in whenever her mother hadn't felt up to having a curious, active only child around. Somehow Aunt Helen had always made time for her. No complaints. No resentment. Women like Aunt Helen were, to use Helen's own expression, "rare as hen's teeth," and this Rissa seemed like one of those. And yet the obviously childless young attorney had tossed off her older sister's concerns about overspending as if Rissa were full of beans, brushed aside how hard it was to be a mother, even joked about adopting a teenager.

She was cocky, this Athena type. So sure of herself. A lot like Adele had been at that age, so sure she'd have forever to find the right man and start a family. How foolish she'd been to postpone that—she'd procrastinated, really, unsure of herself after so many years of being single. At least she'd been able to remedy the man part of the equation by the time she hit forty, but by then, conceiving a child turned out to be impossible. As for Roger, she wasn't even sure about him anymore.

She took a deep breath and let it out, then looked around Pablito's parking lot for Roger's old Volvo. No boxy blue wagon. Had he forgotten their date? Or was he just late? It wasn't quite one-thirty yet, but usually he showed up early. Not today, though.

"Please," she said aloud, "just let him be late."

Fortunately the restaurant was only a few steps away. Besides the pain in her feet and her worries about Roger, she was hungry. Really hungry. All she'd eaten today was a granola bar on her way to work, running late after that long call from Carol Wheaton.

She should have checked her voicemail before leaving for Macy's—Carol might have needed to speak to her. Still, it was unlikely that the custody case had been resolved yet. The judge was probably still deliberating. From what Adele gathered, there were significant parenting problems on both sides.

Not for the first time, she was glad she hadn't gone into law, like that Athena type. The idea of having to rule on a child's future struck her as impossible, not much advanced from the days of King Solomon. She couldn't imagine having to defend one parent at the expense of the other. Still, an attorney like Athena would be a worthy adversary, a real fighter.

At one-thirty on the nose, Adele locked the car and walked into the small, dark restaurant. As soon as she squeezed through the tiny vestibule, the aroma of smoky chipotle peppers hit her nostrils, making her mouth water. She eased around the corner of the bar, where Pablo Montoya, the owner, was mixing a frozen drink.

"Adele," he called out over the grind of the blender. "Welcome to Pablito's."

"Thanks," she called back.

He shut off the blender. "How about a margarita? On the house. In honor of a special long-time customer."

Roger had probably put him up to this. "No, thanks," she said. "I have to get back to work soon."

"Too bad. Your husband will be disappointed." He shrugged and turned to a young woman with pink-streaked red hair standing nearby. "Lindsay, show Dr. Martin to her table. Over there, in the corner." To Adele he said, "A table for lovers."

She followed the hostess to the corner table. Once seated, she strained to read the menu in the dim light.

Pilar, their favorite waitress, came to the table with a bowl of warm tortilla chips and a small black cauldron of Pablito's homemade salsa. "I haven't seen you here in a while," she said.

Adele frowned. "I suppose we haven't been in for quite some time."

"Months, maybe."

"Really? Has it been that long?"

Pilar nodded. "You meeting the mister?"

"Yes. And he's late." Her heart started to flutter again. "You know, I think I will have that margarita Pablo offered me."

"Coming up," Pilar said.

The drink tasted sweet but tart and icy cold, and when the tequila hit her empty stomach, it felt warm and friendly. She took a chip and munched it, hoping to fend off getting tipsy. She had Beth Ann at three, after all.

After she'd taken another sip, Roger came around the bar, grinning and holding a long plastic tube that no doubt contained a set of house plans. She noticed a trace of mud on his hiking boots—he'd evidently come from his earlier appointment at the job site, which he must have rescheduled for later. Or so it appeared, anyway.

When he got to the table, she motioned for him to sit. "Hello, love. Did you run into traffic? Usually you're so punctual."

He pulled out his chair and sat, groaning a little as his backside hit the seat, held up the tube. "I had to go back to the house to get this."

"For your Hilliard job?"

"You'll see."

What was there to see? "You're the mysterious one today."

He grinned. “I have a little surprise. But not until after you’ve had a margarita or two.”

“I shouldn’t even be having one. I have a client at three.”

“I know,” he said, stashing the tube under the table. “I checked your planner this morning. You’re booked up from three till eight tonight.”

“Some of my clients need evening appointments, you know that. And I did keep the morning open—”

“Almost open.”

Lauren, he meant. He’d seen her penciled in. “A rare exception,” she said.

“Not so rare. Adele, you promised.”

She let out an exasperated sigh. “Sometimes my clients have to come first. But in this case, I’ll admit I made a mistake. I won’t let anyone talk me into that again.”

“And you missed lunch with your mother.”

Why was he reproaching her like this? “I’ll go there tomorrow,” she said. “I had a cancellation, so it’ll work out fine.”

Pilar came to the table with a chilled bottle of Corona. A wedge of lime stuck out of the bottle’s long, transparent neck. “Here you go,” Pilar said to Roger. “The usual.”

“Gracias,” he said, his accent perfect.

“And will you be having your usual?” Pilar held a ballpoint pen above her order pad, eyes on Adele.

“Yes. A cup of posole and the blue corn enchiladas. Chicken today, I think.”

“Red or green chile?” Pilar said, pen still poised.

“Christmas.”

“Make that two.” Roger pushed the lime all the way into the bottle.

Pilar scooted behind them, on her way to the tiny kitchen, and Roger took a long pull of his beer. After he'd set down the bottle on the cocktail napkin, he smiled. "Both red and green chile today? Living dangerously."

"I took my pills, Roger. I'll be fine."

"Good. So you're feeling well."

She fiddled with her paper napkin, played with a tortilla chip—anything to avoid his gaze. Finally she looked up, just as Roger was raising one dark eyebrow.

"What's going on, Adele? Something's bothering you, I can tell."

This was her opening, the moment she'd been waiting for. She ought to spill her foolish fears, but she couldn't. Instead, she told him about what had happened at the gas station, where she'd stopped on her way to the mall. "I thought I'd give the clerk the exact change," she said. "It took me a while to get the coins out of my wallet—"

"Your arthritis."

"No. Well, maybe my fingers were a little stiff. But I wasn't moving all that slowly. The woman behind me kept sighing, as if I were spoiling her day."

"I'm sorry, love. That must have been annoying."

"It felt...humiliating." She stopped, shrugged. "I realize I'm not quite as nimble as I once was, but did that give her the right to be rude?"

"You know how some people are. Impatient. Self-absorbed." He shook his head. "But otherwise, you're feeling well?"

"Well enough."

"Glad to hear it. Drink up, then. I want to show you my surprise."

She smiled and picked up the big, bowl-shaped margarita glass with both hands. Her fingers ached a little but she didn't want to show pain. Roger would fret over her and they'd never get to his surprise.

"To my one true love," she said.

Roger clinked his beer bottle against her glass. "And to mine, forever and ever."

His usual reply, what he always said before they drank. He hadn't forgotten their traditional toast. He was fine, just distracted these days—probably by his surprise, whatever that might be. She took another sip of her drink.

While Roger talked about his meeting at the building site and the belted king-fisher he'd seen flying over the nearby lake, she finished her margarita, feeling like a kid who had to drink all her milk before she could have her dessert. Still, it was fun to play the child now and again. When was the last time she'd done that?

"All done?"

She nodded. Her stomach pulsed with warmth now, and her face felt flushed.

"Excellent," he said. "Now for my surprise."

He pushed the chips and salsa aside, along with her glass and his beer. Slowly he uncapped the plastic tube, pulled out a cylinder of paper, and unrolled what looked like a typical set of Roger house plans. "I've been working on this for weeks."

"And what is this?" She helped him smooth the pages, her curiosity mounting.

"A house," he said. "For us."

"For us? But we have a house. A beautiful house."

"This is more beautiful still. At least I think so. And it's a green house. Environmentally friendly. Take a look."

Slowly she lifted each drawing and pored over it, holding up the huge sheets with his help. When she'd seen them all, she stared again at the front elevation. "But it's an adobe," she said. "You've always said adobes won't work in Ohio—too much rain. Surely you're not suggesting fake adobe."

"It's not designed for Ohio," he said. "It's for our property in Arizona."

"But we bought that as an investment."

"Or for retirement, remember? When we bought it, we agreed we might decide to retire there, depending on how we were doing financially. And we're doing well. Very well, in fact. Therefore—" His long, bony index finger jabbed at the drawings. "I'd like to build this on our lot. Soon."

"But my practice—I can't just abandon my clients. And my mother. Who's going to look after her?"

"The people at the nursing home," he said. "And your Aunt Helen."

"Helen?" Adele shook her head. "She has Walter and the farm to look after. The grandchildren. And she's not exactly a youngster herself."

"She's only seventy-three," Roger said. "Not that much older than I am. And she's doing just fine. I spoke to her this morning. As for the grandchildren—"

"You called my Aunt Helen?"

He nodded. "And I told her about this." He pointed to the plans.

How could he go behind her back like this? She took a breath, visualized snow falling. "What did she say?"

"Well, you know your Aunt Helen. She said, 'Tell Dell not to worry. Of course I'll see to Betty's care.'"

"I have a responsibility to my clients, Roger. I can't just pick up and leave. Even if Aunt Helen's willing to see to it that Mom's well cared for, I can't just shut down my practice. Not now."

"When?"

"I don't know," she said. "Not for some time to come." If ever.

His face turned a deep purplish-red. "You also have a responsibility to me, Adele, and to yourself." He lowered his voice. "You have arthritis and acid reflux and who knows what all, and I'm not in top shape any more either. How much time does either of us have left to enjoy a new home?"

Her throat tightened—it was all she could do to get the words out. "You don't...Roger, for heaven's sake, don't tell me you're going to die."

He frowned. "Of course I'm going to die, Dell. We all are. And I'd just as soon die in the bright Arizona sunshine as in a gray Ohio drizzle."

She blinked, trying to take this in. "How long?"

"A year at the least. Depends on how long it takes to—" He frowned again, then started to laugh. "Were you asking me how long I had to live?"

"I...I didn't know what to think. This is all so sudden."

"Sudden? My god, Adele. We're in our sixties. I'm down to one or two projects a year. And you're supposed to be down to a half-dozen patients a week."

She looked at her empty glass. "That's easier said than done."

His face went from reddish to pale. "Okay," he said, rolling up the plans. "I can see I'm wasting my time here. We can talk about this later, at home." He slid the plans into the tube just as Pilar came to their table, balancing a tray of steaming food. She stepped back to let him pass.

When Roger had rounded the bar, Pilar set their food on the table as if nothing had happened. "The mister not feeling too well today?"

"No," Adele said. "Not well at all. And I'm not feeling so well either, Pilar. If you don't mind, I'll just pay and—" She swallowed. And what?

CHAPTER 16

Carol

Carol shifted her weight from one foot to the other, thankful she'd worn her comfortable slip-ons, especially after the four blocks they'd just walked to get to the Chinese restaurant. Her nausea was gone now, but her mood was starting to curdle with each passing minute.

She looked at her watch. If they didn't get a table soon, they'd be late getting back to court. She turned to Wes, who stood beside her on the sidewalk, fiddling with his cell phone. "I thought you said Kung Ho wouldn't be crowded today."

Wes shrugged. "Usually it's not in the middle of the week. The woman who took our name said it would only be ten minutes."

"Well, I'm tired of standing here. Tired of standing period."

Earlier, she'd stood for quite some time outside the courthouse in the fresh air. Then the glass-paned doors to the courthouse had opened, reflecting the noon sunlight like two golden mirrors. Stephanie Powell stepped out, toting her sleek briefcase. Finally, Carol thought as she headed up the steps to savor the good news.

But this was no reprieve. Wes's Amazon-attorney, unsmiling as usual, told her point-blank that nothing had happened. Nothing! Carol slipped past her to find her husband. She needed details, and it seemed clear from Counselor Powell's brisk demeanor that she wouldn't get them from Stephanie.

Things went from bad to worse then. Inside the courthouse, near the foyer, Wes was having a cozy tête-à-tête with a thirtyish blonde in a pink linen suit and high-heeled sandals of iridescent green. The shoes, all thin straps and sharp spikes, reminded Carol of two dragonflies. The blonde was slender as a dragonfly, too.

At that moment Carol felt a jolt of jealousy so strong it made the tips of her fingers tingle. She took a breath, then another, and let the feeling pass. She put a hand on the sleeve of Wes's silk suit and whispered his name.

Startled, he blinked at her. "Carol," he said. "I didn't see you standing there."

"Obviously." Carol tilted her head toward the blonde, who by this time was clattering across the marble floor of the foyer in her dragonfly shoes.

"Oh, that," Wes said. "She's a potential customer."

"In the market for a house?"

"She saw my photo on one of our cart ads."

"The supermarket ads?" Carol pictured her husband's retouched photo—his "rock star" photo, she called it—smiling up at her from a shopping cart at Kroger.

"She said to me, 'You're *the* Wesley Trent, aren't you? Of Wesley Trent Realty?' I said yes and gave her a business card, in case she's looking for a house. She's in the key demographic." He explained, not for the first time, that most home buyers were women. "I was just turning on a little professional charm."

Inwardly Carol winced. Wes was talking about the same professional charm he'd used on her three years ago, after her first husband's death from a heart attack, when she'd had to sell their family home and find a smaller place closer to the college. She'd thought Wes had been love-struck, and that infatuation, in turn, had unlocked in her an emotional door that had never before been opened. Could she have been wrong about Wes's early reaction to her?

"So this was strictly business," she said.

Wes had nodded then and started talking about where they might eat, his voice as smooth and sweet as vanilla custard. Carol had mumbled yes to his suggestion and insisted they walk to Kung Ho—she needed to work off her anger.

But walking hadn't done the trick. Now, as the sun beat down on the top of her head, she wondered again if the concern that Wes had shown for her at their first meeting had been only a show of charisma. Her neck was sweating, prickly underneath her heavy hair. She wished she'd kept her satin-covered elastic band. Even a rubber band would do at this minute—and a cool place to sit down. But the tiny lobby of the restaurant was packed with noisy, waiting diners, and she wanted to be alone with Wes.

"Wesley," she said, her voice tender now. "Do you remember the day we met?"

"What? Oh, sure. You came to the office. You'd just lost your husband, you said. You looked so sad and yet so brave that day. So serious. Determined to get on with your life when it was clear you were barely able to function. I admired that in you. Still do."

She was amazed—they'd been together off and on for nearly two years, yet he'd never told her this before. Suddenly she felt woozy. She grabbed at Wes's arm for support.

"Whoa," he said. "Are you all right?"

"Just a little light-headed." She unbuttoned her jacket and flapped the lapels, to generate a breeze. "Another hot flash coming on, I suppose."

His eyes went straight to her chest. "I meant to tell you earlier. You look fantastic like that."

She looked down at the pale expanse of flesh above the black lace and felt a small smile lift one corner of her mouth. He wanted her. His encounter with that blonde had been just what he'd said, a flash of professional charm. Well, she could turn on the charm, too—with him, at least. She opened her jacket a bit wider and smiled slyly.

"Really fantastic," he said, putting his arm around her waist. He drew her closer and tucked her unfurled hair back behind one ear, whispering what he'd like to do with his Care Bear a little later, using his silly bedroom name for her. Then he paused and leaned back and gave her a puzzled look. "What did you do with your shirt? Weren't you wearing one of your white button-downs this morning?"

"I was," she said, "but the heat was making me queasy, so I took it off." A white lie—a sin of omission, the nuns at her high school would have called it. So was her failure to mention the cigarette-slip, but she couldn't face that now. She'd tell him later, when they were in bed together, after the custody case had been decided.

"You okay now? You look a little flushed. You're not having that nervous-stomach thing again?"

"I'm all right now," she said.

"Good. Because we've still got a long way to go before we win this case. If we win."

"Don't think negatively, Wes. Say 'When we win.' Let your words reflect your confidence." Confidence you apparently don't feel, she thought.

"Stephanie's been reassuring," he said. "She thinks we have a pretty good chance of winning."

"A pretty good chance? We didn't go through all this legal nonsense to lose. Really, Wes, I'm surprised at you. You're not like this when in comes to a real estate sale."

"This isn't real estate."

"True," she said. "And I'm fully aware this isn't going to be a cake-walk. I just hope it doesn't get ugly this afternoon." She grimaced as she imagined the details of their "affair" being trotted out by a desperate Sharon and her smarmy attorney. "If it does, don't forget to remind the judge of the many ways that Sharon's fallen down on the job as a parent."

"I don't know if that's a good idea, Carol."

"What about Tessa's description of her mother's pill problem?"

"I don't know if I'd call it a pill problem."

"But she's taking muscle relaxants. While Tessa's with her." Carol mimicked Sharon gobbling a handful of pills and then "crashing," exaggerating the anecdote that Tessa had told them at the dinner table a few weeks ago. "I hope you make it clear that Sharon is struggling to be a responsible parent right now—struggling and losing. This is about Tessa having proper supervision, not about who loves her most or who's maddest at the other parent. It would be foolish to lose this case because you weren't willing to be candid in court."

Wes nodded slowly. "Yeah, okay, I'll mention it again to Stephanie."

"Please do." Carol was drenched in sweat now. "Why don't we go inside, into the air conditioning?"

Nodding, Wes pulled open the heavy red door that led into the restaurant lobby. After Carol nearly stumbled over the threshold, his gaze went straight to her feet.

"Wearing your comfy shoes," he said. "I thought you were getting rid of those."

Carol struggled to keep from poking him in the ribs. Why did Wes feel the need to editorialize on her shoes? She felt angry, but something else too, a sharp metallic feeling she could almost taste. Guilt! She actually felt guilty for wearing her unisex slip-ons while she was with Wes, knowing he despised them. Now she was doubly angry because she cared that he despised them.

"Actually," she said, "I was planning to replace them with a new pair. The same style, but in a different color." Raising an eyebrow, she added, "Possibly an iridescent green." She felt a twinge of satisfaction at delivering this jab, along with another feeling, a craving of some kind, but not for food or a cigarette. Well, now was not the time for self-psychotherapy. She'd file that away for later discussion at Dr. Martin's.

"Trent for two," the hostess called out.

"That's us." Wes's voice boomed.

The hostess, taking small steps because of her tight red pants and precarious high heels, showed them to their table in the main dining room. Wes pulled out Carol's chair, and when she was settled, he excused himself to use the restroom.

Carol picked up her menu and set it down again. Why did everything upset her so? She closed her eyes to visualize a pond someone had thrown a stone into. The concentric ripples widened and slowed and disappeared. When the pond was like a mirror again, she opened her eyes.

A short, stubby woman in black pants and a white shirt came swooping by with a pitcher. She filled Carol's glass with ice water, which Carol gratefully sipped, dehydrated from the vomiting. That must be contributing to her foul mood.

The waitress asked if she wanted hot tea.

"Yes," Carol said. "That would be wonderful. And bring two cups. Please."

After glancing at the menu a second time, Carol took another sip of water and looked around the jammed restaurant. Businessmen like Wes packed two of the larger tables, conducting lunch meetings of some sort. One or two women sat at each round table, dressed in dark suits or crisp trousers with contrasting jackets. They spoke less often than the men and laughed at the men's jokes. The men, on the other hand, didn't seem to pay much attention to their female companions.

She checked her watch again. How long did it take a man to relieve himself? She set the menu down and went back to people-watching.

At a nearby table sat a family of five—husband, wife, two teenaged boys and a younger girl with straight brown hair. A shiver ran down her spine. The other family—she assumed it was a family from the casual, intimate way they interacted—was a shadow of her newly blended family, a girl and two boys. They were all younger, though. The girl couldn't be older than ten, and the boys appeared to be only about fourteen and fifteen.

A voice echoed in Carol's head: "Fifteen's the worst, if you ask me." The woman with the braids she'd met in the courthouse restroom had been right about that. Her boys had given her fits at that age, especially Eric. And dear Lyle, intense scholar that he was, had possessed only one fatherly weapon in his arsenal—reason. That didn't go far with emotional teens.

Peals of laugher erupted from the shadow family's table. The boy sitting at the end of the curved banquette was laughing and elbowing his sun-streaked blond brother, so like her Eric. The other boy was darker and shorter, like Michael. Her boys were fraternal twins, easy to tell apart yet as intimate as identical twins, with their own catch-phrases and in-jokes and almost paranormal intuition about one another. Tessa had found that fascinating. She loved having two big brothers, though they were away at college most of the time. When they were home, they treated her like a cute, amusing mascot, and she seemed to thrive on the attention. And of course her boys adored their stepfather—he'd rescued them from boredom and grief not long after Lyle's death, dropping by their new house and taking them to basketball and hockey games. He'd even scored tickets to the coveted Ohio State-Michigan football game that fall. Then, shortly before winter break at the college, Carol learned from a gossipy colleague that Wes, by then her lover and the love of her life, was married, with a twelve-year-old daughter.

"Ready to order?" The stubby waitress was back, pouring

green tea into a small handleless cup that she'd set in front of Carol.

"No," Carol said. "My husband—" She motioned to the other chair. "He'll be back soon. Don't pour his tea yet."

The waitress nodded, set down the teapot and bustled away, her thick thighs pumping in her loose microfiber pants, her white shirt buttoned almost to the chin. The waitress was dressed, Carol realized with a shock, exactly as she'd been dressed this morning, minus the black jacket.

Carol stared for a while at the dark rectangle that led to the men's room. She craned her neck to see between the half-closed accordion doors that separated the smaller section of the L-shaped dining room from the main room where she sat. Finally, from the short end of the dining room, a grinning Wes threaded his way between tables, stopping at one of the big round ones. After shaking hands all around, he let his right hand slip into his suit-jacket pocket, where he kept his cell phone. Carol pursed her lips. He'd probably been on the phone in the restroom again, though he'd made a promise not to check it while they were out together at restaurants.

"Hey," he said, plopping down in his chair. "What did I miss?"

"Absolutely nothing," she said. And then, though she tried to hold it in, she added, "Did you get through to whomever you needed to call?"

He flushed slightly, though his expression never changed. "I thought maybe I could catch Tessa between classes."

"And?"

Wes picked up his tall menu and focused his gaze on it. "It went to voicemail."

Carol frowned. "Why were you calling Tessa? It's not as if we have any news to report."

"I thought I'd see how she was holding up today. This is hard on her, you know."

"I know. But life is hard." Carol thought back to her own mother, so eager for her daughter to excel at everything, always reminding her that life was hard but if you worked hard, you could make that hard life a little sweeter. The opposite of Tessa's mother, who was behaving like cross between an indulgent Disneyland Mom and a hovering Helicopter Parent. Nowadays Sharon seemed to feel that life owed her sweetness, and if she didn't get it, woe to he who withheld the goodies. That would be Wes, Carol realized with a jolt. And Tessa, of course, represented the goodies.

The waitress bustled by again. "Ready to order now?"

Carol ordered Moo Goo Gai Pan with steamed rice. Wes said he'd have General Tso's Chicken with fried rice and an egg roll.

"You know," she said after the waitress left their table, "I've been thinking about Tessa and Sharon. Their relationship. What Tessa means to Sharon."

Wes sighed. "Honey, I've told you. Don't get all worked up again about Sharon. She's totally irrational. There's no sense in trying to figure her out."

"I agree," Carol said, though she really didn't. She'd been talking with Dr. Martin about Sharon for weeks now, trying to understand the situation from her rival's point of view. Some of what Dr. Martin had said, while highly unpalatable, rang true. Just last week, Dr. Martin had pointed out that Wes had betrayed both of them. After some argument, Carol had conceded this, adding, "But there's a vast difference in how we handled that betrayal. In time I forgave Wes for not telling me he was married. I healed from my wounds, but Sharon hasn't done that."

"And she may never do so," Dr. Martin said. "Sharon's wounds may run too deep. She and Wes were married for a long time. They have a child together. And Wes betrayed her in what you might call an archetypal manner." Her therapist had gone on to cite Euripides' play Medea as an example of the level of rage such a betrayal might trigger in a trusting wife.

"She does seem bent on revenge," Carol said. "With most of it is aimed at me."

"An innocent party."

Carol nodded vigorously. "But Sharon doesn't believe in my innocence. She seems to assume that I knowingly and willingly threw myself into an affair with a married man. It wasn't as if I broke up his failing marriage."

Dr. Martin had paused then, in that way she had, hoping that her client would fill in the blank. When Carol hadn't, the therapist had said in her cool, even tone, "But might you have hurried its demise?"

"Carol?" Wes was frowning. "You're a million miles away."

"I'm sorry," she said. "It's this custody case." She cleared her throat and spoke the words that had been sticking there for days. "Do you think we're making a mistake?"

CHAPTER 17

Madeline

Madeline glanced at her watch as she pulled into the courthouse parking lot to drop Sharon off—1:45 p.m. Good.

"This should give you plenty of time to meet up with Marcus before court resumes at two," she said.

"You're a doll." Sharon hopped out of the car.

Madeline leaned towards the open window. "I'll be back as soon as possible," she said as Sharon walked up the sidewalk. Sharon waved without looking back.

Madeline watched her disappear inside the glass front doors, then she threw her car into reverse and swung the big SUV back around. She'd get Olivia from day care first, which would leave her just enough time to pick Noah up from kindergarten by 2:30. Typical—her frantic schedule constantly dictated to the minute by those she loved.

Why was the car in front of her going so slowly? She gunned it and zoomed around the tiny sedan.

How much easier life would be if Noah rode the bus. But he didn't like the bus. He'd ridden it a few times, the first week of school, and had gotten picked on by some first-grade boys, so that was it. She worked part-time for exactly this reason—so she'd have the freedom to do things like take her kids to school and pick them up from school if she needed to.

She heard the stack of mid-term papers sliding around in the back. Hopefully they weren't getting all mixed up. She'd been on a high from helping Sharon cope through her tough day, but now she was starting to feel anxious about everything in her life that wasn't getting done. She'd promised her Thursday class she'd have their mid-terms graded by their next class period, but that wasn't going to happen. Not if she had to spend the rest of today back at court. Next week she'd pick up the Tuesday class's mid-term papers to grade. And there was a stack of clean laundry piled up on the couch waiting to be folded. Jack was helpful when he was home—sometimes he'd even load the dishwasher without being asked—but some things, like folding laundry, were just not his strong points.

And she was pretty sure there was some serious soap scum building up in their bathrooms, but she'd been trying to avoid looking too closely. Olivia got the stomach flu Saturday before last, when it was supposed to be Madeline's cleaning day. Instead of her regular cleaning, she'd spent the day cleaning the bed sheets and carpet in various rooms, even a dresser—nothing in a house is safe when a three-and-a-half-year-old hasn't yet gotten the hang of making it to the toilet. Sharon had wanted to come over for a cup of coffee that day and seemed a little put off when Madeline told her it wasn't a good time.

"So I won't kiss her on the mouth," Sharon had said. "It doesn't bother me that she's sick." Madeline didn't have the energy that day to explain that she wasn't worried about Sharon being bothered.

Sharon had no idea what it was like to clean a whole house

and clean up after two little kids. From the time she and Wes were first married she'd had a weekly housekeeper. And although she had Tessa to take care of, well, one kid is just not the same as having two. It's the sibling thing that drives a mother to the brink of insanity. Like trying to keep Noah away from Olivia when Olivia was throwing up. God forbid you ever have two throwing up at the same time. And even just the she touched me, he touched me first scenario that gets played out every day in fifty different ways.

She pulled into the Kids R First parking lot. There were no empty parking spaces up front. Why was it so crowded today? She found a spot in the back and put the gear into park. Then she remembered—Parent's Day! There was supposed to be a luncheon! How could she have forgotten? This court situation had totally thrown her off schedule. Wednesday wasn't one of Olivia's typical day care days since Madeline only taught on Tuesdays and Thursdays. When she got the notice from the day care two weeks before, she remembered thinking she could bring Olivia in that Wednesday for the special celebration, but if it turned out to be inconvenient for them that day, Olivia would be none the wiser.

But then Sharon had called Tuesday evening having a meltdown and begging Madeline to come to court with her the next day for moral support. Then Jack had offered to drop Olivia off. Now Olivia was there for Parent's Day, but no parent of hers was. This was just awful.

Jack was there this morning, so he must have heard about it. Why hadn't he called her? She grabbed her cell phone and dialed.

"Hey, Babe, listen, can I call you back?" he said. "I'm in the middle of something."

"No. Why didn't you remind me about Parent's Day being today?"

"What? Where are you?"

"I'm in the parking lot at the day care," she said. "I've already missed the luncheon. Didn't someone say something to you this morning when you dropped Olivia off?"

"Well, yeah, Miss Henderson said something about seeing one of us at lunchtime, but I said we both had other things going on today."

"Why didn't you call me right away? Or say something when I spoke to you from Panera?"

"Because you promised Sharon you'd be there for her. I thought you remembered the luncheon and just made the choice to help Sharon out."

"No. I did not," she said through her teeth. "If I had remembered, I would have at least asked you to fill in for me at the luncheon."

"Babe, I couldn't have left work today even if I'd wanted to. Remember, I told you IPS is expecting those drawings by tomorrow."

She realized she was shouting now, and that Jack probably didn't deserve it, but she couldn't stop herself. "I can't remember everything for everybody in this family, Jack!"

"Madeline, listen. Olivia is only three years old. There will be many more luncheons to attend. You're a good mother, and a good friend. Don't beat yourself up over this one. Now, like I said, I have to go. I've got tech support with me here right now to help fix my problem with Auto CAD. Can I call you back later?"

"Don't bother!" She punched the button to end the call before he could say another word.

She looked at her watch—1:50 p.m. She'd wait ten minutes and go in on the hour. She'd already missed everything anyway. And she had to pay by the hour on a drop-in day, so she might as well get her money's worth.

She knew everything Jack was saying made sense, but she wasn't ready to forgive herself. Or him. Lately he'd been so preoccupied . He always said the right things to her, that's why it was hard to get mad at him, but sometimes she felt like he was on auto pilot while he was saying it. Like he didn't really see her. He didn't see how much stress she was under, how she felt guilty all the time—torn between the house, the kids, him, her teaching job. Did he even notice that she hadn't been writing lately? The last story she submitted for publication was the baby-weight article.

Like most people who work full-time, Jack thought that because she only worked part-time she must have all of this free time available. Her life must be so easy. Well, her life wasn't easy. Not that she'd trade it. But just because she was able to spend a lot of time with her two young children didn't mean her life was any less complicated than any other woman's.

No one in her life understood her loneliness. While she got huge satisfaction out of loving and caring for Noah and Olivia, it still wasn't the same as spending her days with a peer. Someone who gives back. Sure, she had friends, like Sharon, and, of course, Jack, but they were busy with their own stuff. Moments of true kinship were few and far between.

Madeline reached in her purse and pulled out her wallet. She took out the crumpled up paper with Jack's handwriting that she'd been carrying around since he gave it to her a couple of years ago. She'd been having a particularly stressful few weeks and was feeling pretty down. Jack had left for work early that morning, while she was still sleeping, but when she got in her car to take the kids to day care, sitting on her dashboard was a note written on scrap paper, no doubt scribbled in the early-morning darkness. It read, "I'm with you today." Nothing else. Not even a signature.

She pressed the note to her chest. She had been too hard on Jack. Displacement, he'd call it later. He could be quite intuitive for an engineer. She'd apologize, and he'd forgive her. His logical, no nonsense approach to life annoyed her at times, but it also grounded her. In fact, maybe she needed him too much. Had grown too dependent on his emotional support. When it wasn't there, she didn't know what to do anymore. She could help other people with their problems, but she needed Jack to figure out her own. Part of her didn't like that feeling. But then part of her remembered how in tune Jack was with her because they were so close.

She swore that Jack could read her mind in bed. She never had to ask him to touch her somewhere else for awhile. Or move over a little. Or apply more pressure. Or less. He always knew. Just when she was thinking in her head, faster now, he was moving faster. When she pointed this phenomenon out to him, he'd laugh and say, "I'm just good, Baby." But she knew there was more to it than that. She felt a sort of spiritual connection when she had a good conversation with her female friends like Sharon. With her husband, it was sex that was spiritual.

When had they made love last? Had it been a week? Yes, she would definitely apologize tonight, and then maybe one thing would lead to another.

She checked her watch again. Two o'clock. She started walking toward the front door of the day care. Then the door opened and none other than Libby Larson appeared with her daughter Shiloh. Great. Not her. Not now. When Libby saw her, she stopped, held the door, and waited. "You better get in there!" she said too loudly. She wore her plastic smile of concern. "Poor little Olivia has been so upset!"

Madeline felt her nostrils flare and tried to deep breathe the rest of the way up the sidewalk. Libby was one of those full-time stay-at-home moms who never did one thing that didn't revolve around her kids. She used the day care a few hours a week to get her nails done, or shop, although she said she only used the day care for the socialization, so Shiloh could have playmates. But Madeline knew better. She had heard this from other mothers who used the day care full-time and didn't care for Libby's constant bragging about her motherhood. Libby always pretended to be impressed by Madeline's part-time efforts at the college, but she knew Libby secretly judged her for having a job at all when she had two kids to raise.

When she got to the door that Libby was still holding open for her, she forced a smile. "Thank you. How did it go? I really wanted to be here."

"Oh, it was marvelous! You really missed something special. The kids all sang, and then each one got to present to their mother the most adorable little poem with their handprint on it. You know, about always being there, and everything. You can probably still get that poem."

Madeline noticed, as usual, that when Libby's head bobbed as she talked, her short blond hair didn't move. It was a helmet of hairspray. Was she trying to be mean or was she just that stupid? Madeline preferred to think of her as stupid.

"Thanks for the tip. I'll make sure to ask Miss Henderson for it. You and Shiloh have a nice day."

She looked down at Libby's shoes as she walked past her through the doorway. Libby was wearing the latest style from Skechers that was a combination between a sneaker and a sandal. In fact, they looked like gladiator sandals. The sporty, practical shoe that crossed over a mother's foot and held it securely said I have to be comfortable because my kids might need me to sprint across the yard to save them at any minute. Give me a break.

As soon as she entered the room she looked around for Olivia, trying not to make eye contact with any of the other mothers. As soon as Olivia spotted her she ran to her with that adorable scarecrow run—arms and legs akimbo—and jumped into Madeline's arms. "Mommy, where have you been?"

"I'm sorry, Livvie. Mommy was trying to help out her friend, Tessa's Mommy. She's having a tough time right now." She buried her face in Olivia's neck.

"Oh. What did you help her do, Mommy?" Olivia's blond curls were damp with sweat, but she still smelled sweet. She hugged Madeline's head. Thank goodness little kids are so forgiving.

"Mommy stayed with her, well, just outside the room while she was having a bad day."

"Oh, like when you sit outside of my room when I've had a bad dream?"

"Yes, Peanut, pretty much the same thing."

"I've got a present for you in my backpack."

"I can't wait to see it."

"Are we going to see Tessa now?"

"You bet," she said.

After Madeline got Olivia buckled into her booster seat, she headed over to Noah's kindergarten. She pulled into the pick-up loop at 2:20 p.m. and waved to Noah who was already standing there waiting. He was talking to a little boy that she didn't recognize. Noah walked away from the little boy, opened the car door, and dropped his backpack next to Olivia.

"Hi, Big Guy," Madeline said. "Who was that you were talking to?"

"That's Alexander, Mom. The one I've been telling you about. He got his card flipped to black today!"

"Oh, my. Maybe you shouldn't be hanging out with him then."

"He just wanted to know where I got the fool's gold I brought to class for Show and Tell."

"I see. Did you tell him it was on our trip to Cumberland Caverns?"

"No. I couldn't remember that name."

"Well, how was the rest of your day?"

"Great, Mommy. Mrs. Foley said we can bring our apples home tomorrow."

"The ones we made out of construction paper? For the family tree?"

"Yeah!"

"That's great, Honey. We can put it up in the playroom. Say hi to your sister."

"Hi, Livvie."

"Hi, Noah. We're going to see Tessa run now!"

"Did you bring the bell, Mommy?" Noah said.

"Yes, it's in the trunk."

"And my pom poms?" Olivia said.

"Yes, they're back there, too."

"Yaaaay!" Noah and Olivia said in unison.

Madeline pulled out onto the main road and headed for Patterson Middle School. "Listen up, guys. Do you remember Tessa's friend Emily? The one who babysat with her before?"

"Yeah, she's really nice," Noah said.

"She let me use glitter glue one time," Olivia said.

"Well, she's going to run today, too, and she and Tessa are going to take turns watching you, okay? Mommy has got to go be with Tessa's Mom for awhile longer, but then either Daddy or I will be back to pick you up. This is very important. Are you both listening?" She checked the rearview mirror for compliance.

"Yes," they said.

"When Tessa is running, stay with Emily. Listen to Emily. Do not wander away. Understand?"

"Yes," they said.

"When Emily is running, stay with Tessa. Listen to Tessa. Do not wander away. Understand?"

"Yes," Olivia said.

"Noah? I didn't hear you."

"Yes, Mommy, I understand."

"I just want to make sure you're safe. How much does Mommy love you both?"

"Big!" Olivia said.

"A lot," Noah said.

"Right," Madeline said.

She glanced at her watch. "Now, Tessa doesn't get out of school until three. Since we've got a little bit of time, who wants to swing by McDonald's Playland?"

"Me!"

"Me!"

"I said it first!"

"No, I did!"

"Nuh uh!"

"Did too!"

"Mom!"

"It doesn't matter who said it first," she said. "Both of you better knock it off or nobody will get to play."

Madeline sighed deeply as she turned and headed for the golden arches. Although it was Sharon who was in court, she herself had already been judged twice today. First by Carol Wheaton regarding her professionalism, and then by Libby Larson regarding her motherhood. And neither of those women could fully appreciate all that she was trying to juggle.

CHAPTER 18

Tessa

Mrs. Burns, the eighth grade English teacher, was writing on the board when Em poked Tessa in the back with the eraser end of her pencil.

"Pull that down," Em whispered.

"What?"

"Your shirt. Your skin's showing."

Tessa sighed and pulled hard on the hem of her track t-shirt, which she'd changed into after lunch, after the disaster with the ketchup. No use. It was way too small—she'd shrunk it on purpose, so she'd look hot for Tommy, but now she didn't even want him to glance her way.

Luckily, Tommy sat in the front of the English classroom and she sat in the back, on the other side of the room, in their assigned seats. Mrs. Burns seemed to feel that kids like Tommy, who could be a pain during class discussion, did better if they sat up front where she could keep them "engaged." That meant keeping them on the topic.

Tessa liked Mrs. Burns. Even though this was the last period of the day and Tessa was getting anxious about what the judge was going to say, she was halfway able to concentrate on the discussion because Mrs. Burns made it interesting.

Today they were talking about refining a writing prompt to make it more personal. On the board in big, loopy cursive, Mrs. Burns wrote People Who and then three dots, which she called "ellipsis." Then she said, "Notebooks," which meant they were to write ellipsis in their notes, which was a pain, but it also meant ellipsis was going to show up on a test, so Tessa wrote it down.

Mrs. Burns gave a few examples of ways to complete the phrase, such as people who scare me or people who are my heroes, and asked the class for more examples. Tommy kept looking back at her, but Burnsie was all over him, calling his name and asking for his example. Thank God for Burnsie.

Jenny Schneider raised her hand. "Like, can we do "People Who Suck"?

Everybody laughed, including Mrs. Burns, but a couple of seconds later the teacher waved her hand in front of her face and poof, she was serious again. She always did that when she wanted the class to get back on track, and everyone thought it was hilarious. After a couple more giggles, everyone got quiet again.

"Let's take that a step further," Mrs. Burns said to Jenny. "But instead of using your slang term, 'sucks,' we'll use a euphemism." She paused, which meant, write this down. They raised their pens. She spelled and defined euphemism. Then she gave an example. Tessa wrote that down, too. Euphemisms could come in handy when talking to Mom and Dad. Carol, too. Especially Carol. Maybe she'd use the word euphemism at dinner tonight—it would be fun to see Carol's eyes light up.

If she went to Dad's for Wednesday visitation—that was still up in the air. On Sunday, Dad had said not to worry, one way or another he'd see to it that they had their Wednesday evenings together. It still pissed her off that her mom was messing with that.

"Tessa? How might you refine this phrase further?"

Oh, crap. Caught daydreaming again. "Um, I don't know," she said. "People who make me mad?"

"Not bad," Mrs. Burns said. "You've mentioned an emotion—anger—and that's great. But can you be more specific? This is going to be a short essay. If you're specific, you can write less."

"I like that," Tommy said.

Mrs. Burns smiled at Tommy and said, "So you can say more in fewer words. And as we've learned this year, that's even more challenging." She turned back to Tessa. "Any ideas?"

Tessa so wanted to show Tommy how smart she was, how his stupid stunt hadn't shut her down. "Yeah." She gave Tommy a hard stare. "People who let me down."

"Excellent. I can tell from the passion in your voice that you care about what you just came up with. And that, people, is what you want to find—a phrase that gets you feeling angry or thrilled or lonely or scared. That gets you to feel. Then your writing will show that passion." Mrs. Burns went on about the details of the assignment, writing each point on the board and now and again looking over her shoulder.

Mrs. Burns was totally different from Mr. Schilling. Last

year Schilling had given them worksheets on grammar and vocabulary during the third nine weeks so he could focus on directing the school play, which was called Bye, Bye Birdie. It was about a girl who wins a date with a hot celebrity like Justin Timberlake just before the celebrity has to go into the army. Mr. Schilling explained that in the olden days, when that play was written, young men had to serve their country whether they wanted to or not. "Today," he said, running a hand through his too-long gray hair, "we have an all-volunteer military. No draft." Then he went on for a long time about Vietnam and protest marches and other boring stuff until Ryan Dunn raised his hand and asked if this was history or English. Mr. Schilling sent Ryan to the office. Other than that, Schilling was okay. He'd given Tessa the lead part in Bye Bye Birdie, even though she'd missed the audition, and he'd also encouraged her to pursue acting as a career.

The only other adult who'd ever talked seriously to her about "a career in the theater" was Carol. Her stepmom actually thought that if she worked hard in school, she could get into Yale. Tessa still wasn't sure she wanted to go into acting—modeling sounded like so much more fun, posing in exotic places like Paris and Hawaii—but she always felt so smart when Carol told her she had the brains to go to an Ivy League college.

"You have the rest of the period to work on your drafts," Burnsie was saying. "Write as quickly as you can. Don't stop to fix anything. You'll do that tonight, for homework."

A few kids groaned, but Burnsie made her serious face into a happy one. Tessa knew the hand thing was just a gimmick, but it worked because Mrs. Burns didn't act all fake or lie or send them to the office for minor offenses. She treated all the kids, even the pains and the daydreamers, as if they mattered. Mrs. Burns was the one grownup in her life that hadn't let her down. Not yet, anyway.

Tessa chewed on the end of her pen for a minute and started to write.

PEOPLE WHO LET ME DOWN

by Tessa Trent

People let me down all the time. Like today, my best friend and I were going to dress alike, including our shoes. When she got to my house (we walk to school together) she was wearing a pair of dark brown Mudd platform sandals, which was the exact opposite of the all-white Nike Shox we were going to wear. I know. That's such a little thing. But to me it was huge, because today is a really big day for me. Not only do I have a major track meet after school, but my parents are in court arguing over which one I am going to live with from now on. Talk about stress! So when my best friend showed up in those sandals, I was like, Oh, no, how could you. She so let me down.

At lunch I sat near a guy I've been friends with since sixth grade. We used to be really close, and for a long time now, I have had deeper feelings for him that I have been trying to communicate without being too weird. Today I tried to show him without words that I cared for him (and would even go out with him if he asked me) but instead of either ignoring me in a polite way or showing me that he liked me that way too, he threw food at me. He ruined my favorite t-shirt, and I had to change into an old shrunken tee that I hate. He hurt my feelings and embarrassed me so much! He let me down even more than my best friend. Way more.

But the people who have let me down the most in my life are my parents. That includes my stepmom. It's weird, but even though I'm not all that close to Carol (my stepmom) because she and Dad have only been married since January, she has let me down slightly less than Mom or Daddy. Her problem is she's pushy. She takes Dad's side to the point that he gets mad at Mom and goes overboard. Carol thinks I need to study more and makes me do study table at their house. Also, there's always somebody in the house when I get home from school at Dad's. Carol thinks I need that kind of supervision at Mom's, too, so she talked Dad into calling Mom and asking her to "tweak" my custody schedule. My mom got really, really mad and filed a motion with the court to have me almost all of the time. I wouldn't even get to go to Dad's every other weekend! That is totally unacceptable! If Carol had kept her nose out of it, I wouldn't have to be wondering as I sit here writing this who I'm going home with tonight! So that is how my stepmom let me down.

My dad has let me down even more, though. He says he loves me a lot (and I love him too BTW) and comes to all my meets and buys me most of what I want. But ever since I started middle school, he's been like, "Tessa, ask your mom," or "Tessa, ask Carol" when I come to him with a problem, as if he has no clue how to be a dad anymore. I mean, before the divorce he always let my mom have final say, and okay, he wasn't home much and was on his cell phone all the time, but he's a realtor. That's how he does business. And he's good at what he does. So I was always okay with that when Mom and Dad were married. But now, for some reason, I need my dad to be more than that, and he's all like, "I don't know, Tessa, go ask someone else." Ever since I started having boyfriends and going to dances and all that, he can't handle it, so he turns it all over to my mom and stepmom.

But the person who has let me down the most (and I feel really bad saying this, but it is true) is my mom. I mean, I love my mom to pieces, but ever since Dad left, it's been all about Mom. Like I'm not hurting? Like I don't need special understanding? I lost my Daddy! Now he never comes home. That's worse than when he used to be gone most of the time. Our house feels so empty. It even echoes. And Mom just goes on and on about how hurt and lonely and mad she is. What does she think I am?

The worst part is, even God let me down. I should probably add that I was never all that religious. I mean, I go to church on holidays and some Sundays, but it's not like I pray every night or say grace over my lunch like some kids do. But after Mom and Dad split up, I used to pray they'd get back together. I really believed He would make that happen, because I had always been a pretty good kid. So I thought, God will make this come out all right. That was when I started to feel better. I was really doing pretty good for a while, thinking maybe God really loved me. I hoped that with time, Mom and Dad would quit fighting and get married again.

When Dad told me he was seeing someone, it was like God shoved a sliver of glass in my heart. I could just tell that this "someone" wasn't a girlfriend you take to the Friday night dance or something. This person was clearly someone super-special to him already, plus I also overheard my mom talking about Dad being involved with this older college professor. I thought, Dad's going to marry her! He's just waiting to tell me when he thinks I can take it. And sure enough, a few months later, he told me that he and Carol were getting married after the holidays. I was so upset I threw up.

It wasn't just that Dad was getting remarried. Kids' parents do that all the time. It was that I asked God to put my parents back together over and over, and instead of making that happen, God did just the opposite. He let me down completely. For the first time in my life, I'm beginning to wonder if there even is a God.

Tessa put down her pen and gasped for breath. She felt like someone was sitting on her chest. She forced herself not to panic, turned around in her seat and pulled her Vuitton bag off the back of the chair. Her inhaler had to be in there somewhere.

Em looked up. "You okay?"

She shook her head and unzipped her bag. Where was that inhaler? She knew she'd brought it with her. Crap. Maybe it was in her backpack. But where? She couldn't remember if she'd put it in the outside pocket or inside.

She struggled to get air, making strange little sounds that reminded her of a tiny pipe organ in her chest. Was she going to die here, in Burnsie's classroom, with all the kids standing in a circle around her watching her turn blue? She tried to squeeze out two words, "My...backpack," but she didn't even have enough breath left for that.

Em was now rooting frantically in Tessa's purse. She tried to tell Em the inhaler wasn't in there, but no words would come out. Then Mrs. Burns was standing next to her, pulling her to her feet. "We need to get you to the nurse's office," she said. Em was right behind her, stuffing Tessa's English paper into her backpack and hoisting it onto her shoulder along with the Vuitton bag.

"I'll take her," Em said.

"We'll both take her," Mrs. Burns said. "Keep working, people," she said to the class. "The excitement's over."

But it wasn't. Tessa still couldn't breathe.

CHAPTER 19

Sharon

Sharon was walking up the sidewalk to the glass front doors of the courthouse when she changed her mind. She'd make a quick stop at her car to use her cell phone and leave one more message.

She dialed Tessa's number. "Hi, Sweetheart. It's Mom. I miss you. I'm thinking about you. I just had a nice lunch with Madeline and I'm back at court now. I think we'll be up soon. Now don't worry, I'm going to take care of everything. You just enjoy this gorgeous spring day we're having and I'll see you soon. If you get to stay with me tonight we can do our toenails! Love you! Byeeeee!"

She dropped her cell phone in the front seat and headed back up the sidewalk. She was a good mother. She always tried to be upbeat, encouraging, and fun around Tessa. But still, as Madeline had suggested, time apart can make the heart grow fonder. If Tessa stopped going to Wes's on Wednesdays and only went one weekend a month instead of two, she wouldn't get as many chances to miss Sharon. She did seem to appreciate her mother more after she came back from Wes's. Was more interested in spending time with her. At least she didn't balk when Sharon dragged out the nail polish and popcorn for their pajama parties in front of the TV.

She walked through the metal detectors for the second time that day. On the other hand, if she won at court today, Tessa would be home this weekend, so she wouldn't have to record *Desperate Housewives* for them to watch later. It would be a celebration. She hated sitting at home alone knowing their show was on, thinking about Tessa being with Wes. And The Evil-Know-It-All. Especially she hated thinking about Tessa with The Evil-Know-It-All. At least she didn't have to worry about The Evil-Know-It-All trying to watch *Desperate Housewives* with Tessa, or trying to be her girlfriend. That pseudo-intellectual would never lower herself enough to participate in pop culture. Didn't she get that she drove Tessa crazy by riding her all the time about her grades?

When she'd made her way through the halls to the courtroom doors, Sharon found Marcus standing just outside of them.

"There you are," he said. "Have a nice lunch?"

"As a matter of fact, I did," she said.

"Good. We'll probably be up next. Are you ready?"

"As much as I'll ever be."

They sat close to the front this time. The judge wasn't back yet, but there were far fewer people waiting now. She felt a surge of hope. Maybe this would all be over soon.

She turned to look when she heard the doors in the back open. It was Wes and his stick-figured attorney. What had they been doing over the lunch break? Whatever it was, certainly The Evil-Know-It-All had supervised.

Judge Francis and the bailiff entered from the side doors.

After the bailiff asked everyone to stand and announced that court was now in session, the judge called for the Trent vs. Connor case.

Wes's attorney jumped up. "Here, Your Honor."

Marcus took her arm and they stood. "We're here also, Your Honor," he said.

The four of them walked forward and stood in pairs on either side of the bench. Sharon straightened her back.

Judge Francis looked back and forth and studied them for a moment.

"So there are two motions today. Am I to understand that Mr. Trent—" She looked at Wes and raised her eyebrows.

"Yes, Your Honor?" his attorney said.

She continued. "Mr. Trent has requested a change of physical custody?"

"Yes, Your Honor. My cli—"

"And Ms. Connor—" She glanced at Sharon. "—has filed a counter motion requesting that the existing parenting time of the teenage child with her father be reduced?"

"Yes, Your Honor," Marcus said. "We feel that Mr. Trent and his new wife have been alienating Tessa from her mother. Tessa is confused right now and needs the stability of a more regular routine. And since Tessa has spent the majority of her life in the care of my client, that environment is her comfort zone and is where she should be."

Judge Francis looked at Wes and then at his attorney. "And Mr. Trent?"

"We believe that Ms. Connor is only requesting that parenting time be reduced as a retaliation to my client's motion," the stick figure said. "The truth is that Ms. Connor works a lot and just doesn't have the time to spend with Tessa that Mr. Trent and Ms. Wheaton have—"

"Are you suggesting that my client should be punished for being a single mother with a career?" Marcus said.

"Furthermore, Ms. Wheaton holds a doctorate degree and is a respected educator."

"That means Ms. Wheaton makes a better candidate for motherhood?" Marcus said. He sounded as outraged as Sharon felt.

"What we're suggesting," the stick figure said, "is that Ms. Connor has grown more and more unstable over the past couple of years and that it would be in Tessa's best interest for her to spend the majority of her time with her father."

Marcus turned to her. "Are your referring to the past couple of years since your client cheated on my client during their marriage and then married the woman he was having an affair with?"

There it was. The zinger. Sharon wanted to kiss Marcus. She watched Wes's face so she could enjoy the full effect. He looked like he needed a bucket.

"Your Honor," the stick figure said, "Mr. McDermott's client knows perfectly well that Ms. Wheaton was not the reason for the breakdown of the marriage. And the issues Mr. Trent has with Ms. Connor's mothering now are some of the same issues he had with her during the marriage. As well as a few new ones."

This couldn't be happening. Sharon took a breath to speak, but Marcus put his hand on her arm to stop her. "If Ms. Powell is going to even attempt to suggest there is negligence on my client's part, she'd better be able to back it up."

Wes whispered something to his attorney. She nodded and then said, "Your Honor, we are not accusing Ms. Connor of negligence. And we are willing to consider a compromise, but reducing Mr. Trent's parenting time to only one weekend a month is completely unacceptable. Ms. Connor has no real basis for claiming that this is in any way in Tessa's best interest. She is close to her father and gets along well with his wife, Ms. Wheaton. They provide a loving, stable home for her. Your Honor should definitely consider giving him more, not less time."

Judge Francis looked back and forth between Marcus and Wes's attorney. "Counselors, I'm going to give you time to try to work out a compromise between your clients. It sounds to me like there is no compelling reason to make a significant increase, or decrease, of parenting time on either side. If I'm forced to rule, I will, but then neither of them may be happy with my decision. Please encourage them to try to reach an agreement."

"Yes, Your Honor," Marcus said.

"Thank you, Your Honor," the stick figure said.

The two attorneys whispered to each other as they started walking toward the back doors. Sharon and Wes followed, trying not to walk directly beside each other.

When they stepped into the small waiting area, The Evil-Know-It-All was sitting there by herself reading a book. Sharon wished Madeline was there. She must still be trying to get the kids to Tessa and Emily. Sharon stayed focused on Marcus to avoid eye contact with any of the rest of them. She was glad when he quickly he took her by the arm and led her down the hallway.

The only sound on that awkward trek was the sharp rapping of the stick figure's high heels on the concrete flooring as the three of them followed behind—Wes and the two dominating women in his life. At least he'd stopped the dominatrix in the black high heels from trying to ruin her reputation in front of the judge. But the real question was would he ever be able to control the dominating woman he'd married.

Whispering started up back there, then stopped abruptly. No doubt The-Evil-Know-It-All was dying for details. Why did she have to be in on this?

Before they reached the metal detectors, they turned left down another hallway. In a few yards they came upon two rooms, one on the left and one on the right. Marcus led her into the room on the left. She turned to see the stick figure leading Wes and The Evil-Know-It-All into the room on the right.

When Marcus had closed the door behind them, Sharon sat in one of the metal chairs around the conference table. In the cramped room with the overhead fluorescent lighting, she might have been waiting for a cop to come in and interrogate her until she confessed to a crime. In fact, this whole experience was making her feel like a criminal fighting for her life.

"What are you thinking?" Marcus said as he turned the chair next to her to face her and sat down.

"I. . .am. . .so. . .angry," she said, allowing a full emotional response to wash over her now that she was away from the watchful eye of the judge. "I can't believe they suggested that I'm unstable and that Wes has issues with my mothering. He knows damn well I'm a fantastic mother!"

"It seems like they have a card they're thinking about playing. Do you have any idea what that might be?"

"No. I can't imagine what he thinks he's got on me."

"Think for a minute what Tessa might have told them that you don't even realize has been discussed at their house."

She fiddled with the Tiffany & Co. ID tag on her choker.

"Sharon, you might as well tell me everything you can think of. I'd rather find out now from you than be blindsided in front of the judge." Marcus took a pen and legal pad out of his briefcase.

"Well," she said, trying to keep her voice from shaking, "Tessa knows I've been taking Valium to help me sleep. I had a tough time when Wes first left me. A lot of anxiety and insomnia, you know, like anybody would when something traumatic happens. My doctor prescribed them for me, though, so how can he possibly use that against me?"

"It has been two years since your divorce, right?"

"Right," she said and then swallowed.

"So Valium isn't supposed to be used long-term. Do you take it during the day or just at night?"

"Usually just at night."

"Usually?" Marcus said, furrowing his brow. "So that means you're out of it sometimes during the day when Tessa is around, and when you're driving her?"

"Why are you talking to me like this?" she said. She couldn't believe this was happening. Suddenly even Marcus thought she was a bad mother because she was human and needed help coping sometimes. She was a single mother, for god's sake. No one had her back.

"Sharon, I'm not judging you. I'm just trying to show you how the other side can twist things."

"So what do you suggest I do? Fold? Do you think I should just give them what they want?" She knew her voice was shrill.

"I'm not saying that. But maybe we should consider offering them more than one weekend a month. If we throw them a bone, I don't think they'll go after your pill problem."

Sharon wanted to say I don't have a pill problem, but she was too defeated to protest.

There was a knock at the door. Marcus jumped up, cracked the door, and peeked out. He turned back to her. "It's their attorney. I'll be right back." Marcus grabbed his legal pad and pen and slid through the crack in the door without opening it much, then carefully closed it behind him. She wanted to laugh at the absurdity. It was as though they were children playing a game of espionage. When Marcus came back with a message from across the room, maybe it would self-destruct in five seconds. A Mission Impossible. That's what this was. How could she live her life like this, constantly fighting with Wes and his new wife, pulling Tessa back and forth between them?

The door opened slightly and Marcus slid back through. "They have a compromise." He looked down at his legal pad. "They don't want Tessa with them full time, but they do want to see her more during the week so they can help supervise homework. You're at work during the afternoons anyway. This way Tessa won't be home alone. Wes can adjust his appointments to be there when she gets home from school. Then you can pick her up in the evenings, either before or after dinner. You can think about which works best for you.

You could still alternate weekends. Although—" He scratched something out on the pad. "Wes is so busy on the weekends because of the nature of real estate, so he may want some Thursday nights instead of Saturday nights. What do you think about alternating—"

"Stop. Just stop." She put her hands over her ears and closed her eyes. "I can't do this right now. I can't think about it any more today. My head is going to explode!"

When she opened her eyes again, Marcus said, "Here's what we're going to do. We'll tell the judge we can't reach a compromise today. We've been here since early this morning and it's almost three o'clock now. We are going to need a continuance. She'll probably give us 30 days to try to work it out before she makes her own ruling."

"Fine." She couldn't think of anything else to say.

"I'll be right back," he said. He shut the door softly behind him.

She closed her eyes again and tried not to think about the fact that more than anything right now she wanted to swallow a little white pill.

CHAPTER 20

Carol

"Unbelievable!" Carol's voice bounced off the hard walls of the cramped conference room where they'd worked so hard to hammer out a compromise, as directed by the judge. Sharon, of course, had rejected it. Worse, she'd refused to provide a counter-offer.

"The woman is simply unstable," Carol said. "She has no center, no sticking power. She's all feelings and no thoughts—"

"Carol." Wes put his finger to his lips. "Let's talk about it in the car."

Stephanie turned to Wes and said she'd finish up and call him on Monday.

Carol grunted and reached under the chair for her bag. "Then what? We'll discuss Sharon's latest round of ridiculous demands? Let me guess. She'll ask for yet more child support and to be with Tessa every other leap year day."

"Please," Wes said, "wait till we get in the car."

She knew that tone. "All right," she said.

They made their way to the courthouse parking lot, Wes squeezing her upper arm lightly, as if to keep her quiet, but in the most gentlemanly way possible. When they got to his Mercedes, he reached in his pocket, frowned, and turned to her, a look of confusion on his face. "You still have my key, don't you?"

"What? Oh. Yes, just a moment." She unzipped the inner pocket of her bag, nudged the tampon holder aside, and pulled out the keyless remote he'd tossed her this morning, when she'd volunteered to take their cell phones back to the Benz. That seemed like an eternity ago.

"Thanks," Wes said. "I ought to get you one of these. One of your own. This is your car, too, now." He pressed remote, opened her door, and helped her up into the tall SUV.

"Why don't we drive through campus," she said as he settled in behind the wheel. "The meet won't start for an hour or so, and I could use a little time to decompress."

Wes shrugged and started the car.

"I'm so disappointed," she said.

He turned left out of the parking lot but said nothing.

She tried again. "We were willing to give up so much."

"Carol, we're really not giving up anything we don't want to give up. We talked about that at lunch."

"True. But we responded with an offer of genuine compromise—Tessa would spend afternoons with us, after school, until Sharon gets home from work. Otherwise, the same schedule she has now. No change in child support or holidays. How can Sharon pass that up?"

Wes shrugged.

Why would he not say what he was feeling? It was irritating that he kept so much inside. She'd been amazed he'd revealed so much of himself at lunch. Perhaps that was all he had in him. On the other hand, perhaps she could draw him out again.

"Why is she dragging things out?" she said, trying to sound as if she were musing to herself. Sometimes that drew a response from Wes. Not this time.

She turned to him and said, with some passion, "I think she just wants to make us sweat, Wesley. She actually enjoys seeing us twist in the wind."

"I don't know." He sounded as if he were pulling the words out of hardening cement. "Sharon can be pretty spiteful when she's hurt, but usually she'll jump at the chance to get what she wants. I think she was blindsided by our offer. She's been fighting so long she doesn't know what to do when someone gives in."

"Not that we gave in, exactly."

"Not at all," he said. "I wish that was how Sharon saw it."

As they entered campus through the south gate, she took a deep breath and exhaled slowly. "Wes, if you don't mind, I'd rather not talk about Sharon or Tessa right now. I need to clear my thoughts."

He nodded.

She took another deep breath and focused her attention on the scene outside, one that never failed to calm and yet inspire her. The university campus was at its most beautiful in spring. Two weeks ago its beauty had peaked, though. She recalled the crabapples bursting into bloom, their fragrance wafting in through the open window in her office. She'd breathed in their scent the way she breathed in Wes's, like a lover's musky cologne, and wished the trees could stay that way forever.

But they hadn't, of course. It wasn't in them to last. They had no fight in them—they refused to cling to what they loved, those sturdy but delicate branches. Every year the blossoms withered and blew away in the wind like pastel confetti, replaced by tiny apples and pointed, oval leaves the color of Madeline Greenfield's pants. The leaves and fruit grew all summer long, getting fuller and heavier. Eventually fat crabapples would drop to the ground and rot, and the leaves would die and blow away as the blossoms had. All winter she'd stare out at the bare branches—dark and shiny after a late November rainstorm, gray-brown beneath a light coating of snow—and imagine another spring.

Now, in their spring phase, the chartreuse leaves stood out in sharp contrast to the dark orange-red brick of the campus buildings. Late tulips and a few withering daffodils still bloomed here and there in well-tended beds. "Narcissus," her mother had called the little daffodils she'd planted in their yard. "So beautiful, like that young man who fell in love with his own reflection."

Carol recalled a time when she was eight or nine, a little stick of a thing, too skinny to hold up her taffeta Easter skirt without the velvet suspenders her grandmother had made for that purpose. She and Mother had walked hand in hand through Mill Creek Park while her father and brothers played ball near the picnic shelter. "Look at that," her mother said, pointing to a nearby hill, which was not green but bright yellow. Carol squinted to make out whatever had turned the hillside that hopeful color. "Daffodils," her mother said, pointing. "Thousands and thousands of daffodils. God's promise fulfilled." It was the only time she'd ever heard her mother, who'd converted to Catholicism to please her father, speak about God in her own words.

She turned her attention back to the campus outside, streaming by as if in a travelogue viewed in slow motion. She rarely saw it this way. Usually she walked to campus from their home a few blocks away. When one walked, the buildings stood out as individual entities. The steeple-topped chapel, which lent a New England flavor to the central quadrangle. Crandall Hall, as square and squat as a reddish-brown toad. The Charles P. Fessler Library, its central tower thrusting up into the Dresden-blue sky, looking as proud and tall and hard as Stephanie Powell. Peebles Hall, the English building, with its mismatched wings, alike but not alike, like her twins.

This part of the college, the historic part, had been built in the nineteenth century and reflected the more linear, no-nonsense lines of the Queen Anne period. Carol was grateful that the college's founders had avoided the frippery of later Victorian excesses. She was even more grateful they'd stipulated that all buildings erected henceforth must conform to a similar style. Every class building and dormitory—even the newer Chandler Auditorium—was composed of rust-colored brick, in simple lines, with stone lintels and sills and glinting multipaned windows. The composite effect was one of harmony, simplicity, and—she had to admit it—charm. The college, viewed this way, had charm.

It wasn't a small college any more, though. Tiny Fessler College became Central Methodist College near the turn of the twentieth century, and morphed again, toward the end of the 1970s, into Fessler University. Not long after that, she and Lyle had found positions here, he in the history department, she in English. Had he lived, he'd still be holed up in Crandall Hall, in his dusty corner office, poring over old books the library messengers had just trotted over to him, like eager servants. He'd had charm, too—a quiet charm. Not like Wes's more dazzling charisma.

She looked at her husband while he drove, his perfect profile superimposed on the sunny spring day. How had she gone from Lyle to Wes? Alpha to Omega—or was it the other way around?

Carol shifted her gaze to the bicycling students speeding to class while Wes maintained the absurd fifteen-mile-per-hour speed limit required on all central campus streets. They too had been built of bricks but had been paved over with asphalt and striped in a garish yellow that reminded Carol of the chair she sat in when she released her frustrations at Adele Martin's office.

She slid her hand into the glove compartment and pulled out her cell phone. Dr. Martin would no doubt be in session now, but Carol thought she'd let her know that the hearing—such as it had been—was over, at least for now. She felt an odd calm descending on her, as if the barometric pressure in her head had dropped. It would feel good to hear Dr. Martin's voice, if only a recorded version.

"Who are you calling?" Wes said, averting his eyes from the road for a second.

"Dr. Martin. I thought I'd let her know what...Wes! Watch out!"

Wes braked to avoid hitting a tousled student on a bicycle. "Damn," he said. "He never even looked up."

She slipped her cell phone into her bag. She'd call Dr. Martin later, perhaps during one of the many tiresome lulls at the track meet. Wes didn't need any more distraction right now.

And Wes was right about the cyclist. Even now, the boy pedaled on, oblivious, with his shaggy head nodding rhythmically, a pair of white wires dangling from his ears. Like Tessa—always plugged into "her" music, her culture—or lack thereof.

Still, Carol had to admit that Tessa had style. Other girls copied from their peers. Tessa chose her clothes based on some other aesthetic, something internal. Something she'd learned from her mother. Her real mother.

"Wesley," she said, pointing. "Turn left here, will you? There's something I need to pick up at the Satin Giraffe."

"What?" Wes's forehead wrinkled.

"A pair of shoes, actually. I've had my eye on them for some time."

CHAPTER 21

Madeline

Madeline watched all of the kids running around McDonald's Playland. She scanned the passersby for signs of her two, and occasionally, she actually spotted one of them.

There was Noah's white sport socks coming out of the tube slide, then the rest of him. His butt skidded across the floor. Rather than land on his feet, he preferred a dramatic finish. If the rough and tumble landing hurt, you'd never know it. He laughed, bounced back up, and was off again.

Madeline caught sight of Olivia as she inched her way backwards down the levels of one of the towers. That was Olivia, cautious and deliberate, careful not to injure herself. Roll to the tummy, let the feet down first, secure them on the level below before releasing the upper body.

Madeline took her cell phone out of her purse and dialed Jack. More ringing and voice mail picking up. Why wasn't he answering? He'd said he was busy today, but he usually picked up when he saw from the Caller ID that it was her, even if he could just talk for a second. Maybe she'd underestimated how upset he'd been when they last spoke. His voice stayed even and calm. But she had hung up on him at the end. Maybe he was punishing her by not returning her calls. She'd already left a quick message that she was trying to get in touch with him. She wouldn't leave a second. She would wait.

Olivia wandered over to the table where Madeline was sitting. "Mommy, is it time to go see Tessa yet?"

Madeline checked her watch. Ten minutes until three o'clock. "It just about is, Baby. Five more minutes, okay?"

"Okay, Mommy." Olivia lay her head in Madeline's lap. Madeline patted her back, then ran her fingers through her daughter's damp, tangled hair.

When Olivia straightened back up, Madeline leaned in to kiss the top of her head. She caught a whiff of that babyish scent she loved so much. Both of her kids still had that perfect, sweet smell about them. Their hair, their skin. She shoved her nose into the folds of Olivia's neck and sniffed loudly, like a dog. She rooted her nose around Olivia's neck and chin as Olivia rode waves of laughter.

"Mommy!" Her head was thrown back in ecstasy.

"Okay, go play now," Madeline said, before she got her daughter too far out of control. "And tell your brother five more minutes when you see him."

"Okaaaay," Olivia sang as she skipped back toward the play structure.

At the table across from Madeline, a woman sat down with her tray. She had no children with her, which was odd, since most adults wouldn't go anywhere near a Playland if they didn't have to. Madeline couldn't help but stare at her. She'd never seen anyone like her around Columbus. Could she be in town for the upcoming powwow at the county fairgrounds she'd just read about in the Dispatch? According to the article, the annual event was named after a Sioux woman who founded the Native American Center of Central Ohio in the seventies. Must be a small group of members in this area.

She had no idea whether this woman was Sioux, but she had long, perfectly shiny, straight black hair. Her skin was as rich and creamy as a Starbucks cappuccino. She wore blue jeans and a white shirt with snaps down the front. Her body was lean and strong. Her nose was perfectly straight, her high cheekbones sculpted. All features Madeline coveted but did not possess. She had her squatty, featureless German ancestry to thank for that.

On the woman's feet were moccasins. Actual moccasins. Not the knock-offs you can buy almost anywhere. These were impressive. Completely covered with orange, white, and blue beads.

The woman was so striking, she could have been the model for Disney's Pocahontas, Olivia's current favorite of the Disney movies. She also could have been the actress in the movie she and Jack saw during their trip to Niagara Falls. The Maid of the Mist. That was the name of the tour boat they'd ridden around in at the bottom of the falls. The name referred to the Native American maiden who legend said disappeared into the mist. That overwhelming mist. They were given disposable blue raincoats to wear on the journey because it's impossible to pass by the torrential falls without getting soaked.

After their boat ride, she'd insisted that she and Jack stop by the nearby Imax Theatre to learn more about the legend. In the movie, Princess Lelawala, daughter of the chief of a tribe that lived near the Niagara River, was being forced to marry an elderly tribesman of her father's choosing. She decided to run away rather than marry a man she didn't love.

Wearing moccasins and an animal-skin shift, Lelawala stepped into a canoe and paddled her way down the river, which eventually led her over the falls and to her death. Her spirit lived on, and she was forever after referred to as the Maid of the Mist. Madeline had been drawn to the woman in that legend as she was now drawn to this woman. She'd never wanted a pair of moccasins in her whole life, until now.

She picked at Noah's leftover fries. Of course the kids had to order Happy Meals, even though they'd both already had lunch. She took the last bite of Olivia's cheeseburger. Since her children had been on solid food, her meals usually consisted of their scraps piecemealed together. She rarely ate a full meal of her own anymore.

She could relate to Princess Lelawala. She, too, would never marry a man she didn't love. She'd rather go over the falls. Once she knew the love was gone, she'd run away from Reese as fast as if she were shooting down a river on a canoe. And that ride had landed her at Jack and a new life. A better life.

She threw the kids' trash away, careful to save their Happy Meal toys, and found their shoes in the red bins by the play structure. One pair of Stride Rite slip-on sneakers—Noah hadn't learned to tie his shoes yet—and one pair of pink Stride Rite Mary Janes with a velcro strap and the word "Munchkins" printed on the soles.

"Noah and Olivia Greenfield, time to go!" she said, trying to project her voice over the chaos. After only a few protests, she soon had them corralled and their shoes back on.

On the short ride over to Patterson Middle School, Noah said, "Is Daddy coming to the game, too?"

She didn't realize she hadn't answered until Noah asked again. "Mommy? What about Daddy?"

"He's supposed to come later, to get you and Olivia, if I'm not back. How about we try to call Daddy right now?"

She dialed Jack's cell number with one hand while she drove with the other. She reached behind her to hand the ringing phone to Noah.

"I want to talk to Daddy, too!" Olivia said as Noah took the phone.

"After Noah," Madeline said. "Shhhh!"

"It's Daddy's voice, but it's not him," Noah said, sounding dejected.

"Leave him a message. Tell him you're looking forward to seeing him at the track meet when he gets off work. Don't forget to wait for the beep."

"Daddy? Um, I see you look forward here at the meet. Love you!"

"Now hand the phone to your sister."

"Hi Daddy!" Olivia said, then she waited.

"Livvie," Madeline said, "remember, it's a message. You have to talk."

"When are you coming, Daddy?"

"Tell him you'll see him later."

"I'll see you later!"

"Tell Daddy you love him."

"I love you, Daddy!"

"Okay, now hand the phone back to me."

Madeline put the phone to her ear just as she was pulling

into the Patterson Middle School pick-up loop. “Hi Babe. I still haven’t heard anything from Sharon, so I guess once I find Tessa and Emily I’m headed back to court. Fun, fun. It may be hard for me to call you again since I can’t take my phone into the courthouse, so don’t wait to hear from me, just plan on coming over here to PMS after you get off work. I love you.” She chuckled at her inadvertent reference to pre-menstrual syndrome in the message. She and Sharon got a kick out of exploiting the acronym for Tessa’s school.

As she pushed End Call she wondered why she hadn’t said, “Sorry about earlier.” She’d been thinking it. But it hadn’t come out of her mouth.

She waited at the curb while middle school students came out and either jumped on a bus or jumped in their parent’s car. She thought of Princess Lelawala again. Proud, strong, independent, unafraid.

“Mommy, can you turn on Radio Disney?” Olivia said.

“Sure.” She pushed the ON button and a rap version of the Little Red

Riding Hood tale came on. Noah and Olivia were singing along. They knew every word. She had to admit it was catchy, but also bizarre—a fairy tale from the hood. Nothing like the music she had listened to as a child. An image of Kermit the Frog singing “The Rainbow Connection” leapt to her mind.

Cars were pulling out of line behind her and swerving around her to leave. She watched the last few kids wander out of the doors. Still no Tessa.

She drove out of the pick-up loop and around to the parking lot. “Come on guys, let’s go find Tessa.”

She unbuckled Olivia while Noah hopped out of the car

on his own. She grabbed both of their hands—Noah was famous for darting off in a parking lot. When they were inside, she led them into the main office. The secretary was shuffling papers, probably finishing up her daily tasks. She looked like she'd already had quite enough for the day. Both kids were pulling and tugging on Madeline's arms to get away, but she had a firm grip on them.

"Hi, I'm Madeline Greenfield," she said and waited for the secretary to look up. "I'm looking for Tessa Trent. I'm a friend of her mother's."

"I believe Tessa is still in with the nurse," the woman said.

"Is she okay?"

"She had a little scare. Mrs. Burns brought her down here at the end of last period. You can go on down there if you want. At the end of the main hallway make a right, then the next left. The nurse's office is the first doorway on the right."

"Thank you." Madeline backed up and turned around, moving herself and the kids together in one fluid motion, and headed in the direction of the nurse's office.

This was not what Sharon needed today.

CHAPTER 22

Tessa

Tessa sat in the nurse's office, on the edge of the chair, trying to relax. Her heart had stopped thumping, but her chest was still tight. On the nurse's desk a few feet to her left was her pink backpack. On her lap was her Vuitton bag, and in her hand, her albuterol inhaler, which she'd found in the front pocket of her cargo shorts just as the nurse was telling Burnsie and Em she could take it from there. She should have looked in her pocket first—that was where her mom liked her to carry her inhaler—but she'd been so freaked out by the asthma attack that she'd forgotten she'd slipped it in there this morning.

Now, a few scary minutes and two puffs of albuterol later, she didn't feel quite so panicky, but for once she didn't feel like talking, either. Instead, she watched while the nurse bustled around her office, tidying up her files at the end of the day.

"You're gonna be breathing a whole lot better real soon," the nurse said, nodding her beaded, braided head. "Just take it easy for a few minutes, rest up." The nurse opened a file drawer, took out a folder and started writing.

Tessa had never seen this nurse at Patterson before. That

had freaked her out at first, because Nurse Musgrave was this one's total opposite, short and sort of chubby, with long, feathered hair the color of ballpark mustard—not her best color, especially with her pasty white complexion. This new nurse looked amazing in her tight, coppery braids and golden tan that didn't look like it came from a booth.

And those beads! Each tiny braid was strung in every pastel shade imaginable. Some matched the mint green of the nurse's scrubs, which was another thing that made her different. Nurse Musgrave would never have worn scrubs. She usually wore khaki pants and cotton knit twin sets and loafer-y mules, much less medical-looking. The new nurse was wearing scrubs and lavender Crocs clogs and even had a stethoscope draped around her neck. She looked like she could get a job acting in Grey's Anatomy and never need a wardrobe change.

Tessa had been thinking about getting a pair of Crocs for herself—she loved all the styles and colors the plastic shoes came in. She'd first seen them at the University of Kentucky bookstore. That was the weekend they'd all driven down to Lexington visit her stepbrother, Michael, who was studying to be a pharmacist.

"All the med people wear them," Mike said as they passed the display. Of course he didn't. He still wore the same black leather Adidas he'd been wearing when she'd met him last fall.

The purpose of the trip to UK, her dad said, was to spend some time with her "new family." She'd wanted to say something about him coming back to his old family, but she didn't want to act like a total dork in front of Eric, her other stepbrother, the hot one. Eric was also the handy one, the guy who fixed the family's messed-up computers and broken furniture. He was going for an associate degree in some techno field after dropping out of the University of Michigan. Carol was super-disappointed that Eric wasn't in a real college studying a real major, but she never said so. She just kept leaving brochures from Ivy League schools on his desk in his room, even though Eric now lived in an apartment in Columbus and hardly ever came home.

On their way to and from Lexington, Tessa made sure she sat in the backseat, next to Eric. Mike was smart and nice and all that, but he had that over-the-top Carol seriousness. Eric was a lot more fun—the way Carol would be if she wasn't so busy bossing Daddy around. Eric was the kind of guy she'd like to go out with some day.

Not that she'd ever consider going out with Eric. For one thing he was her stepbrother. For another he was way too old for her. Lately, though, she'd been thinking about how great it would be to go out with somebody a little older than the guys who went to Patterson. Like Tommy. God, he was immature. That ketchup stunt had been totally childish. So had the way he'd been acting in English today. Maybe that's what had set off her asthma attack. Well, that and what was going on in court. She was so keyed up over how the hearing would come out that she could hardly concentrate on the track meet, let alone her school subjects.

Could she even compete today, after the asthma episode? She took a deep breath and then another—she was definitely breathing easier now.

"I was just wondering," she said to the nurse. "Can I run

later? In the track meet? I'm doing relays, and the other girls are sort of depending on me."

The nurse looked up over her half-glasses, which had the cutest pink plastic frames. They reminded Tessa of her mom's "cheaters," the drugstore glasses her mom wore at home only, so she didn't have to hold close print way out at arm's length.

"I don't see why not," the nurse said, "if your lungs are back to normal." She took the stethoscope from around her neck and put the ends in her ears. "Let's see how you're doing now."

The nurse told her to take deep breaths and listened first to her chest and then to her back. She draped the stethoscope around her neck again and smiled. "You're just about there. But to be on the safe side, I want you to sit here a while longer."

"Not too long, okay? I'd really like to make my track events."

The nurse stood in front of her with her hands on her hips and grinned. "Just so you know, I've got another gig to get to, so no, I am not going to be keeping you one single second longer than you need to be here. You hear that? Cause if not, I'm gonna have to check your ears, too."

She laughed. "My ears are fine."

"Okay, then, you sit here for a little while. And no laughing. That might set you off again." The nurse grinned even wider, showing off a space between her front teeth.

Tessa stifled a giggle. She liked this new nurse a lot better than Nurse Musgrave, who always acted as if Tessa was the most pathetic person in the world when she came into the nurse's office wheezing. She wondered if the new nurse was here to stay—she hoped so. "Um, did Nurse Musgrave quit?"

The new nurse shook her head, which made her beads rattle. "She's out on leave. Maternity leave is what the temp agency said, but they don't always get things right, so don't start any rumors. I'm Nurse Charles." She turned and stuck out her right hand.

Tessa shook the nurse's long-fingered hand the way her dad had taught her to, firmly, but not too hard. "Tessa Trent," she said.

"I already know your name." Nurse Charles tapped her folder, which she'd set down on the corner of her desk.

"Oh, yeah. Duh." Tessa shifted around in her chair. "Do you really have another job to go to, or is that just, you know, nurse talk, to get me to sit still?"

Nurse Charles laughed so hard at that she got tears in her eyes. "You're a smart one. I have a real job to get to, at the Retreat at Duck Creek. That's a nursing home. Any other afternoon and I could sit here with you till four, but not on Wednesdays. That's the only night I can work, when my daughter's at her dad's."

"Really? I go to my dad's on Wednesday nights. Well, I used to. Now I don't know where I go. My parents are battling it out in court today. It's so lame." She shook her head. "They act like they're the only ones whose lives matter."

"You think?" Nurse Charles took off her half-glasses and set them down on her desk. "Let me tell you something, Tessa Trent. I'm guessing your mom and dad are hurting every bit as bad as you are, maybe more. You ever have a boy break up with you and you don't know why? And no matter what you do, you can't get him back. And maybe he's not even sorry he hurt you? Well, maybe your parents are feeling some of that."

Although Tommy hadn't exactly broken up with her, she got what Nurse Charles was trying to say—her mom wasn't over her dad. She nodded.

"And I'm also guessing you spend more time with your mom than your dad. You think it's easy for him to go from seeing his daughter anytime he wants to seeing her once or twice a week?

Tessa looked down at her Vuitton bag. "Not really."

"Of course not. Says in your folder you're fourteen. You're too young to think like that yet. But your parents have been fourteen, just like you. They know what you're going through. Now, correct me if I'm wrong, but you've never been forty, have you?"

Tessa shook her head. "My dad's almost fifty, actually."

Nurse Charles reached for the stethoscope again. "Breathe deep now, that's a girl. And again. That's good. Point is," she said, "you've never been their age. You've never walked a mile in your parents' moccasins, as the saying goes. And, pardon me if I'm opening my big mouth once too often, but you've probably been feeling just a bit sorry for yourself, haven't you? Just the tiniest bit?"

Tessa rolled her eyes. "Maybe a little."

"Okay, now, there you go." The nurse draped the stethoscope around her neck again. "Your lungs sound clear." She pulled her chin in and looked Tessa up and down. "You know, sometimes you just gotta have a little faith, Tessa. Wait things out. You gotta be open to receiving what's given, you know what I mean?"

Tessa didn't quite get what Nurse Charles was talking about, but she nodded.

"You sit tight for just one more minute," the nurse said. "I have to make a couple more notes in your folder and file them."

Tessa nodded again, but she was so anxious to leave that her left foot started pumping up and down on its own. She had to concentrate hard to get it to stop, and even then it would start up again. On her third try, she got it stopped just as her mom's friend Madeline looked in through the window in the nurse's office door.

"Hey, Tessa, how are you doing?" Madeline said, pulling the door open. She walked in, holding on tight to her kids' hands, one kid on either side of her kiwi green chinos. Madeline was such a cool dresser.

"Tessa!" Olivia squealed.

Tessa held her arms out and Noah and Olivia jumped into them.

"Hey, guys," she said. As she squeezed them tight, all she could think about was what must have happened at court. She looked up at Madeline, hoping for a hint.

Then Madeline, who was such a total mom-type, said, "Your mom's still at the courthouse, Tessa. Nothing's happened yet."

How could that be? She was about to ask when Nurse Charles looked up from her notes, as if she was just realizing there was somebody else in the room. She had her half-glasses on again and looked at Madeline over them.

"So," the nurse said, "we meet again."

Tessa frowned. How did Nurse Charles know her mom's

friend? Even her mom didn't know the new nurse yet, and her mom always made it a point to get to know the nurses, on account of Tessa's asthma. This was just too weird. She wanted to interrupt, but Nurse Charles went on talking to Madeline, asking her, "Are those women still angry?"

What women, she wanted to yell. Her mom and Carol? Had they gotten into a catfight at court? Is that why the case hadn't gone before the judge?

"In that book you were reading," Nurse Charles said.

Tessa exhaled hard with relief. Just a book—Madeline was always reading a book. Carol, too.

"I'm not sure," Madeline said to Nurse Charles. "I had to quit reading to go pick up these two." She motioned to Livvie and Noah.

Then Nurse Charles said, "That's a pair of nice-looking kids you've got there," and Madeline smiled like she was starring in one of those teeth-whitening ads.

"Um, excuse me," Tessa said—her dad didn't like her interrupting adults. "But I have to get to my event?"

"I'll stay with Noah and Livvie," Madeline said. "Until I find Emily."

"Thanks." Tessa turned to Nurse Charles. Something told her you didn't leave Nurse Charles's office without permission. "Can I go now?"

"If you've got your head on straight," the nurse said. She sounded serious, but she was smiling, too.

Tessa slid her inhaler into her purse. "I do. Seriously."

"Then get out there," Nurse Charles said. "Make your parents proud."

"I will," she said, and for the first time in a long time she actually meant it—she wanted to make her parents feel proud of her, in a gazillion ways.

CHAPTER 23

Adele

After cancelling her appointments for the rest of the day, Adele swiveled in her desk chair to watch the fish tank, hoping to induce some calming alpha waves before tackling her Roger problem head-on. The graceful angel fish and darting neon tetras didn't calm her, though. She turned back to the open appointment book on her desk and marked a line through each name, methodically printing the word Reschedule underneath. Even that didn't help. She was hopping mad, as angry as Carol Wheaton.

Had Carol called while she'd been out? She checked her voicemail. Sure enough, there were two calls—one from Beth Ann, saying she wouldn't be coming in at three, and one from Carol.

"I wanted to let you know how things turned out," Carol's voice said. "Nothing's been decided. Wes and I offered a perfectly reasonable compromise, but Sharon turned it down, and now the case has been continued for a month. See you at two tomorrow."

The message was typical—brisk and to the point when Carol had no live audience. Had Adele been on the other end, she'd have heard another version, full of bile and passion, and in her current mood, she might have snapped at her client, undoing weeks of progress. She'd been smart to cancel her appointments today. Maybe she ought to think about cancelling tomorrow's, too. But Carol was vulnerable at this stage of therapy, like a hermit crab that had just shed its shell. She ought to come in to the office tomorrow to work with Carol, at least.

That was what Roger failed to grasp. Yes, she ought to stop taking new clients, and she probably ought to start thinking about tapering off into semi-retirement, so they could travel more. But to pick up and move to the Southwest so Roger could build his adobe palace while some of her clients were on the brink of a breakthrough? Tapering off wasn't as easy as it sounded.

In this office, she had power. But when she went out into the larger world—to the mall or the gas station or even to the college, to take an evening course or attend a poetry reading—people didn't see her for what she was, a Wise Woman, a sort of junior Elder, to be consulted and revered for the wisdom she'd accumulated and could dispense. She had at least a full decade left in which to lead her clients to insights, to promote healing. She was Healer, for heaven's sake. That wasn't her job but her calling, what she did, who she was. Without it, who would she be? Just another old lady?

She closed her appointment book and pushed back in her desk chair, let her eyes roam over her bookshelves. Her gaze went to the box of peanut brittle she'd meant to take to her Aunt Helen over a month ago, along with a stack of crossword puzzle books she'd bought for her mother. Could Roger be right? Had she become so caught up in her clients' needs that she'd been neglecting her family and her personal life?

That might explain Roger's forgetfulness. Maybe he'd "forgotten" their anniversary this year because he was angry with her. Passive aggression—she'd seen it in clients hundreds of times, but maybe she'd missed it in her husband. Maybe he wasn't answering the phone for the same reason. She rarely gave a client her home number, but sometimes she made an exception. Did Roger resent these intrusions into their private world? If she asked him, he'd chalk it up to being busy with his house plans and not wanting to be bothered picking up. They had a machine, after all. Maybe he had a point.

She thought of phoning him on his cell, but she needed more time to think things through. So did he. Roger could be stubborn and closed-mouthed when he was angry. It would be better to let him work through that on his own. She should be processing her own feelings, too. If she'd been neglecting her loved ones and her personal life, as Roger claimed, the only way to find out for sure was to do something about it.

She looked at the bookshelf clock. She had plenty of time to drop off the peanut brittle at Aunt Helen's, visit with her aunt for a few minutes, and have dinner with her mother at the nursing home before heading back home after rush hour. By then, she'd know what to do—shut down her practice and move away into the sunny unknown of retirement, or inform Roger that his plans would have to change. She slipped the candy and the crosswords into her briefcase and locked the office.

The drive across town took longer than usual. It was mid-afternoon when she finally turned off the congested highway onto the rural road that led to Aunt Helen and Uncle Walt's farm. She wouldn't miss this awful traffic if they moved away.

Gravel crunched under her tires as she pulled her sedan up to the old farmhouse. She grabbed the peanut brittle, her aunt's favorite, and stepped out of her car.

The screen door opened. Aunt Helen stepped out onto the front porch, dressed in her usual elastic-waist jeans, a white t-shirt, and over that, a faded chambray work shirt that looked like it had once belonged to her son Shay, who farmed part of the property. Her long gray hair was twisted up into a bun bobby-pinned on top of her head, and on her feet was a scuffed pair of riding boots. There wasn't a thing about her outfit that looked typically feminine, yet Aunt Helen was the most feminine woman Adele knew.

Her body, for instance. Aunt Helen was broad and a little fleshy, like the droopy-breasted fertility statues that prehistoric peoples had revered. And certainly she'd given birth three times, decades ago. But Aunt Helen was still fertile in another sense. She had the power of life in her, a sort of invisible green thumb that made everything she touched bloom longer and everyone she fed get stronger.

Adele looked down through the middle portion of her lenses at her new flats, which still felt odd after her high-heeled pumps. It was as if she retained a felt memory of her body uplifted, tilted forward, her weight on the balls of her feet. In the flats she felt closer to the ground, lighter and more nimble yet somehow less powerful, as if she'd been demoted. She sidestepped the bright pink bleeding hearts that nodded over the edge of the front flower bed and mounted the porch steps, unsure of what to say to her aunt. It'd been so long since she'd visited. Should she apologize or breeze past that, as if nothing had happened?

She'd just opened her mouth to say I'm sorry it's been so long when Aunt Helen interrupted. "Why, Adele. What brings you out here? I thought you and Roger would be celebrating." Aunt Helen grinned like a child let in on a grownup secret.

Adele held up the box of peanut brittle. "I brought you a little present."

"How nice. You're always so thoughtful. Well, come on in. Shay'll be here pretty soon, after he gets done in the barn, and Walt should be home shortly. You're welcome to stay for supper. Venison chili. One of your favorites."

"Thanks," Adele said, "but I can't stay long. I'm planning to have dinner with Mom."

"Oh, she'd love to see you. And today's a good day for a visit. She was quite lucid this morning."

Aunt Helen held the door open, and Adele stepped over the threshold into what her aunt called the parlor. Reproduction Early American furniture in gold and orange and brown crowded the small living room. One of her aunt's crocheted afghans was folded neatly over the back of the sofa, and the old woodstove jutted out from the fireplace opening. Was Walt still splitting his own firewood? And did Helen still stoke the fire, as she had in years past? No wonder Roger assumed Helen could take care of her mother for the years to come.

"Here," Adele said, pressing the box of candy into her aunt's veiny hands. "Enjoy."

Aunt Helen grinned and set the peanut brittle on the scratched maple coffee table. "Make yourself comfy." She motioned toward a pair of his-and-hers velveteen recliners. "I need to stir that chili. Be back in a jiffy."

After her aunt had disappeared into the kitchen, Adele sank down into the recliner closest to the front door, tugged on the lever to extend the footrest and elevated her feet. Though hardly her style, the old chair felt like home. How many lazy summer days had she spent on this farm, riding horses and spending time with her cousins, learning to clean a fish or put up forty quarts of peaches in a day? Her mother hadn't always had the energy for that, or the inclination. In fact, Aunt Helen had been as much a mother to her as her own mother had, yet she'd always taken her aunt's love for granted. Maybe being a surrogate parent, as Aunt Helen and that Rissa woman at Macy's had been, was a lot like being a stepmother. Carol Wheaton had talked about that in some of her sessions.

In fact, Adele was now beginning to think that Carol was so angry at Wes's ex-wife—and so pushy about the custody issue—because she resented the strong bond that Tessa shared with her mother. Carol was jealous, and the custody motion was her way of striking out at her enemy. As for Carol's over-the-top reaction to Madeline Greenfield and her "silly shoes," that was displacement, anger transferred from Tessa's mother to her friend, Madeline.

She ought to make a note of that for tomorrow's session, but, oh, the squishy recliner felt divine, easing the pain that now radiated from her left hip to her lower leg. Sitting all day in one position—even in the Aeron chair that Roger had bought her—was ill-advised for a woman with arthritis, but she couldn't very well stand or walk while her clients sat. And now, despite her efforts to stay alert, she was getting drowsy. She let herself become one with the recliner.

When her eyes flickered open again, Aunt Helen was pushing through the kitchen door, humming and carrying a tray that held a pitcher of iced tea, two glasses, and a plate filled with homemade oatmeal cookies and four triangular sandwich quarters. Egg salad on whole wheat, each with a ruffle of homegrown lettuce. Her favorite childhood lunch.

"Let me help," Adele said, struggling to collapse the recliner.

"Help with what? You relax."

She reclined again while Helen poured iced tea and handed her a glass. "It's already sugared. I hope that's all right."

Adele took a sip. "It's wonderful."

Aunt Helen set the plate of cookies and sandwiches on the maple end table. "Have some, Dell. Come on now. Don't be shy."

"But I'll be having dinner with Mom soon and—"

"This is a snack."

"You won't let up till I eat something, will you?"

"Probably not." Aunt Helen smiled and flopped down on the sofa.

Adele ate one sandwich quarter and then another, followed by one of Helen's luscious cookies. Meanwhile her aunt broke open the peanut brittle box, which she passed first to Adele, who shook her head. "Bad for my teeth," she said.

Aunt Helen broke off a small triangle of brittle and examined it. "Did Roger show you his plans? He was so excited when he called this morning." She popped the brittle into her mouth and bit down hard.

"Yes." Adele felt her anger flare again, took a breath. "And I must admit I was sorry he approached you first. You must have felt pressured to say yes."

"Adele, you ought to know me better than that. If it was a problem for me to look after your mother, I'd have said so from the get-go. Now, tell me, what did you think of the plans?"

"They're lovely, like all of Roger's house plans. Spectacular, actually."

"Of course. Roger's a talented man. When will the house be done, then?"

"That's hard to say. Roger says it'll take at least a year."

"And I imagine he'll be right on the money with his estimate, as usual."

Adele set her iced tea glass on top of a crocheted coaster and tugged on the lever to bring the recliner upright. "Most likely."

Aunt Helen broke off a second piece of brittle, this one larger than her first. "So by this time next year you'll likely be moving into your new home."

"Maybe so." She brushed the crumbs off her trousers. She didn't have the heart to tell Aunt Helen she didn't want to go to Arizona. "Thanks for the snack," she said, rising from the recliner. "Delicious, as always."

"Going so soon?" Aunt Helen said through a mouthful of peanut brittle.

"I'm afraid so. You know how early they serve dinner at the nursing home, and I'd like to visit with Mom for awhile first."

"Oh, she'll love that. She thinks the world of you."

"And I think the world of you, Aunt Helen."

Her aunt cocked her head to the side. "Why, Dell, what brought that on?"

"I've been doing some thinking—"

Aunt Helen laughed and patted Adele's cheek. Her hand smelled of celery and almond-scented hand lotion. "That's my Adele," she said. "Always thinking."

Adele sucked in her lips and bit down on them to stifle a smile, but she could feel her cheeks plump up and her eyes crinkle. "I'd better go," she said.

She stepped out onto the old porch with its creaky swing and often-painted metal chairs, tipped forward against the railing so a sudden rain wouldn't pool in their indented seats. She pictured mosquitoes breeding in the stagnant water, Aunt Helen bustling outside with a scrub brush in one hand and a broom in the other. Aunt Helen was woman of action, not thought. Or, rather, a woman of swift thought followed by equally swift, deliberate action. How wonderful it must be not to think so much, to just do.

"Thank you so much," she said to Aunt Helen, who still stood in the doorway, her face softened by the gray mesh of the screen door. "For everything. All you've done for me all these years. I really do appreciate it, you know."

Helen smiled and shook her head. "Oh, for heaven's sake, Dell. Of course I know. Now get going, will you? You're going to be late."

CHAPTER 24

Stephanie

Stephanie was on the interstate again, this time driving south, back to her neck of the woods. It had been a frustrating day at court. She knew she'd lost ground when Marcus played the single mother sympathy card in front of the judge. No one ever looks good when they attack a mother. All the way back to the Virgin Mary, society has wanted to believe that mothers are pure, holier than other people. If you can prove a mother is really bad you might have a shot, but Wes wouldn't let her go there. Still, maybe it was for the best. Maybe Sharon would come around and they'd be able to settle this thing in the next few weeks before it further degenerated into something Tessa would never be able to recover from.

Thank goodness traffic wasn't as bad on the way home as it had been that morning. She was sailing along. Probably due to the fact that it was well before five, in addition to the fact that most suburbanites headed north out of the city after work.

She'd been waiting since lunchtime at the mall to be free so she could go see Max. But first she needed to stop by her apartment. It was time for Riley to go out again. Besides, she missed him. She'd first brought him home for protection as much as for companionship. Didn't all single women need a dog? But then she'd fallen in love. No matter how long she'd been away he'd run to the door, his nub of a tail wagging like crazy, body quivering with excitement, each time she came home. It could have been five minutes or eight hours, it didn't matter. He was all about her.

She loved the way he looked, too. He wasn't one of those model dogs with a long, elegant nose and fluffy hair, like the Golden Retriever, the dumb blond of the dog world who appears in all of the advertisements and calendars. Instead, she'd chosen a lesser known breed, a fawn-colored boxer. She'd been intrigued by his asymmetrical coloring, the random brown-and-white splotches all over his body. His face didn't make sense either. A quarter of it was white, the rest black. His nose was smushed and his jowls hung in a perpetual frown. His hair was so short you could see every line of his anatomy. His ribs were definable underneath his barrel chest. His rear end was skinny. No surprises. What you saw was what you got. And Stephanie liked that. She also liked how expressive he was. He would look at her with those penetrating brown eyes, his head cocked to the side and brows furrowed while she talked to him. She swore she could tell what he was thinking.

Her stomach cramped, but that was okay. She liked the feeling of being hungry, hadn't thought twice about skipping lunch to shoe shop with Marisa. As long as her stomach felt flat and tight, she was happy. There was nothing worse than that bloated feeling after eating or drinking too much. She never bothered to weigh herself either. Her hip bones were her measuring stick. If they stuck out far enough, she knew she was doing all right.

She pulled into the parking lot of her newly-renovated apartment complex. She'd chosen to live and work in an artsy area near the Short North. Well, as artsy as could be found in the Columbus area. Sometimes she fantasized that she was really a young, single attorney practicing in downtown Chicago, or better yet, Manhattan. Then maybe she'd be able to promenade down ornate hallways with murals on the ceiling and marble on the floor, instead of those of the generic 1970s institutional building she'd been in today. If it weren't for Marisa, she'd never stay in Columbus.

She did have a pretty cool law office, though. It was only blocks from her apartment. She'd rented the space and decorated it with interesting pieces she'd found here and there, an old architectural table for her desk, a lamp in the foyer from an old bank. With a credit card she'd bought an eclectic array of paintings by local artists to scatter throughout, from the foyer to the conference room in the middle to her office in the back. Then she'd hung a stained-glass shingle outside with her name on it in cursive letters, Stephanie J. Powell, Attorney at Law. How she loved looking at that sign.

The only undesirable part of her life was that every month she held her breath until she'd made enough money to cover the overhead on the office, the rent on her apartment, and the minimum payments on her credit cards. Fortunately, she kept getting so many clients on referral that she was busy enough to bring in more money than she'd imagined for having a relatively new practice. Her clients loved the fact that she didn't have much of a life outside of practicing law. They told their friends how she worked around the clock. In fact, most of her clients were friends of previous clients. And new clients were constantly pouring in. Still, her apartment was sparse, she needed a better car, and although her wardrobe was designer, she didn't have as many outfits as she would have liked.

She jogged up the steps to her apartment. She'd barely cracked the door before Riley was leaping up and down at her like a Mexican jumping bean. She leaned over so he could lick her face. It was the only way to stop him from jumping.

"Okay, okay, that's enough kisses, Boy," she said.

Squeezing through the doorway around Riley, she set her briefcase on the kitchen counter. She kicked off her heels—that felt better—and plopped down in her oversized chair. Riley rested his head on her leg. While she rubbed between his ears with one hand, she pushed her answering machine playback button with the other.

"Hi, Steph, it's me. Uh, Justin. I was wondering if you were ever going to call me back? I thought we'd been having a really good time, but then I haven't heard from you in awhile. I don't know if you've been getting my messages, but—"

She hit Delete.

The next message was from Marisa.

"Hey, Steph. I just saw you, but after you left I called Max and told him you might be stopping by today. Thanks again for talking to him. And for listening to me. And for suggesting I get these boots. I love them! I've got to run. Talk to you later."

Stephanie put her hands under Riley's hanging jowls and lightly tugged on them, pulling him in close to kiss his flat nose. "After I change and you take care of business, wanna go for a ride to Mad Max's house?"

Soon she was pulling into Stonehurst, Marisa's subdivision. Although they lived in towns that bordered each other, Marisa was further west, away from downtown, so their neighborhoods looked worlds apart. In fact, Marisa's town reminded her of where she'd just been for the court case. And both small towns were similar to where she and Marisa had grown up near the Ohio/Michigan border. Town Hall in the center of town, surrounded by older homes and family-owned businesses, then fanning out to newly-built, or remodeled, local schools, and then finally to the newest housing developments on the outskirts of town. One of these new subdivisions— with baby trees planted throughout the mini lawns of similar houses with open floor plans— was where Marisa lived.

Stephanie put Riley's leash on him then led him out of the car. She rang the doorbell and waited for Max to answer. It took a few minutes, but then there he was, pajama bottoms and sock feet, no shirt, reddish-blond hair tousled. He was rubbing his eyes. Had he been napping in the middle of the afternoon?

"Hey, Mad Max, Maxamillion, To the Max!" She ran through every nickname she had for him each time she saw him.

"Hey."

Riley jumped at Max, but she jerked his leash back. "Riley, down!"

Max reached over and petted Riley's head.

"Wanna walk Riley around the neighborhood with me?" she said.

"Sure, let me get some clothes on." The screen door slammed shut.

Riley nosed around in the freshly cut grass while they waited. Max was back out in a flash in jeans, a T-shirt and sneakers.

They took off down the sidewalk, Riley out front practically dragging her, and Max beside her, hands in his pocket. Although he was only sixteen, Max was almost as tall as she was, which put him near six feet.

"So I hear you had some trouble at school?" she said.

"You're not gonna lecture me, too, are you?"

"No, that's not my style. You know that. I just wanted to find out how you're doing."

"All right, I guess. I don't care about being suspended from school. I'm mostly bummed about baseball. "

"I can imagine," she said. "You know, it could be worse, though."

"You think so?"

"Sure. You should see the situation I dealt with at court today. My client has a daughter who's a little bit younger than you. She runs track. Anyway, she's being pulled back and forth like a piece of taffy between her parents. Her dad's remarried, her mom's popping pills. They can't agree on anything when it comes to setting up her weekly schedule."

"Brutal," Max said.

"She went all day today not even knowing whose house she was going to be at tonight. It's really ugly sometimes watching adults at their worst. You're lucky your parents are so normal, Max."

"You think they're normal?"

"They love you and they love each other," she said.

"That's what normal is?"

"I would have settled for that when I was little. Once there's a divorce, the children become wards of the state. Isn't that a disgusting way to describe a child, a ward? Anyway, the parents are no longer in charge, the courts are."

"That sucks."

"For everybody involved," she said. "If parents stay married, the courts can't step in and make decisions for them, like where you live, or whether your child takes ballet or baseball, or what type of school you send them to. But as soon as you divorce, they can decide anything and everything for your child. The government is now the one who makes decisions in the child's best interest and allows each parent to have certain rights. But your parents are still a team, Max. Your family is intact. Mine wasn't."

"Where are my grandparents these days?" he said.

"Last I heard your grandmother was somewhere out west, trying to make a living painting sunsets."

"Has she sold one yet?"

"Who knows? I'm sure if being an artist doesn't pan out for her she'll find a new identity for herself. Maybe belly dancing in Nepal."

They rounded the next block.

"What about Grandpa?" Max said.

"I think he's still living in Florida with that Marie."

"The one he brought with him when he visited a few years ago?"

"I think so," she said. "Your mom talks to your grandparents more than I do, you should ask her."

"I don't think she wants me to ask her anything right now. She's pretty mad at me."

"She'll get over it. If your worst high school experience is having to sit out of baseball for one season, when the season is almost over anyway, then you're not doing too badly."

"Yeah, I guess," Max said.

"And I'm sure you've learned your lesson. About underage drinking."

"Yeah, it's not worth it."

Except for the sound of Riley panting, they walked in silence for a few minutes. She'd done her duty. Max was going to be okay. His shoulders were already looser than when they'd first left the house.

A school bus passed by them, bringing kids back from where Max would have been on a normal day.

"Hey, whatever happened to that guy you brought to my last game?" he said.

"Oh, he's out of the picture now."

"He was nice."

"Yes, he was."

"Geez, I'm glad I'm your nephew and not your boyfriend."

"Why would you say that?" she said.

"You stomp all over every guy you go out with," Max said, matter-of-factly.

It stung, but she kept walking. She pictured herself dancing around in red cowboy boots, like in Jessica Simpson's music video for the Dukes of Hazzard movie, singing the remake of the old Nancy Sinatra hit, "These Boots are Made for Walking." In the video, Jessica stomps across the bar right before cold-cocking a guy.

CHAPTER 25

Sharon

Sharon started her car and let the engine run. She opened the glove box and took out the pill bottle. This would be the last time. "Damn!" she said out loud when she realized she didn't have anything in her car to take it with. She threw her head back and popped the pill in, swallowing it dry. It left a metallic taste in her mouth.

She pulled out of the courthouse parking lot and headed toward Patterson Middle School, which was only a few blocks away. She plucked her cell phone off the passenger's seat. Maybe she could catch Madeline before she left to come back to the courthouse.

Madeline answered right away. "Share, are you out already?"

"Yeah, we got to go up right after lunch, but then the judge sent us to these rooms to try to work out a compromise. It was getting so complicated, so I had my attorney ask for a continuance. Now we've got 30 more days to try to work it out."

"Oh."

She could hear the disappointment in Madeline's voice. "Where are you?" she said.

"I'm still at PMS. There was an incident at the end of school today. Let me start by saying Tessa's okay."

"What happened?" She tried not to think worst-case-scenario, something Wes always accused her of doing.

"Tessa had an asthma attack in English class, right before the bell rang. Mrs. Burns walked her to the nurse's office. But she's much better now. She couldn't find her inhaler—"

"I'm always telling her to keep it in her pocket—"

"She did find it in her pocket eventually. The nurse checked her lungs a few times and watched over her until she was back to normal. Tessa's doing great now. In fact, she's already gone off to her track meet."

"Does the nurse think she's okay to run?" Sharon's heart was pounding right out of her chest.

"Sure, it's like it never happened."

"Thank goodness." She allowed relief to wash over her. Or was that sensation the Valium kicking in?

"Just a minute," Madeline said. "Noah, put your sister down. Somebody's going to get hurt. Okay, sorry. Share, it's the weirdest thing. You'll never guess who the nurse was."

"Who?"

"The woman from court today, the one with all the braids."

"The one who got custody of her daughter back?"

"That's the one," Madeline said. "She just took over for Nurse Musgrave. Her name is Nurse Charles. She was very nice. When I pulled up to drop the kids off I couldn't find Tessa, so I parked my car and we walked into the school—"

Sharon rolled her eyes as Madeline went on and on about

how she ended up at the nurse's office where Tessa was. Madeline tended to babble when she got nervous or excited.

"—then when we walked in everything was already pretty much over, but when Tessa saw me I could tell she was anxious to find out about court, so I told her right away that nothing had happened yet. Nurse Charles must have put two and two together when she saw me and I mentioned court because she said, So we meet again. Then, get this, she said, Are the women still angry? At first it completely threw me, I wasn't sure what she meant, but she was talking about my book.'"

Sharon didn't care about any damn book right now. "What did Tessa say? Did she seem upset?"

"Not really. She just said she had to get to her event. I told her I'd stay with the kids in the stands until I caught up with Emily after her race. Tessa hugged on Noah and Olivia for a minute, then she dashed off. In fact, she left so quickly she forgot her backpack. Nurse Charles found it and ran out of the school after me. I told her I'd get it to Tessa."

"Thanks. I'm almost there, by the way."

"Good, because I think there's something you should see."

"What?"

"When Nurse Charles handed me the backpack, it wasn't zipped all the way and there was a paper falling out of it. I just caught a glimpse of it but I couldn't help but notice the title: PEOPLE WHO LET ME DOWN."

"I'm pulling in right now. Where are you?"

"In the bleachers, on the west side."

"I'll be over there in a sec."

After Sharon left her car, she almost raced to the bleachers, at least as much as she could in two-inch heels with a Valium buzz. She had to read that essay. She spotted Madeline sitting there with Olivia next to her jumping up and down clapping her hands and Noah climbing back and forth from one row to the next. With careful deliberation she stepped her way up the rows of seats and settled herself beside Madeline.

Madeline gave her a quick hug hello. "Emily was just here, but I told her not to worry about babysitting. I told her we were here now and could stay for the rest of the meet."

"Where's the essay?" she said. It was all she could think about.

"Right here." Madeline turned to Tessa's backpack that sat on her other side and pulled it out.

Sharon read each line quickly once. Then she started over again and read it slowly this time. Thankfully Madeline left her alone and didn't ask any questions. She was busy enough trying to control Noah and Olivia. Sharon stopped at one paragraph and read it again and again: But the person who has let me down the most . . . is my mom. . . . ever since Dad left, it's been all about Mom. Like I'm not hurting? . . . Our house feels so empty. . . . And Mom just goes on and on about how hurt and lonely and mad she is. What does she think I am?

How could she have been so blind? How could she not have known her daughter's feelings? She was glad Tessa pointed a finger at Wes and Carol in the essay, but at her? As the one who let her down the most? Her daughter thought she was selfish? She, who had loved her daughter with all of her heart from the moment she was born, was now selfish? She, who had been so hurt and betrayed by Wes? How could Tessa write these things about her? Was that what had prompted Tessa's asthma attack? Why was everything falling down around her now? She didn't deserve this. She didn't.

She pictured Tessa swaddled in the hospital blanket, the nurse handing her to Sharon for the first time. Tessa had screamed with a determination far beyond any newborn she'd ever seen.

She remembered Wes's panicked face in the middle of the night. "What's wrong with her? Why does she cry all the time?"

"It's probably just colic," she'd said with the newly discovered confidence of motherhood. Rubbing her back, she'd rocked Tessa until morning. She hadn't minded the lack of sleep. She was needed.

It had been the same when Tessa was five and had been hospitalized with her asthma. Sharon had taken off work and stayed by her hospital bed the whole week. Although he'd called every day, Wes had only stopped by to see them a couple of times.

She glanced up from the essay, but Tessa still wasn't out on the field. She struggled to tune out the Greenfield kids, who were shrieking in her ear.

Holding the essay to her chest, she closed her eyes. It had been she who'd wanted to have kids in the first place. Not Wes. He would have been happy to keep the dual-income-no-kids lifestyle. Dinks, he'd proudly referred to them as before Tessa. Sharon was the one who felt something was missing without a child. And she'd never been able to convince Wes to have another after Tessa was born. He wasn't even bonded with the one child they already had until after they'd split. THEN he suddenly became interested in being a father.

Sharon was thrown forward with a sudden force. There was a sharp pain between her shoulder blades. She opened her eyes and spun around. Noah had fallen into her and Madeline was trying to pull him back up. She had no patience for little kids right now. Not today. In fact, she wished she could click her heels together three times and send herself home.

CHAPTER 26

Tessa

From the nurse's office, Tessa went to the girls' locker room to change. As usual, it smelled like spray deodorant and stale sweat, with a little sunblock thrown in.

Nothing had happened at court yet. Incredible. But maybe that was a good sign in disguise. She thought about what Nurse Charles had told her, to be open to receiving what was given. But what, exactly, was being given?

She unlocked her locker and pulled out her new Air Max 360's. The premium running shoes had cost over a hundred dollars, which Carol said was highway robbery, but Tessa knew the shoes would make a difference today. She'd definitely make her parents proud while running in them.

She kicked off her Shox and took her inhaler out of her purse and put it on the bench behind her. Because they weren't allowed to wear jewelry out on the track, she took off her earrings and necklace and slipped them into the zippered pocket of her purse. Then she put her Shox and Vuitton bag in the bottom of her locker.

After checking to be sure nobody else was around, she undressed, grabbed her track shorts and Patterson tank top from the top shelf of her locker and put those on, then slid into her new running shoes. They felt even better than her Shox, light but strong. She could run at least ten seconds faster in these babies. They were worth every cent Dad had paid for them. She pulled hard on the laces and tied them tight but not too tight, the way the clerk at Runner's Edge had shown her. She would win today, she could feel it.

She slipped her inhaler into the waistband of her track shorts and arranged the loose tank top so the inhaler didn't show. She looked down at her shoes and clothes and purse in the bottom of her gym locker. She hated to leave her stuff there, even with the lock. Especially the Vuitton bag. Kids were breaking into lockers all the time, stealing stuff.

Still, her parents weren't here to look after her super-special purse, and Madeline would probably be leaving as soon as she found Emily. No, she'd better lock her stuff up and hope for the best. You've got to have faith, Nurse Charles had said. Okay, she'd try to have a little faith. Not too much, though.

As the lock clicked shut, she felt a surge of panic. Where was her backpack?

"Crap," she said out loud. She'd left it in Nurse Charles's office.

What if somebody else found it—the janitor or maybe the principal? She cringed at the thought of someone reading her essay. Hopefully Em had shoved it down deep in her backpack. It didn't matter if it got all wrinkled—she was planning to rip it up and redo it tonight. "People Who Have Walked a Mile in Your Shoes." That would be a way better topic. She could say something nice about her parents for a change, or at least have fun trying to imagine them at her age. It was hard to think that her parents had been kids like herself, though. Was it possible they'd had crushes on people who weren't right for them—on each other, maybe? Did they get scared before tests? Nervous before track meets?

She definitely needed to stop daydreaming and get out to the track. She could get her backpack later, after her first relay. Or maybe Madeline had picked it up. Madeline was always looking out for everybody.

As Tessa walked through the locker room and into the gym, she wondered if Madeline was getting sick of looking after her mom. If people would only quit sympathizing with her mother, maybe her mom would stop feeling so sorry for herself. Like mother, like daughter, Tessa thought. They were both guilty of feeling sorry for themselves.

With the side of her thigh, she pushed on the door that led out to the track, leaning hard against the crash bar. It was cool how you could never get locked in a school building, even if it was locked from the outside. That made her feel safe somehow.

A whoosh of hot, humid air hit her as the door opened. Not the best weather for running. It felt more like summer than spring.

Her mom didn't really like Ohio and was always making nostalgic remarks about going back to her hometown, Chicago. She'd better not try to move them both there, to get away from all the divorce craziness. Not after Tessa had found her niche here at Patterson, and she'd already planned to fill a similar niche in high school. She was the style diva, and guys liked her—followed her around, even.

Like now. Ryan Dunn was coming up to her, probably about to ask her out, even though he was three inches shorter.

Tessa changed direction and cut through the boys' shot put area, being careful not to get in their way. Tommy Leonetti was on deck, waiting for his turn to throw the shot. She was tempted to ignore him when she walked by, but there was something about the way he was standing there, trying not to look her in the eye, that told her she'd better speak up now.

"Hey, Tommy," she said as she passed behind him. "I didn't appreciate what you did at lunch today."

Tommy looked down at his feet. "Listen, I'm sorry, okay? Kyle thought it would be funny."

"Well, it wasn't. Now you owe me a new shirt. Ketchup stains, in case you hadn't heard."

"Okay."

Okay? He was going to buy her a new shirt, just like that? "It's from Hollister," she said, and before Tommy could say no way, she hurried on to where the other girls were gathering for their races.

Em was sweating from doing warm-ups and guzzling a flavored water.

"Hey," Tessa said.

Em's eyes got big. "Are you okay? Your lungs were, like, making accordion sounds."

"I'm better now. That new nurse is awesome. I found my inhaler, by the way. It was in my pocket." She patted her waistband. "So I'm all good."

"You had me so scared."

"I know. You were freaking out."

Tessa thought about how scared her mom had been when she'd first rushed her to the hospital for a breathing treatment. The nebulizer-thing they'd used on her had sounded louder than a 747, and the doctors were all "Stat," and "Check her pulse ox," but after that first crazy time, her mom totally had it down. God, she wanted to hug her mom right now. If only the stupid hearing was over and everything was back where it had been before she left for school, like in that movie Groundhog Day, only in a good way.

Okay, she was clearly feeling sorry for herself again. She ought to think of others who needed her, like Noah and Olivia.

"Hey," she said, frowning. "Where are the Greenfield kids? I thought Madeline was bringing them out to you."

Em jerked her thumb at the bleachers behind them. "She said she didn't need us to babysit after all."

Maybe Madeline had decided to quit babysitting her mom, too. That could be a good thing, like when she'd stood up to Tommy.

"Guess what," she said to Em. "I just ripped Tommy a new one."

"Seriously?"

"I told him he owed me a new t-shirt, and he goes, 'Okay.' Just like that."

"Wow. You go, girl."

"I know. I can't believe I did that."

"That's so awesome."

"Oh, and when I was in the nurse's office? Madeline told me nothing's happened in court yet. Can you believe it?"

Em frowned, as if she was thinking this over. "That might

not be all bad. Maybe the judge told your parents to go work it out. That happened to mine once."

"Did they?"

Em shook her head. "But they've got more issues than yours do."

"Somehow I doubt that."

"We'd better head over to Coach Stanley." Emily tossed her empty water bottle into the trash can.

Tessa nodded, but her eyes were now on the west bleachers. "Hey, Em," she said, pointing. "Over there, next to Madeline? Does that look like my mom to you?"

CHAPTER 27

Madeline

Madeline was trying not to look over Sharon's shoulder while Sharon read Tessa's school essay. She busied herself with Olivia, who was standing between her legs. "Let me see another cheer, Livvie."

"Go Wildcats! Yaaay!" Olivia jumped up and down, shaking her pom poms.

Sharon's eyes were closed now, and she clutched the essay to her chest.

Noah, who had been climbing back and forth on the rows, lost his footing and fell into Sharon. She pitched forward, then turned and shot Madeline an annoyed look.

Madeline quickly pulled him up. "Watch what you're doing, Big Guy."

Sharon went right back to reading.

Madeline scanned the athletes on the track below looking for any sign of Tessa. She still wasn't up. It had been over an hour since Madeline had arrived with the kids, and they were starting to get restless. So was she, for that matter.

She looked to the left just in time to see Jack walking toward them from the parking lot. He hadn't returned her calls, but he had come. How did he get here so early, though, on a busy work day? Her elation turned to anxiety when she saw the look on his approaching face.

She watched as he made his way up the bleachers.

"Daddy!" Noah said.

"Daddy, you're here!" Olivia said.

He scooped each of them up with an arm. "It sounded like Mommy could use some help today, so I brought some work home to finish." He was definitely in martyr-mode.

Without looking at Madeline, Jack turned to Sharon. "How'd everything go today?"

Sharon looked up from the essay only for a second. "It didn't," she said. "We go back in a month."

Jack moved on. "Madeline, I'm going to go ahead and take the kids home with me. Could you walk us to the car?"

"Sure," she said, jumping up. Instinct told her not to argue. "I'll be right back," she said to Sharon.

Jack didn't say a word to her the whole walk to his car. He asked the kids about their days and casually bantered back and forth with them. They didn't question why all of his attention was on them, they just reveled in it. Watching Jack be the father that he was only made her feel guiltier.

After Jack had gotten the kids tucked into his car and she'd kissed each of them goodbye, he closed the car door and turned his attention to her for the first time.

"What is with you today?" he said. "You're not usually this selfish and rude." That was Jack. Dead on aim. Just not usually with her. He looked so intently at her she squirmed.

"Look, I just got overly stressed, okay? I've got all of these papers to grade, and I really didn't have time to be at court all day, and then there was forgetting the parent luncheon with Olivia, and then trying to get the kids to Tessa and back to court—"

"I know you have a lot on your plate," Jack said, "that's why I'm here. Even though you hung up on me."

"Only I get here and Tessa's had an asthma attack, so I stay, and then Sharon shows up and is all upset about this school essay Tessa wrote. And you've been really busy lately, coming home later and later from work. Sometimes it's just too much for me to handle, you know? I can't take care of everybody!" She willed herself not to cry. She hated her own tears.

Jack threw his hands up. "Who said you have to take care of everybody?"

"Everybody in my life seems to think I have an endless supply of patience and generosity to pass around. Why am I just support personnel, there to make everybody else's life easier? When is it ever going to be about me?"

"You're doing this to yourself, Madeline. You don't have to be perfect, you know. Learn to set limits with people."

"Set limits? Oh, okay, I'm sorry Noah and Livvie, Mommy doesn't feel like making your breakfast this morning, or picking you up from day care today, or attending your little school thing—"

"You know that's not what I'm talking about. I just mean that it's okay to say no once in awhile to the people you love. They're not going to stop loving you because you said no."

She turned and looked at Noah and Olivia through the car window. Olivia put her hand up to the window. Madeline touched the glass and smiled.

"Madeline? Are you hearing me?"

"Yes, I hear you."

"And then there's Sharon. When she asked you to come to court with her, you could have told her it just wouldn't work out for you, that you'd be thinking about her today, and to call you when she got done to let you know what happened. You didn't have to give up your whole day to go over there."

"Yeah, I guess. I don't know if I can do that, though."

Jack looked at his watch. He was probably thinking about the Reds game. And how this was taking too long.

"Just go on," she said. "I don't want you to miss your precious game." She turned her back to him and waved to the kids through the window.

"That's not fair and you know it." Jack grabbed her wrist and spun her around. "Yes, I want to get home in time for my game, but I'm willing to take the kids with me. Isn't that enough?" He looked so vulnerable. "What do you want, Madeline?"

"I don't know." She leaned against the car and crossed her arms, staring straight ahead at nothing. She heard Jack sigh.

He was right. She knew she should be grateful that, unlike some husbands, his particular hobby enabled him to be at home and didn't cost a fortune. He didn't golf. He didn't like to go to bars.

Although, sometimes it annoyed her that their lives seemed to revolve around baseball and football. In the spring and summer it was the Cincinnati Reds, in the fall and winter it was the OSU Buckeyes . He needed to be home to watch the games, and sometimes games were every night. Sure they had TiVo, but if he recorded it to watch later, some insensitive jerk at work would be talking about the scores the next day.

And he wouldn't be able to turn his laptop on, or his ESPN screen might inadvertently show him the scores of a game before he'd had a chance to watch. And the whole family had better watch out if Daddy found out the score to a game before he'd seen it.

But he was there when they needed him. He loved them, and they knew it. They felt it every day. She knew from her first marriage that this kind of devotion in a man was not so easy to find.

He repeated his question. "What do you want? Do you need more help with the kids? Do we need to get somebody in to help with the house?"

"No, no. That's not what I want. I don't think I want anything to be different, really. Sometimes I just need a break. And sometimes I don't know I need a break until it's too late and I've had it."

"And then you hang up on me."

"You're right. It was unfair of me to take it out on you. You've done nothing but try to help."

"That's more like it." He stroked the side of her arm. After six years of marriage and two kids she still loved his touch.

"And you're right about Sharon," she said. "I shouldn't have gone to court. I wasn't even in there with her. I was by myself all morning. Well, sort of. I'll tell you about the new friend I made later."

"Well, I'm not going to get in the middle of you and Sharon, but she has been a little self-absorbed lately. You might want to let her know that you have needs, too."

"I know. I will. But not today. She's got too much to deal

with already today." She nodded towards the window. "You'd better get them home, and I'd better get back to Sharon."

Jack took her hand. "You know I'll always try to help meet your needs. I can't always do it perfectly. And sometimes other things get in the way, like work. Which pays for our house. And that SUV you're driving. But you need to tell me when you're starting to lose it, and we'll figure something out, okay?"

"Okay," she said. She leaned in and put her face on his chest. She loved his scent, so woodsy, manly.

"You're lucky you're hot," he said.

"No, you're lucky I'm hot." She smiled and buried her face deeper. She knew she wasn't drop-dead gorgeous in most people's eyes, but to this man she was, and that's all that mattered. This was what Sharon was missing. Being loved makes you beautiful.

Jack gripped her forearms and held her back to look in her face. "You didn't mean what you said about the Reds, did you?"

"No, of course not."

"Because I was hoping you'd wear your Reds hat for me later."

"And nothing else, right?"

"Yep."

She leaned up and kissed him then turned to blow kisses at her children through the window. They were waving and blowing kisses back. Jack reached around from behind her and cupped her right breast where the kids couldn't see. It was more of a playful squeeze, but she could feel herself turn warm. Yeah, life was pretty good.

She walked back towards Sharon in the bleachers and looked up at the sky. Clouds were moving in.

She wished she was wearing her new navy J. Crew critter wellies, the rubber boots with the dogs printed on them that she just had to have, even though had Jack told her she wouldn't have many opportunities to wear them. Well, this was the perfect opportunity, but she hadn't had a clue this morning when she put on her fabric slingbacks that the sunshine would be departing. But that was spring for you. You just never knew what it would bring.

CHAPTER 28

Adele

Adele walked through the airy, pastel lobby of her mother's nursing home. About two dozen seniors were enjoying a Big Band sing-along, some seated in wheelchairs, some in faux-leather armchairs. The sounds of Glenn Miller vibrated from a boom box set on top of the white grand piano, where the youthful recreation director with her bright smile and shiny brown bob sat, encouraging the residents to join in. "Come on," the woman at the piano called out, "let's hear everybody's voice this time." Had her mother ever attended these sing-alongs? Probably not—Mom had been more of a Tony Bennett girl in her day.

Adele turned left, down the corridor that led to her mother's room. Though spotless and stylish, the Retreat at Duck Creek always smelled vaguely of urine, and the staff, though friendly and hard-working, seemed almost too efficient to be truly caring. Still, it made more sense for her mother, who now used a walker or a wheelchair, to live here rather than with her and Roger, in their less-than-accessible post-modern home.

She reached the end of the hallway and slipped into her

mother's room, which was decorated in soft tones of beige and rose and faded green. A wide bank of windows overlooked a courtyard, and beyond, a corn-and-soybean farm that a developer was turning into a condominium complex. Today the vertical blinds at the window were closed, probably because her mother's roommate was sleeping.

Her mother, though, was awake and staring at the window, as if she could see through the opaque blinds. She was dressed in a short-sleeved floral print shirt, slate blue knit slacks, and a pair of Ecco oxfords in the softest mahogany leather with three slim Velcro closures. The shoes had been Adele's Mother's Day gift from last year, an ironic one, since her mother rarely walked anymore. Still, a woman of any age needed nice shoes, and the staff certainly appreciated the convenience of Velcro.

Today her mother's sparse white hair was tucked behind her ears, and her oversized glasses frames made her look like a slightly confused owl. She sat not in her wheelchair, but in the room's lone wing chair, upholstered in vinyl, to protect against toileting accidents. To the left of her chair was her walker, decorated with cheery crocheted flowers, Aunt Helen's handiwork.

Adele rounded the bed and leaned down to kiss her mother's cheek. "Hi, Mom."

Her mother looked up and blinked, then smiled. "Well, hello, sweetheart."

"How are you doing today?"

"Oh, I could be better." Her mother's standard reply. "How are the kids?"

Her throat tightened. "It's Adele, Mom. You're thinking of Helen. She's the one with the kids."

Her mother adjusted her glasses. "You're right. You two look so much alike in this light. Could you open the blinds a little?"

"Of course. I don't think your roommate will mind." Adele reached for the wand and pulled the blinds back.

"Oh, that's better." Her mother squinted at the bright orange earth-moving equipment in the distance. "What's that?"

"A backhoe, I believe."

Her mother looked down. "Are those new shoes?"

"Why, yes, they are," Adele said, pleased that her mother had noticed. "I just bought them today."

"How you loved getting new shoes when you were little. I used to take you down to Slayton's shoe store and have your feet x-rayed in that little machine, to check the fit. How you loved that."

"I remember. I'm here to have dinner with you. I'm sorry I missed lunch."

"Oh, that's all right. I know you're busy with the farm."

"I'm Adele, Mom."

Her mother looked up, blinked again. "Of course you are." She turned back to the window. "What's it like outside? Are those storm clouds? We'd better take in the patio furniture before it gets drenched to the bone."

"The Retreat staff will do that."

"The Retreat?"

What was wrong with her mother today? Occasionally she got confused—she was in her eighties, after all, and had a few symptoms of mild dementia—but never before had she seemed so thoroughly discombobulated. Could it be her medication? Adele made a mental note to check with the nursing staff before she left today, to review her mother's chart.

While her mother stared out the window, Adele walked around the room, peeking into the closet, the bureau drawers. Everything was clean and tidy, the short-sleeved spring tops placed on the top of the stack, the pastel double-knit pants hung in the front of the closet. Aunt Helen's touch.

She set the stack of crossword puzzle books on the bedside table and thumbed through the easy puzzle book she'd brought last time. It didn't look as if it had been opened, much less filled in. Her mother had been a whiz at the toughest puzzles in her day, even anagrams. Now she seemed to have lost interest in even the simplest ones.

"What's this, Mom? Over your bed? This sign?" It was handmade—probably by Walt or Shay or one of the grandchildren—clumsily painted and hanging at an angle from a push pin by a satin ribbon. "Getting Old Is Not for Wimps," it said. Wasn't that the truth?

"What? Did you say something, Helen?"

Adele tried to swallow the growing lump in her throat, tried again. A part of her wanted to scream, "I'm your daughter!" What was wrong with this place? Had a careless nurse double-dosed her mother?

She looked at the bulletin board opposite her mother's bed, to be sure it was up to date. The staff set up one for every resident, to aid in short-term memory. Each day they changed the date and the menu, and they encouraged families to bring in current photos of themselves with their names written in bold capital letters. ADELE and HELEN were flanked with photos of Helen's kids and grandchildren and Walt. No photo of Roger, though. Why hadn't she brought in a recent picture of him? She'd told herself she'd do it when she had the time, but she hadn't made time.

Adele pointed to the menu. "I see we're having meatloaf for dinner."

"Meatloaf," her mother said with a grunt. "They serve meatloaf every night. I want to go home now. Can I please go home?"

Adele managed to swallow, took a breath, forced a smile. "Let's have dinner first."

"I don't want dinner," her mother said. "I want to go home."

Adele squeezed her eyes shut, trying to come up with the right response. When she opened them again, her mother was staring out the window. She knelt down and steadied herself on the arm of her mother's wing chair.

"I'll be right back, Mom," she said. "I need to talk to your nurse."

At the nurses' station around the corner from her mother's room, she looked for Sandra and Chuck, the two she usually spoke with on her lunchtime visits, but their shift had already ended. In their place she found two unfamiliar nurses, Julie and Monique, according to the photo ID badges that hung around their necks. Julie was pale and birdlike and nervous, all shaky hands and shuffling feet. Monique, a statuesque woman with a headful of braids, seemed more approachable.

"I'm wondering," she said to Monique, "if you can tell me

whether the doctor's been in to see my mother recently? She seems...well, confused. Could she be overmedicated?"

Monique smiled, showing off a gap in her upper incisors. "And your mother is?"

"Betty Hollenback."

"Let me see if I can release that information."

"I'm her daughter."

"Oh, I reckon you are. But now we've got all these privacy laws and confidentiality procedures."

"Yes. I'm aware of those. I'm a psychotherapist."

"Okay, then. So you know what I'm up against. I'll see what the folks in charge have to say." Monique took off down the hallway, humming a tune, her pastel-beaded braids clicking in rhythm to match her strides. On her feet was a pair of rubbery-looking plastic clogs in a pale shade of purple.

Adele leaned against the counter of the nurse's station, her back to the fluttery Julie. She had no desire to interact with anyone right now, not unless they had information about her mother, hard data, facts. There had to be a rational explanation for this confusion, and that nurse with the purple clogs had better have some answers when she got back.

CHAPTER 29

Stephanie

Stephanie sat in one of the purposely mismatched wooden chairs she'd found to add to the décor in her office. Her feet, clad in black BCBG slip-on sport shoes, were propped up on her shiny black conference table. She enjoyed these times when she could relax in her office after hours with the front door locked and enjoy the world she'd created for herself. Only this time she wasn't alone.

After their walk, Max had agreed to come with her. For some reason she didn't want to leave him home alone. She'd taken Riley back to her apartment and changed into her black velour Juicy sweatsuit, the only one she owned.

"This is some fascinating reading you've got here," Max said. He was walking beside her bookshelves scanning the titles of her law books.

"It sure is, smart ass," she said. "Do you want a pop or something? You can help yourself to my fridge over there."

"Sweet. You keep pop in here all the time?" he said as he walked over to the kitchenette across from the conference table. He opened the black refrigerator next to the black countertop and cabinets and helped himself to a Coke.

"Well, yeah. I like to be able to offer my clients something to drink when they're sitting here going out of their minds about whatever it is they're here to see me about."

"Your office rocks, Steph."

"I know," she said. "Grab me one of those, will you? But make it a Diet."

"Right on."

"Do you want a glass and some ice?"

"No. Do you?" he said, stopping halfway back to her with the pop bottles.

"No, that's okay. I can drink it like that."

Max sat down next to her and propped up his dirty sneakers, with the laces untied, next to her BCBG's on the conference table. They sat there and sipped with an easy silence between them.

"Is your mom okay?" she said. "She didn't look good when I saw her today."

"I think something's going on. They've been spending a lot of time talking in their bedroom with the door closed."

"You mean after what happened with you at school on Monday?"

"Before that. They've been looking all serious lately, talking in low voices. A few times when their door was shut I heard my mom yell a little."

"How long has that been going on?"

"I don't know, a month maybe."

"That long?" Why hadn't she noticed that her sister was troubled? She wanted to ask Max if he thought his mother was sick, or if his parents' marriage was in trouble, but she didn't want to be the one to put those thoughts in his head. Instead she said, "I'm sure it's nothing."

"Yeah."

She watched Max crack his knuckles. She wanted to talk to her sister, but that would have to wait.

"So, why did you say you're glad you're not one of my boyfriends?" she said.

"Well, I mean, it's not like you're not hot. You are."

"Thanks, doofus," she said, kicking at his feet next to hers on the table.

"No, I'm serious, even if you are my aunt and all. It's just, well, Mom even says you have a hard shell."

"She does, does she?" She continued to sip her Coke. She was good at playing relaxed under pressure. She was an attorney, after all. "What else does she say?"

"She thinks you protect yourself from ever getting hurt again. The way my grandparents hurt you guys when you were little."

"That's interesting," she said.

Max was on a roll now. "She thinks you don't allow yourself to care for anyone except Riley."

"That's crazy, I care for you and your mom and dad."

"Yeah, but that doesn't count because you don't have your own family."

There it was. He didn't know it, but there was nothing he could have said that would have hurt more.

"I suppose I don't. I guess I've just been tagging along with your family for all these years." She forced a laugh.

"It's not like we mind or anything," Max said. "We like having you around and all."

"Gee, thanks," she said, kicking at his feet again.

So her sister thought she was pathetic. She wanted to get mad, but every time she thought about what might be wrong with Marisa, worry took over. What would she do without her sister?

Her cell phone started ringing from the next room, so she went to the front waiting area, where she had left it on top of her secretary's desk with her purse, and answered it.

"Steph? It's Marisa. Is Max with you?"

"Yeah. I brought him by the office with me since nobody was home yet. Where have you been?"

"Listen, Paul and I wanted to take you and Max out to dinner tonight. Can you just bring him with you and meet us at Outback?"

She took a breath. She wasn't sure if she felt like being agreeable. "Which one?"

"The one on Dublin-Granville Road." Marisa said.

"What have you been doing up that way all afternoon?"

"I just had some errands to run. Anyway, can you meet us?"

"But we'll be fighting rush hour traffic." Did she sound as petulant as she felt?

"Please, Steph. It would mean a lot to me."

"I'll see what I can do."

After ending the call, she chewed on the antennae and walked over to the windows to look out. The whole outside wall, except for the wooden door, was windows. In fact, this was the only room in the place that had windows. When she was in either her conference room or her office, she had no idea what was going on outside, she was in her own little world.

Standing there she could see that the sun had left. There was a low rumble of thunder in the distance. She leaned forward, turned her head to the side, and looked up. Yes, indeed. There was lightning in the northern sky.

CHAPTER 30

Carol

When the first crack of lightning split the dark clouds, Coach McAllister said something to the assistant coach, who then pulled the girls' relay team aside. The coach lifted his bullhorn and turned to the bleachers, where Carol sat beside Wes, as far from Sharon and Madeline Greenfield as they could manage.

"The meet is called for fifteen minutes," the coach said to the crowd. "If there's no more lightning after that, we'll resume."

A fat drop of rain fell on Carol's nose. She turned to Wes. "And if there is more lightning?"

"Then we go home."

"Good," she said, wiping off the raindrop. Another fell, then another. A woman with two-toned hair—dull brown interspersed with bleached-blond stripes—rose from her spot in front of Carol and said to the woman next to her, "Come on, Mindy. Let's wait it out in the car."

Most of the runners were heading for the narrow opening in the fence on the other side of the track. Carol was about to elbow Wes and point this out when the sky opened up. Rain pelted the bleachers in sheets, blown by a chilly wind. Soon the other spectators began clogging the gated exit nearest the parking lot behind them, to their right. In another minute they'd be soaked. Carol reached for Wes's hand, but he was already on his feet. "Head for the Benz," he said. "I'm going to go get Tessa. I don't want her out in this."

Carol nodded and took off for the car, in the opposite direction. She would have preferred to have run with Wes, hand in hand, like two lovers fleeing a storm, but she was glad to see him finally taking the initiative with his daughter.

Two lovers fleeing a storm—that was the painting they'd seen in the Cleveland Museum of Art before they'd married. He'd bought her a postcard reproduction, which she'd propped up on her desk at work. How she wished she was in her cozy office at this moment, with Chekhov and a cup of tea. Instead she was running amidst of a gaggle of track moms dragging their whining toddlers and pre-teens.

She focused her attention on the opening in the chain link fence up ahead, trying to recall where Wes had parked. Her feet, bare to the elements in her new open-toed, high-heeled sandals, were wet and cold. "Strappy sandals," the clerk at the Satin Giraffe had called them. "Burnished with gold" had rounded out the sales pitch.

Why had she worn her new strappy sandals to a track meet? They were highly impractical. Still, as she splashed along the path that led to the parking lot, she realized that she was able to run in them. She had made a good choice. Her feet felt so much lighter in these sandals. She'd be in Wes's Benz in no time.

Except that she didn't have the key. She looked around for

Wes, who stood on the other side of the track, at least fifty yards away, sheltering Tessa with his suit jacket. Under her breath she cursed and hurried through the narrow opening in the fence, her heels tapping out a slower rhythm now. Why rush? She'd be thoroughly soaked by the time Wes got Tessa to the car in the far corner of the parking lot and unlocked it so they could all get in. Certainly she knew no one in this crowd she could beg shelter from.

No one except Sharon Connor.

There, in the handicapped parking space next to the fence opening stood Sharon, who was indeed handicapped in her own way, fumbling in her bag. Sharon pulled out her keys and looked straight at Carol. Her eyes widened. Then she blinked.

"Get in," she said.

Without thinking, Carol ran around the front of Sharon's pewter-colored sedan. The automatic locks clicked and when Carol pulled open the door, the new car scent hit her in the face. The luxury sedan had been paid for, no doubt, with Wes's generous child support. She lowered herself in the passenger seat and, through tight lips, thanked Sharon, adding, "I'm sure Wes will be along with Tessa in a moment."

Sharon said nothing.

Carol shrank down in the passenger seat and wrapped her arms around her chest. One of her chills had overtaken her. She had to hug herself hard to keep her teeth from chattering.

Sharon started the car and reached for the heater controls, her rose-colored nails bright and shiny against the soft grays of the car's interior. Her movements were slow and labored. With exaggerated care she turned the heater up to its highest setting.

Within seconds, the windshield fogged up. Carol's view of the track blurred, the runners and coaches nothing more than indistinct smears of red and yellow and blue on a green background. The sky was as gray as Sharon's new Lexus, and the rain beat down on the roof of the car like muffled drumbeats. She wished Sharon would turn on the windshield wipers so she could see but was still grateful for the heat—even if it was Sharon who provided it.

"This is awkward," Sharon said, still staring straight ahead.

"Indeed." Carol wasn't in the mood for chitchat, especially with Sharon. She turned her head toward the window, willing Wes to trot across the track to rescue her, conjuring up his handsome face, his broad smile, the dear little mole on the side of his chin.

Suddenly Sharon's voice boomed over the steady rat-tat-tat of the rain. Carol turned to face her, but Sharon kept her eyes on the windshield, as if she were talking to someone out on the track. "Since nothing has changed through the courts yet, I suppose Tessa will be having the usual Wednesday dinner with you and Wes."

Carol wanted to pretend she hadn't heard, but that would make things more awkward still. "That's what we'd planned," she said. "But with this delay—" She gestured toward the foggy windshield to the track beyond. "I doubt we'll have time to take Tessa out to dinner and have her back to your place by eight, which, as I recall, is the time you usually insist on."

"Well, she does have to eat," Sharon said, still without turning her head. "I'll think about letting you bring her back a little later tonight."

"How much later?"

"I don't know." Sharon's enunciation was indistinct, mushy. "I'll talk to Wes about it after the rain stops."

"I'd like to be included in that conversation," Carol said, purposely ignoring Sharon's sloppy articulation.

Sharon kept her gaze trained on the windshield.

Was Sharon baiting her with this silence? Or should she just go on, say what was on her mind? She wriggled her bare toes, stinging now in the hot blast from Sharon's heater. She pulled her feet back and yearned for her comfy unisex slip-ons.

"Actually," Carol said, "I'm glad you brought up Tessa's schedule. I was disappointed we weren't able to reach an agreement in court today. I felt the compromise Wes and I crafted was more than equitable. Furthermore, it would meet Tessa's immediate needs—and yours."

"What needs are you referring to?"

Carol licked her lips, straining for the right words. "Tessa's academic needs," she said, keeping her voice as soft and calm as Dr. Martin's. "Tessa does well in school when someone sees to it that she focuses on her assignments. When she's left to her own devices—"

Sharon's face tensed. "You do not tell me what my daughter needs. You are not her mother."

Carol felt her hands clutching at the edges of her seat, her fingertips digging into the soft leather. "Nor have I ever tried to be. Do you have any idea what it's like to be a stepparent? I care every bit as much for Tessa as I do for my twins, yet when she's hurt or needs advice or wants to talk about breaking up with a boy, Tessa goes to you. Oh, she's polite enough to me, even affectionate. But I fully understand that no matter how much I love Tessa, I'll never replace you in her heart."

For the first time since they got in the car together, Sharon turned to face her. "You expect me to feel sorry for you? You've already raised your own kids. Now you have my husband, and you're trying to get my child as well. Haven't you taken enough away from me?" Tears welled up in her gray-blue eyes.

Carol struggled to get her mind around the depth of Sharon's hurt. Was she the archetypal home-wrecker Sharon thought her to be, a middle-aged jezebel who'd snatched both husband and daughter? Certainly she hadn't set out to be. Or perhaps Sharon simply didn't know that Wes had deceived them both, his wife by taking a lover and his lover by neglecting to mention he had a wife. Was Sharon therefore stuck, unable to move on because she thought she had Carol and Wes to blame for all her problems? If so, someone needed to set her straight.

"Sharon," she said softly, "you need to understand something. I didn't set out to ruin your life. I didn't even know about you until long after I'd fallen in love with Wes. I thought he was single and childless. I thought I was doing nothing wrong. I'm not some character in a bad TV movie. Don't project that image onto me."

Sharon blinked several times as she searched her face, as if seeing her for the first time. Carol wondered how much of their history Wes had shared with Sharon during their last few breaking-up showdowns.

"So," Sharon said slowly, "we actually have something in common." It wasn't a question.

Carol didn't want to have anything in common with Sharon. Still, the woman was probably right. As Dr. Martin had said, Wes had betrayed them both. "I suppose we do," she said. "Besides the obvious, I think we both tend to see what we want to see at times."

"What do you mean?"

Carol raked her fingers through her damp hair, guiding it up off her sweating forehead. "When Wes and I were first...starting to spend time together, I didn't question him about his family life. I let him tell me what he wanted me to know. And I was still grieving when I met Wesley, a widow of less than a year. He seemed so relaxed and open that I never dreamed he had a wife and daughter. Still, I never asked, 'Are you married?' Not even, 'Have you ever been married?' That's not like me. Usually I insist on getting all the facts, but not this time. I saw him as single because I wanted him to be single." She shrugged, feeling helpless and stupid. "I know what it's like to long for a man you loved and lost, Sharon. I don't know if you're aware of this, but my first husband died quite suddenly, unexpectedly—"

"That's hardly the same thing." Sharon's lips were compressed, her eyes hard.

"I wasn't suggesting that it is," Carol said. "Still, I know how sad and lonely a person can feel after losing a loved one. And how angry. It's irrational, I know, but there were times I was furious with Lyle for having died."

Sharon was frowning now, but her face had lost that tense, combative look. She sat back in her seat and looked upward, at the car's ceiling. "Listen," she said after a pause, "I'm not going to pretend like we're friends. We're never going to be friends. But now that you're in the picture—" Sharon made air-quotation marks with her pink-tipped fingers. "-it looks like, for better or worse, we're in this together. And I will tell you this—I know that Tessa hasn't been happy lately. And her grades aren't where they should be. If you think you can help her with that, I'm willing to let you try."

The car was hot as an oven now. Sweat was dripping down Carol's neck, but she would not ask Sharon to turn off the heater. Not now, not at this moment. "I appreciate that," she said. "And I promise you, I'll do my best."

Sharon sat back in her seat and stared at the blurry windshield again. She reached toward the gearshift and turned on the wipers. One swipe and their view cleared.

CHAPTER 31

Sharon

The rain had stopped and Carol was gone, but Sharon still sat there. She wasn't sure what impulse had caused her to invite Carol into her car, but she was glad that she had. She'd never seen Carol so vulnerable. Sitting there soaking wet and shivering, Carol had looked as pathetic as a drowned cat. She could tell that Carol had wanted to spring out of the car several times, but she hadn't. She had stayed. She'd taken what Sharon had dished out. Unlike Wes, who would dart away from her when there was an issue to resolve rather than digging in and dealing with it.

Sharon was glad she hadn't cried. The Valium probably helped. She'd watched the rain slide down the window behind Carol's head and realized tears should be sliding down her face as well, but the pill had taken enough of the edge off to allow her to maintain her composure. Still, she wished she hadn't taken the pill after she left the courthouse. Carol might have noticed she was slurring her words a bit. She looked at her glove box—she would throw that bottle away as soon as she got the chance. But it didn't matter as much now anyway. The full-scale war was off.

So Carol hadn't known Wes was married. She still couldn't believe it. It had never occurred to her that Carol wasn't the villain in all of this. Carol was just a woman. A woman who could be fooled. A woman who could make stupid judgment calls for love like anyone else. Still, maybe there wasn't complete stupidity to her relationship with Wes. She could see from one angle how the two of them probably made a better match than she and Wes had. Carol was a fighter. She'd given up with Wes long ago, she just hadn't admitted it. But Carol would keep hanging in there with him. She could see that. Carol had the energy to help him be a better husband and father.

Sharon drummed her manicured nails on the steering wheel. She thought about her favorite character from *Desperate Housewives*, Susan Meyer, the one she could relate to the most. Susan was a writer, Sharon worked for a magazine. Like Susan, Sharon was a single mother to a teenaged daughter. Susan and her daughter Julie also lived together more as sisters than mother and daughter in their big house in the suburbs. They watched out for each other, gave each other boyfriend advice. Every week Sharon watched the show with Tessa as though they were watching their lives unfold on the screen. She wasn't sure what her own future held, yet somehow it was comforting to see what was next for Susan and Julie.

But their lives weren't a TV show. This was real. And she had been screwing it up. Tessa's school essay showed her that. Damn, she wished that pill would wear off. She didn't want to be fuzzy anymore.

Maybe she finally could start thinking of this shared custody arrangement as an opportunity for her instead of a punishment. While Tessa was with Wes and Carol, she could start doing things for herself that didn't relate to Tessa. She could take ballroom dancing, for instance. That was another show on TV she liked to catch- *Dancing with the Stars*. During their coffee chats or when they took walks together, she and Madeline enjoyed speculating about which star was going to be eliminated next. She also had really learned to appreciate the skill involved with the different types of dances. She loved the ballroom dances - the waltz, tango, quick step. But she adored the passion of the Latin dances - the rumba, the cha cha, and the samba. She could even see herself taking salsa lessons. Now that was sexy. What a way to meet guys, too.

All she needed was a pair of those ballroom dancing shoes - the high heels with felt on the bottom so they could slide across the floor. She'd always marveled at how the women were able to dance around like acrobats, so agile in high heels, while the men pushed and pulled them as they stood there in their comfy flat shoes. Now wasn't that just like real life?

Maybe she could talk Madeline into taking lessons with her. Or maybe she shouldn't even ask. Madeline was happily married after all. Maybe she should find a single friend who could be her back-up out there. In fact, maybe she should let Madeline be off-duty for a bit. She'd certainly put in her time lately. Madeline had fled the track meet when it started to downpour. She should call to thank her right now.

"How wet did you get?" she said when Madeline answered the phone.

"Wetter than I wanted to be."

"Where are you?"

"The parking lot at Kung Ho. I'm sitting in my car waiting on a take-out order."

"That sounds delicious."

"I was already in the parking lot at the cleaners, and once I smelled the food, that was it. Now the whole family has to eat Chinese food."

"Aaah, picking up the husband's dry cleaning. I remember those days."

"When I left PMS I realized I needed to pick up Jack's suits before they closed or he'd be going to work naked tomorrow!"

"Please don't talk about naked men to your divorced friend."

"Sorry. Where are you?"

"Sitting in my car in the school parking lot," she said. "I'm waiting to see if the meet is going to start back up."

"I broke my new J. Crew umbrella trying to get in the car with the suits," Madeline said and deep-sighed.

Clearly it was time for something to be about Madeline.

"Listen," Sharon said, "I'm sorry your day got so hectic because of me. That was really nice of you to spend so much time trying to support me."

"You're welcome," Madeline said. "Of course, I probably won't be able to hang out all day at court like that the next time you go. Maybe I can just keep my cell phone handy in case you really need me."

"Absolutely," she said. "And who knows if there's even going to be a need to go back to court. I'm thinking maybe Wes and I will be able to come up with an agreement by then."

"That's great. Did Tessa's essay help you reach that conclusion?"

"Yes, partly. As well as a conversation I had with Carol in my car during the storm."

"No way. The two of you trapped in a car together? What was that like? Hey, did you just call her Carol?"

"Yeah. It was an interesting conversation. Oh, and you're going to love this, she had on strappy sandals."

"No way. She changed out of those clunkers in the middle of the day?"

"Apparently you made an impression on her."

"Do you think?"

"One can only hope."

"Do you think it'll last?"

"One can only hope," she said. "Hey, Mad?"

"Yeah?"

"Do you remember me telling you about the time when Tessa was a baby and I had to go to Chicago on that business trip?"

"When Tessa got sick?" Madeline said.

"Yes. Remember, Wes had to call me to get her pediatrician's name? And I flew back right away, even though he said he could handle it?"

"Right, and then later he accused you of not trusting him and it blew up into this big thing."

"Well, I wish I had let him handle it."

"You know that probably wouldn't have made a difference."

"I know. I'm not saying that one thing would have saved our marriage or anything. And I'm not saying I wish we were still together. I just wish I had let him take care of her on that day."

"I understand," Madeline said. "Hey, tell me about what you and Carol talked about in the car."

"I will, but another time. Over coffee, okay?"

Sharon could see through her windshield that the athletes and parents were reconvening on the field. She'd better get back up there before she missed everything.

CHAPTER 32

Tessa

The rain had let up, but Tessa's new Air Max shoes were soaked, heavy and squishy and sure to slow her down. Any advantage she might have in her race was gone. At this point, though, she didn't much care. She finally had some alone-time with her dad, and that was feeling really good, better even than winning her heat and making her parents proud.

It was weird how it happened. Just as she was about to take her place for the 400 relay, it had started to rain like crazy, and her dad had loped across the track with his big old daddy long-legs. When he got to where she was standing, he whipped off his suit jacket—his good silk one—and held it over her head.

"Quick," he said. "Let's run for the car."

Tessa shook her head. "The gym's closer."

So they'd headed for the gym, her dad holding that jacket over her head the whole way. When they got to the door—which was unlocked, thank God—he also held the door open for her. That was so like her dad, so polite, even in a thunderstorm. He always said that good manners lubricated relationships the way oil lubricated an engine, and when manners went, so did the relationship.

Now, as she watched some of the other kids and parents who'd taken shelter in the gym straggle back onto the track, she wondered if that's what had happened to her parents. Back when they were married, they'd said please and thank you to each other, and her dad had opened doors for her mom, but it was like they were just going through the motions. And now, since the divorce, they were ice cold to each other though they still said please and thank you. So it was more than manners that made relationships break down.

She sort of wanted to ask her dad about that, but it didn't seem like the time. Her dad was hard to talk to sometimes. Like now. They'd started up three conversations so far, all of them lame, about sports and real estate and her getting her ears double-pierced. But that wasn't really what was on either of their minds. Maybe she had to be the one to bring it up—what had happened in court today. She was dying to know, but it felt weird asking her dad about it. He looked so nervous standing there, brushing the raindrops off his jacket.

"Um, Dad," she said. "Can I talk to you?"

"What? Oh, sure. One second, though. I need to phone Carol and let her know where we are." He reached in his pocket for his cell.

A dark feeling started pulling her down, like a rickety boat filling up with water. "Is that really necessary?" she said. "I'd sort of like to talk to you about what went down at court today. I've been waiting all day to find out."

And then it happened, her own personal miracle—her dad, Mr. Cell Phone, actually slid the phone back into his pocket. He finally turned to her and looked her straight in the eye. "To tell you the truth," he said, "it's on hold for now.

We're still trying to work something out, but it might take a while." He cleared his throat. "But I want you to know, Carol and I had a long talk at lunch. We realize that you've grown up spending most of your time with your mom—"

"So you want me to go live with my mom full time?" Her voice came out in a loud, high squeak. "Like, you're almost totally out of the picture now?"

Her dad shook his head. "No, that's not what Carol and I want at all. We're trying to work out a compromise between what your mom wants and what we think is best for you."

So nothing had been decided yet at all—what a waste, this whole day shot. Well, maybe they'd go back to court tomorrow and finish it up. She watched as other runners and parents left the gym. When everyone had gone and they were alone in the big, echoing room, she said. "So what happens to me now?"

"I don't know, exactly. The judge is giving all of us a month to sit down and work things out."

Another month of waiting and wondering? "No," she said. "That's not going to work. I am not going to sit around and wait for you guys to divide up my time any way you want. Not any more. I've had it with you guys, all of you."

"Tessa, please." He put his arm around her shoulders and lowered his voice, even though there was nobody around to hear them. "I think you'll like the changes Carol and I are going to suggest."

"What changes?" She crossed her arms over her chest. She was starting to shiver in her thin tank and shorts and wished she'd brought her warm-ups.

"I don't want to get into specifics right now, but it won't be too different from what you have now."

"Really? Like what?"

"As I said, that's up in the air right now. I think what's more important, though, is how we feel about each other. This has been a rough two years."

Could this really be her dad talking? "Tell me about it," she said. "But it's been hard for you, too, I guess."

"You'd better believe it." He draped his damp jacket over his arm.

"These last few months have been a total bear for me. Since you married Carol." She looked up at him to see if he was freaking out before going on. "For me and for Mom."

"I know it was tough, honey."

"But you never said that. Well, just that once. You talked about how it would be an adjustment for me. Like I'm supposed to be over it, just like that." She snapped her fingers.

Her dad stroked his chin, like he was checking to see if he needed a shave.

"Probably wasn't the most sympathetic way to handle the situation, huh?"

"Not really. And then you let Carol make me do study table—"

"Hang on, Tess. I'm in agreement with Carol there."

"Now, maybe. But at first it was all Carol all the time."

"Sounds like you have a problem with that."

"Well, it sort of creeps me out that you'd let Carol have so much say when it comes to me. I mean, you're my daddy. You should be the one to decide stuff that has to do with me."

"I do."

"Not the custody thing. I heard Mom tell Madeline it was in Carol's handwriting."

Her dad's face got tight and frowny, then loosened up again. "I'm going to have final say on that, Tessa. Not Carol. We talked about that, too."

"Seriously?"

"You've got my word." Her dad put out his hand to shake on it. It was corny, but that was her dad, Mr. Manners, Mr. Business, Mr. Let's Make a Deal.

Tessa put her hands behind her back. "I mean it, Dad. No more of this back and forth crap. I don't want to be shuttled back and forth between you and Mom when it's convenient for you, and I don't want you guys to go back and forth in court anymore. If you and Mom can't work this out between you, then I want one of you to give in."

Her dad frowned. "That's a hard one, honey. I've already given up a lot. I only see you a couple of weekends a month—"

"And half the time you're on the phone when I'm with you. I don't mean to be rude, but when I am with you, I'd like your full attention. Not like we'd be hanging out all the time, but if I ask you to help me with my relay handoffs or a problem with a boy, please don't send me to Carol."

"Deal," her dad said. "But if it's English, Carol gets the last word. I don't know a semi-colon from a colon, sweetheart."

"That's different," she said. "Carol's the expert in that. I'm talking about the stuff dads normally do."

"I guess I have been, uh, distracted lately. Carol and I also talked about that."

Tessa leaned against the painted concrete blocks of the

north gym wall, her face at a right angle to her dad's, her left foot against the wall. She wanted her dad to feel how much she disapproved of what he'd been doing, but she didn't want to be a total dork about it, either. Waiting could be horrible, but sometimes, like now, it was the best thing to do. Just wait and say nothing and let her dad react.

"I'm sorry, baby," he said at last, looking down at the maple flooring. Then he looked up. "I did a bad thing. I hurt you and your mom."

"You totally did," she said. "Big time."

"Can you forgive me?"

At the opposite end of the gym, in the open doorway, Ryan Dunn and some of the other guys were horsing around and yelling to one of the assistant coaches, who stood with his dripping whistle in his mouth. The meet was being called off, he was saying. They could all go home. Any other day she'd have been disappointed, but today she was glad. She felt really tired and droopy all of a sudden, like the old Raggedy Ann doll that Grandma Connor had made for her when she was a little kid.

She nodded her head toward the open doors. "Looks like I'm not going to get to run today."

"I guess not," her dad said.

"So will I, like, go home with you tonight? Like usual?"

"Uh-huh. Carol and I were going to take you out to dinner after the meet. We thought you'd be hungry."

"I am hungry," she said. "Can we go to Outback?"

"Oh, boy."

"What?"

"That's not our favorite."

Not Carol's favorite, he meant. "Please," she said. "I love that Blooming Onion."

Her dad sucked in his lips, which meant he was working hard not to say the wrong thing. "Okay," he said after a pause. "Why not? Carol enjoys a good steak, and so do I."

"Awesome," she said, wondering if she should get it all out, everything that had been bothering her for so long. "Um, I do have one question, though."

"Shoot." He was grinning now, like he felt good about giving in on dinner.

"I, um, the reason you and mom are in court...it's not because of something I did, is it? Because my grades are coming up now and—"

Her dad put his hand on her shoulder and looked her in the eye. "It's nothing you did, sweetheart. This is between your mom and me, nobody else. This is not your fault."

"Seriously?"

He nodded. "I've never been more serious."

"Then yeah," she said, finally cracking a smile.

"Yeah what?"

"Yeah, I can forgive you."

She put both arms around his waist and squeezed him hard, and he wrapped his arms around her shoulders and squeezed her too, dropping his jacket on the gym floor in the process. He didn't even pick it up until after she let him go, which was the way it was supposed to be.

CHAPTER 33

Carol

Carol scanned the track again. Where in God's name were Wes and Tessa? From Sharon's car, she'd headed for the track, along with a number of other bewildered parents, now equipped with plastic ponchos and colorful golf umbrellas. She'd stood for some time with the others in front of the bleachers, waiting and tapping the toe of her new shoe on the wet asphalt, not wanting to sit in the damp. Finally Coach McAllister had jogged out of the gym. Through his bullhorn he'd told the assembled crowd that he had to call the meet "on account of the severe weather," though the storm clouds were blowing away in a stiff wind. Now the bleachers were emptying out. Still no Wes and Tessa.

She shook her head. From her big purse, she took a wad of tissues to sop up the water, sat down in the small, dry spot on the chilled aluminum bleachers and pulled out a slim volume of Chekhov. She opened it to the engraved silver bookmark, yet another gift from Wes, and turned the page, determined to lose herself in "The Lady with the Pet Dog." After her talk with Sharon, she could use a short literary vacation to nineteenth-century Russia.

Just as Gurov spotted his married lover's fluffy white Pomeranian, a voice interrupted her vacation.

"Good book?"

She looked up to see Wes standing beside her, his wrinkled suit jacket hanging over his arm, a big grin on his face.

"There you are," she said. "I thought for a moment you'd been struck by lightning." She felt foolish once the words were out of her mouth, but Wes just smiled and assured her that he and Tessa were both fine.

"Tessa and I had a long talk," he said.

"Oh, Wesley—"

"No, it went okay. She's changing in the locker room, that's all. But why are you sitting here?"

"Your car was locked."

"Sorry," he said.

"Actually, it might have been a good thing."

"I don't understand."

"Sit down." She patted the space on the bleachers beside her. "I'll tell you why."

Wes's face twisted up into a frown, but before she could reach into her bag for more tissues, he shrugged, tossed his jacket down beside her and sat on it.

"Your jacket," she said. "You'll ruin it."

He laughed. "It has to go to the cleaners anyway. At least this way my pants stay dry. Now, what's this about the locked car being a good thing?"

"You'll recall," she said with a wry smile, "there was a cloudburst? And of course I couldn't get into your car."

"Sorry again."

"Not your fault. I ought to carry my own key. In any case, I was getting drenched, far from shelter. I looked up, and there was Sharon, parked in the handicapped space again."

Wes shook his head. "I wish she wouldn't do that. It sets a bad example for Tessa."

"That's not my point, though. Sharon took one look at me, soaked to the skin, and said, 'Get in.' And, Wes, I did get in. Don't ask me why. Certainly I was wet and chilled, but that wasn't it. Something seemed to propel me into her car."

Wes's eyes were wide, unblinking. "You actually got in with her?"

"I did. And even more amazing, we started to talk."

"Honey, I wish you'd gone into the school building or something. You know how Sharon always sets you off."

"Usually," she said. "But not this time."

"No?" Wes was smiling, but she sensed tension in his neck and face. He didn't seem to want her talking to Sharon.

She decided to ignore his discomfort and push on. "Not that it was an easy conversation. Sharon started the ball rolling, talking about where Tessa would go tonight. She said she'd talk to you about the details. I'd say that's progress."

Wes shrugged. "In a manner of speaking. I'd rather have this all decided, though."

"So would I. That's why I stayed in that car. I thought if she was going to bring up the custody issue, I had a responsibility to see it through."

"So what happened?"

"I told her I was disappointed we didn't reach an agreement at the courthouse. I explained that our concern was with Tessa, not ourselves."

"Uh-huh." Wes was rubbing his palms together, as if he was cold.

"Then I assured her that I'm not trying to usurp her role as Tessa's mother."

"Good."

"And—" She paused. "I made it clear I did not have an affair with you. Not in the conventional sense of the word, at least. Apparently she didn't realize I hadn't known you were married when we first met—or for some time after that."

Wes frowned. "I thought we agreed not to talk about that any more."

"We're not. I'm telling you what I said to Sharon. I assumed she knew, Wesley. But she didn't—or if she did, she hadn't accepted it. Which might explain why she's so angry all the time. So unreasonable."

"I told her, Carol. I said you were as much of a victim in this as she was. But she didn't believe me. I swear to you."

She put her hand on his forearm. "I believe you, Wes. But perhaps she wasn't ready to hear it. And later, when she was ready—" She stopped short of pointing out how he'd failed to finish the job.

He nodded and looked down through the bleachers. Bits of trash had blown there during the storm, empty water bottles and Power Bar wrappers. For a moment she thought he was going to reach down to pick it up, so he didn't have to face her. He did look her way, though.

"I don't know why I do that," he said. "When the going gets tough—" He shrugged. "I guess I get going the other way."

How long she'd waited to hear him admit that he avoided

conflict. "That does seem true," she said. "At least in personal matters. Now, in business—" She let her voice trail off, the way Dr. Martin sometimes did, and waited while he stared out onto the drenched track, where one of the coaches was still stacking hurdles.

A minute or two passed. If Wes got the connection, he wasn't going to talk about it now. Well, fair enough. Perhaps they'd discuss this later, after she'd made a confession of her own, about the smoking.

"Everyone makes mistakes," she said. "Would you like to hear what else happened? Between Sharon and me?"

He gave her a small smile. "Only if it was good. If you two just sat there talking about me, then maybe not."

She laughed. "It's not all about you, Wes."

"I know, but—"

"She said if we think we can help Tessa after school, she's willing to give us a chance to try."

"Sharon said that?"

She shot him a smug smile. "She did. Can you imagine?"

Wes was shaking his head, eyes still wide. "In a word, no."

"And, you know, I think she will be more reasonable from now. But Wes, I think she was...on something. Slurring her words. She really shouldn't be driving."

Wes sighed. "I'll talk to her about that tomorrow. But not now. She's had a tough day. We all have. This isn't the best time to get through to her."

"Please do, though, and soon. I worry about Tessa's safety. And Sharon's."

Wes's eyebrows lifted, as if he was surprised.

"But now it's your turn to talk," Carol said. "What went on between you and Tessa?"

"We ended up in the gym," he said.

As usual, he was abridging, so she prompted him, asking what they'd talked about. "The custody schedule?"

"Not in so many words. I wanted her to know how much I love her, that I want to spend more time with her. I guess you were right. I do need to step up and say what's in my heart. Thanks for giving me the heads-up at lunch."

"Certainly," she said, hiding her surprise. Their conversation at lunch had been tense, at best.

"Turns out Tessa wants me to be more of a dad. Not send her to you all the time. Or to her mom. I guess I've been sort of missing in action." He gave her a sidelong glance. "I probably need to be more focused on the weekends when Tessa's with us. After school, too. That means I'll have to rearrange my work schedule."

She drew back and studied his face. A smile twitched on his lips—he was proud of this decision. "Well, you are her father." She smiled and slipped her arm through his.

"Also, Tessa wants us to work something out with Sharon," he said. "She doesn't want us to go back to court in a month."

Carol thought of Sharon saying they'd never be friends. Well, they didn't need to be friends—they needed not to be enemies, and that had already come to pass. "I think we'll be able to do that now," she said.

To their right, the gym doors opened with a bang. Tessa walked out, taking long, confident strides, her multicolored designer purse dangling from her elbow, incongruous with her loose-fitting cargo shorts and pale pink tank top. A ray of sun hit her like a spotlight, turning her hair golden. Her jewelry sparkled, along with her lip gloss. She was a beautiful girl, really. Carol could understand why she wanted to be a model or an actress. Still, there was so much more to her than that. Perhaps with time—

Tessa waved when she spotted them and jogged up, all smiles now. She hugged her father and gave Carol a one-armed girlie hug, which Carol returned. Tessa smelled of Burberry perfume—a gift from her father. She'd piled on the eyeliner again, though tastefully. Carol wondered how she'd look in liquid eyeliner. Perhaps Tessa wouldn't mind showing her how to apply it.

"You look lovely," she said.

"Thanks." Tessa's eyes went straight to Carol's new high-heeled sandals. "Cool shoes."

"Do you like them? I saw them at the Satin Giraffe last week and I thought they might suit me."

"They're amazing," Tessa said. "Really."

Amazing. It was hard to believe a pair of silly shoes had elicited this response.

A car door slammed. Carol turned toward the parking lot. She wasn't sure what made Sharon wobble like that. She hoped it was the heels.

Sharon walked toward them, her steps growing steadier. Without looking at her or at Wes, she told Tessa she was sorry the meet had been cancelled. Turning, she asked Wes what time she should pick Tessa up that night, a first in Carol's experience. Usually Sharon told, not asked. Then Sharon did something more amazing—she actually nodded to Carol as she said it. Was she deliberately trying to include both of them in this decision? Carol had to lock her jaw in place to prevent it from dropping. When she'd recovered, she looked up at Wes and reminded him they'd planned to take Tessa out to dinner.

"Dad said we're going to Outback," Tessa said.

Raising one eyebrow, Carol looked over at Wes, who shrugged and smiled. She smiled, too. She could stomach a mediocre dinner in exchange for the look on her husband's face. He seemed in charge again, a father who knew what was best for his daughter and wasn't afraid to say so.

"I sure did say that," Wes said to Tessa. Then he turned to Sharon. "What about 8:30 tonight?"

Carol braced herself for the fireworks—ordinarily Sharon complained about having to pick Tessa up at eight, the legally agreed-upon pickup time, saying that was too late. But no fireworks exploded. In fact, the impossible happened.

"Fine," Sharon said. "I'll see you then."

Sharon Connor was actually smiling. Tessa must have noticed this, too, because she drew her head back and blinked.

"Oh, Tessa," Sharon said, turning back to her daughter. "I have your backpack. It's in the trunk of my car, safe and sound. I'll take it home for you." She leaned forward and hugged her daughter.

"Um, thanks, Mom," Tessa said. She looked relieved.

"Bye, honey." Sharon stepped back. "Have a nice dinner." Again, Sharon smiled.

It was the first time Sharon had ever responded this way. Even Wes stood staring. Surely now there would be some follow-up jab from Sharon, a sly comment about how generous she was being or how difficult this was for her. But no jab came. Sharon headed to the parking lot without looking back.

Carol looked at Tessa. Her stepdaughter's mouth was half-open. Wes was staring at his ex. The three of them stood motionless, taking this all in. Sharon got into her car and drove away with only a cursory wave, as if she did this every day.

Tessa seemed to come back to herself then. She smiled and said, "Let's go, you guys." And before either of them could speak, she started running toward Wes's car, challenging them both to a shorter version of the race she hadn't been able to run. A relay of sorts, with Sharon handing off her daughter to her father and stepmother for a while. Then it would be their turn to hand Tessa back to her mother. Handoffs were the trickiest part of a relay race, Tessa often said. Sharing custody was as well, apparently.

Wes took off jogging after his daughter, but Carol walked slowly in her new high-heeled sandals. The narrow straps were starting to dig into her toes, but she wouldn't slip back into her unisex slip-ons. As her mother always said, "It hurts to be beautiful." Was she beautiful? Perhaps. Certainly her feet were starting to hurt.

When they got to the Benz, Tessa slid into the back. While Wes started the car, Carol turned around to face Tessa. "We're going to work something out," she said. "With your mother."

"I know," Tessa said. "Dad told me. Plus, you guys must be doing something different. Mom wouldn't be acting like this if you weren't."

Carol nodded and turned around in her seat.

They were quiet on their way to Outback, listening to one of Tessa's girlie-pop CDs. Although the parking lot that surrounded the restaurant was crowded, it didn't take long to get a table, a booth toward the front. Father and daughter sat with their backs to the entry. Carol sat opposite, barely able to see over the top of the booth. Tessa insisted on ordering something called a Blooming Onion, which turned out to be rather tasty. They all ordered too-large steaks. Then Tessa excused herself to use the restroom, probably to slather on more makeup. Well, so be it. At least the girl knew how to do it skillfully.

Carol took a sip of water, looking up just as Tessa emerged from behind the plant-topped partition that separated the entry from the dining room. Taking slow strides, Tessa walked past a tall, broad-shouldered boy with reddish blond hair, then turned around and looked back. Her gaze lingered on him for a moment as he walked in the other direction, disappearing behind the partition.

Carol wondered if Tessa knew him, or if she was just attracted to a stranger. The boy hadn't seen Tessa noticing him, thank God, but it was only a matter of time until an older boy asked Tessa out. What would Wes do then?

"Your daughter's growing up," she said to Wes, who was flipping through the dessert menu.

He nodded without looking up. "Growing up too fast, if you ask me."

She laughed and recalled herself at fourteen, short and slat-thin and more than a bit pimply. The ugly duckling, her mother had called her. Maybe there was still time to become a swan. Well, a smart swan. The world didn't need any more dumb swans.

CHAPTER 34

Stephanie

Stephanie was glad the rain had stopped while they were still driving. She didn't have an umbrella in her car, and she didn't feel like eating her dinner soaked. When they walked into the Outback, she told the girl at the podium—how old was she anyway?— that she and Max were with the Hendrickson party of four.

"Right this way," the girl said as she led them around the bar and through the restaurant to the back. As she followed, she couldn't help but notice that the girl's pants and shirt didn't meet. Her narrow waist broadened into fleshy but firm hips that were visible long before the waistband of her too-tight, bargain-basement slacks took over. Peeking out of the waistband was the beginning of a tattoo, which must have extended across her cheeks. Stephanie was all for low-riders, but this was a bit ridiculous. She glanced back and noticed that Max was having a different reaction to what he saw. Typical. She suddenly felt self-conscious in her modest sweatsuit, even if it was designer.

Marisa and Paul were waiting at a table in the back corner.

"Hey, Kiddo!" Paul said to her. "Hello, Son," he said to Max.

Max nodded to his dad then kissed his mom on the cheek.

Stephanie gave Paul and Marisa each a quick hug, then she and Max sat across from them. She was having a hard time looking at Marisa.

"How was work?" she said to Paul.

"Fine," he said, flashing his white smile. "Same ole number crunching. What about your day?"

"The best part was hanging out with Maxamillion here." That was part lie, part truth. She'd enjoyed being with her nephew, but she also felt worse than she had in a long time.

Crossing her legs, Marisa put her foot out in the aisle.

Stephanie looked down. "Your Birkenstocks?" she said. "Where are your new boots?"

"They didn't match the dress I have on today."

"I know. I was hoping you'd buy a new outfit while you were at Macy's and retire that old thing." She was always bugging Marisa to stop wearing those shapeless, ankle-length dresses.

"I'm comfortable in this dress. And you know Birks are my favorite shoes."

"I know, I know," she said. "It's like you're not even wearing shoes. The recessed foot bed lets your feet spread out, yada, yada, yada."

"I think she looks great," Paul said. Max was playing with a sugar packet.

"I mean, the whole idea of Birkenstocks—feet walking around in a bed," Stephanie said. "How lazy can feet get?" She knew she was being mean, but she couldn't stop herself.

Birkenstocks were appropriate for her sister, though. Marisa was far more grounded than she'd ever been.

The waitress stepped up to take their drink orders. Paul told her they were going to need some time to look over the menu.

After the waitress left, Marisa sighed. "Well, there's a reason I'm especially interested in being comfortable right now. And it also has to do with why Paul and I wanted to meet you two for dinner."

So they were going to talk about it here. Marisa's somber tone only fueled Stephanie's anxiety. "There's nothing wrong is there?" she said.

"Well, you know I told you I had other errands to take care of up here today?" Marisa said.

"Yes." Her throat was dry, but she didn't pick up her water.

"I saw my gynecologist."

This was it. This was why she'd been uneasy all afternoon. Her sister had cancer. Was it breast, ovarian?

"I'm pregnant," Marisa said.

Stephanie blinked. She couldn't take this in. She looked at Max who had his fingers poised in mid-air where he'd been about to flick the sugar packet like a football.

"You're pregnant?" Stephanie said.

"It's not like we planned it. You know we tried to have more kids after Max, but when it never happened, we just assumed we couldn't get pregnant again, so we stopped doing anything to prevent it."

"Too much information," Max said as he squeezed his eyes shut.

"Why didn't you say anything before?" Stephanie said. She glanced at Paul. His smile only made her feel more betrayed.

"The timing wasn't right. Not with what's been going on with Max lately." Marisa turned to Max. "Honey, are you okay?"

"I can't believe you're springing this on me here," he said, twisting in his seat. "I can't believe you're doing this to me at all!"

"All we're doing," Paul said, "is having another child. He glanced at Stephanie as well. "I think this is going to be a good thing," he continued. "Mom was just starting to feel a touch of the upcoming empty-nest syndrome, now she doesn't have to."

Spoken like a true man. Let's just fix everything.

"I'm going to the bathroom," Max said.

"Okay, Sweetheart." Marisa tried to pat him as he walked by but she missed.

Stephanie waited until Max was out of earshot. "I thought you were going to do something with your life after Max graduated. Like go back to school, start a new career."

"How can you, of all people, say that to me?" Marisa said.

"What's that supposed to mean?"

"Like being a mom isn't enough? Well, it certainly was good enough when you needed one."

"I never asked you to be my mom," she said.

"That's what I've been trying to tell you. You didn't have to ask."

"Girls, girls," Paul said.

"No, Paul. She needs to hear this," Marisa said. "I might as well have been your mother. I sacrificed for you like a mother, something you'll never understand until you have kids of your own. Oh, that's right, you're not going to have kids. Ever. You couldn't possibly sacrifice for someone else like I sacrificed for you."

"I never said I didn't want to sacrifice for anyone!" She saw from the faces at the tables nearby that her voice had gotten loud.

"No, you never said that. But that's what it is. You cut people off, Steph. As soon as the relationship gets difficult, requires something too tough for you to give, you end it."

"Here we go again with Justin."

"Not just Justin. You break up with every guy that gets too close. And you don't even talk to Mom and Dad anymore."

"Why do we have to bring them into this?" She looked at Paul for help.

"I don't think this discussion is going anywhere productive right now, and Max will be back soon," he said. "Why don't we put this on hold until a better time?"

"Fine," Stephanie said.

"Fine by me," Marisa said. She opened her menu and scanned it from front to back as though it were the most interesting reading material she'd come across in years.

Stephanie looked at Paul and raised her eyebrows. He just shrugged. She hadn't noticed it until now, but he looked as worn out as Marisa. The baby news had to have hit him hard, too. He must be trying to stay positive for Marisa's sake. She had to give him credit. He'd always been a trooper, up for whatever life sent them, including Stephanie herself.

She watched her sister continue to be fascinated by the menu. Max came back from the bathroom just as the waitress showed up to see if they were ready. They fumbled around as they placed their orders.

When the waitress left, Marisa turned to Max. "How do you feel, Honey?"

"I don't want to talk about it," he said and looked the other way.

Marisa looked like she'd just been slapped. It drove Marisa crazy when someone wouldn't look at her.

They waited for their food in clumsy silence. Was Stephanie really going to become an aunt to another kid? She tried to picture Max taking care of a baby and the thought of him up to his elbows in a poopy diaper made her chuckle.

"Hey, it's not so bad having a little one around," she said, rubbing her knuckles across his head. "I helped raise you, after all. When I was about your age. Like your parents did for me when they weren't too much older." She caught Marisa's eye and gave her a tight-lipped smile. Marisa gave the same smile back.

"Yeah, I guess that's what we do in our family," Max said. "We raise other people's kids for them."

Our family, he'd said. It was true, she was comfortable being a part of this family. And until Max, and then Marisa, pointed it out, she'd never thought there was anything wrong with that. But maybe she was making a mistake by clinging only to them.

Perhaps she had briefly enjoyed family life when she was a toddler and Marisa was ten or eleven. She could vaguely remember happy moments. Apple cider simmering on the stove while her parents snapped pictures of her in her Halloween costume. Marisa walking her down the staircase to find their smiling parents waiting by the Christmas tree with presents. Then, after the age of five, she couldn't remember her parents bothering with anything as trivial as holidays or photo albums again. She couldn't even remember either parent bothering to smile at her again.

When she'd moved in with Paul and Marisa at age twelve, they'd shown her how life could be. But the ages of five through twelve were still a blur. She'd spent them longing to be grown up. A therapist would probably tell her that her own blurry childhood was the reason that children, and the idea of having her own children, frightened her so. And maybe it was time to let go of that. After all, she had an example of how to forgive and move on right in front of her.

She looked around the table at the Hendricksons. Each of them was staring in a different direction. Each, no doubt, pre-occupied with private thoughts. Max worried about becoming a big brother, Marisa worried about Max, Paul worried about Marisa. Yet they were making it work. Not perfectly. But they were happy, for the most part. They were a family.

"Steph, I'm sorry about all those things I said to you," Marisa said. "A lot of it is the hormones talking."

"What are you guys talking about?" Max said.

"Your mom and your aunt had a little discussion while you were in the bathroom," Paul said.

"Your mom was elaborating on the discussion we started at my office," Stephanie said. "The one where you told me she said I needed to get my own life?"

"Max?" Marisa said.

He bolted forward. "I nev—"

"Relax, you two," Stephanie said. "Both of you have made a couple of good points."

"You know we all adore you, Kiddo," Paul said.

"Yeah, I know," she said. "But I'm not such a kid anymore."

"Please don't act like twenty-nine is old, or I'll have to hurt you," Marisa said.

"I just mean that I realize I've been avoiding a few grown-up things that I need to face."

Marisa's warm, familiar smile was back.

"Oh good, the food's here," Paul said as the waitress set the plates down in front of them. Everyone started digging in.

"Do you really think I can do it all over again, Steph?" Marisa said. She wiped her mouth with her napkin.

"Of course you can. You're already a great mom—Max and I should know—and you're going to be a great mom to the next one, too." She turned to Max. "Hey," she said, "you think this baby is going to look like me, too?"

"I hope not," he said. "It was hard enough for me to grow up with freckles and red hair." He still seemed pissed.

"I survived it," she said. "And I actually kind of like it now. I used to want to blend in, but not anymore. It makes us special."

"I would be perfectly happy if the baby looked like the two of you," Paul said. Max had already gone back to eating.

"Mad Max," Stephanie said, "How about you and I go shopping for baby booties after this?"

"Whatever," Max said.

"I just assumed since you don't have your driving privileges back yet that you were at my disposal."

"Skank."

"I'll take that as a yes," she said.

She thought of the little boy in the pirate hat she'd seen at the mall earlier that day—the one that reminded her of Max—and smiled. She would help Max learn how to become a good big brother.

She looked at Marisa's stomach. How long before she started showing with this one? In spite of the boxy dress, her soft middle already bulged. Her stomach had been flat before she'd had Max, but not since. Yet Rissa had gladly paid that price, never complaining about the loose flesh or stretch marks childbirth left her with. She admired her sister for that. If only more mothers were like Rissa.

She thought about her exhausting day in court. Did Sharon Connor also think it was all worth it? Was she glad she'd decided on motherhood, now that things had gotten so complicated?

Was Tessa back with her mother tonight? If so, was she feeling torn, like she didn't know where she belonged? She would call Marcus tomorrow and try harder to help Tessa's parents work things out. Tessa deserved to have both of her parents in her life.

Stephanie stopped eating before the rest of them, careful not to reach the point of starting to bloat. When she set her napkin on top of her plate to hide the rest of her uneaten food, she looked up just in time to see Paul and Marisa watching their son who was shoveling a fistful of fries into his mouth. Then they glanced at each other with that knowing look of fondness that parents sometimes get.

Maybe she would call her own parents and invite each of them to come see her office the next time they were in town.

And maybe she'd give Justin a call. She had to admit, she did get lonely sometimes. And he possibly deserved one more chance.

CHAPTER 35

Sharon

Sharon walked down the street toward Wes and Carol's two-story colonial near the campus. Thankfully the Valium had worn off. And now that the rain was over the humidity had lifted. Sharon was enjoying the exercise in the fresh evening air.

Buzzing street lights illuminated the neighborhood. It really was a lovely area, older and with more history than her own housing development. She'd never walked over here before. Usually she was in a great hurry during pick-ups and drop-offs and preferred to blow through in her car as quickly as possible.

She'd assumed it would take her about twenty minutes to get there on foot, and she was just about right. She stepped onto Wes and Carol's front sidewalk at exactly the time they said they'd be back from dinner.

When she'd been so agreeable during the dinner and pick-up discussion, Wes had stared at her as though she were an alien. She liked that she'd surprised him. She was surprising herself, in fact.

As she was pulling her hand back from ringing the bell, the

door opened. Tessa stepped out with her purse on her shoulder, ready to go. No long wait on the porch, staring at a closed door, as was typical when Sharon arrived for a pick-up. This was different. And nice.

"Where's your car, Mom?" Tessa looked up and down the street.

"I didn't bring the car," she said. "I thought we could enjoy the walk back together. Remember when you were little and we used to take long walks and talk the whole time?"

Tessa shrugged. "Okay."

As they walked down the sidewalk, she put her arm around her daughter's shoulders. "Are you feeling okay? After the asthma attack earlier?"

Tessa nodded.

"I know this has been a hard day for you. And I'm sorry for that."

"Yeah. It's not exactly fun to have your parents duking it out at court while you're at school. And you don't even know which house you're going to be at that night."

"I'm sure that's true," she said. "Listen, I wanted to tell you something."

"Okay." Tessa turned towards her. Her face looked the same as when she was three years old—the furrowed brow and narrowed eyes looking up at her mother. Only now she was about Sharon's height, so they were eye-level.

"Remember how you left your backpack in the nurse's office after school? And Madeline got it for you? Well, it was unzipped and your essay was falling out of it. I couldn't help but notice what it was about."

"So you just read it?" Tessa said, pulling away from her. It was more fear than accusation.

"Yes, and I'm glad I did. I needed to hear those things, and if that was the only way you could express yourself, then I'm glad it happened that way."

"Oh," Tessa said. They kept walking, side by side, looking at the pavement.

"Not that I enjoyed what I read. In fact, it was really upsetting."

"I didn't mean to hurt your feelings, Mom."

"I know you didn't, but I've decided that you're right. I'm going to try harder to not make it all about me anymore," she said. "And, I'm going to try to be nicer to your dad and Carol."

"Don't you mean The Evil-Know-It-All?" Tessa smiled.

"So you knew about that, huh?"

"Mom, when you talk to Madeline you forget I'm in the same house. Your voice isn't exactly soft, you know."

"I suppose not. Sorry about that, too. Carol's not so bad, I guess."

This time Tessa put her arm around her mother. "Dad and I had a talk at the meet."

"Oh, yeah?"

"He and Carol decided things are going to be different at their place from now on. Dad's going to step it up, and Carol's going to back off."

"Really?" This she couldn't wait to hear. "Did he say anything else?"

"Uh huh. He said he was sorry he hurt us."

"He included me in the apology?"

"He did."

Sharon couldn't believe it. Wes had made apologies before, when they were first splitting up, but never in a way that sounded sincere. It was more like something you say when you accidentally step on someone's toe. But for him to say it now, to Tessa, a couple of years later - maybe the distance had helped him think things through. Maybe he had grown.

"And he wants to try to work things out with you," Tessa said. Then she quickly added, "About my schedule, I mean."

"I know what you mean." She chuckled. "Don't worry, I'm not looking for a reconciliation with your father. I'm past all that. I hope your father and Carol have a nice, long life together."

"Do you really mean that?"

"Well, no. But some day I will."

Tessa squeezed her mother tightly as they walked. "Mom, what do you do when you like a boy and he's just mean to you?"

"Who are we talking about here?"

"Well, there's this boy at school I kind of like. One minute he's checking me out, then the next he's pretending he doesn't know me."

"Ah, the age-old dance of love."

"Huh?"

"I just mean, it's always been that way between the sexes. Showing interest, but waiting to see if that interest is returned before owning up to it. Like a dance, see, back and forth until the two people figure out what to do with each other."

"You're not suggesting I want to do anything with Tommy—"

"No, no. There's a lot more to a relationship than physical affection."

"I can't believe I'm walking down the street talking about sex with my mother."

"We're not talking about sex, knucklehead. We're talking about the other stuff that goes on in a relationship."

"I don't think I'm ready for any of that stuff yet, Mom."

"Good," she said, trying not to show just how relieved she was. "I hope you take it very slowly when it comes to boys."

"So I don't turn out divorced, like you?"

"Hey, my life's not so bad. You don't need to feel sorry for me. I've got a lot to look forward to. I'm still young."

"Well—"

"No commentary required, thank you very much. And besides, just because Dad and I got divorced doesn't mean you'll be divorced some day. Everyone's situation is unique. And you'll be wiser about marriage than I was because you will have learned from watching my mistakes."

"You didn't make that many mistakes, Mom."

Sharon slid her arm around Tessa's waist and they kept walking like that, locked arm in arm.

"So, what would you like to do when we get home?" Sharon said.

"I know you wanted us to do something together, but I have to finish this book for a report that's coming up in English class."

"That's fine," she said. "You go ahead and read. I've got other things to do."

She ached for Tessa's company, but she wouldn't let on. She would just walk with her daughter.

"Mom?"

"Hmmm?"

"I love you."

"I love you, too," Sharon said.

She still felt fragile, but she knew she'd get stronger. She would no longer allow herself to be the proverbial princess fleeing the ball, leaving her glass slipper behind for Prince Charming to find. It was time for Cinderella to rescue herself. She was a mother now.

CHAPTER 36

Adele

Adele drove through the rain-washed streets, past the college, and turned left into their subdivision. She was torn by two desires, equally compelling, a situation she'd come across many times in her counseling practice. Her mother hardly knew her anymore. She knew that rationally, and Roger had seen that all along. So had Aunt Helen, when she'd said her mother "was quite lucid this morning."

And yet this afternoon she hadn't picked up the surprise in Aunt Helen's tone, hadn't read between Roger's lines. The people at the nursing home would take care of her, he'd said. He knew that soon it wouldn't matter if her mother was bathed and dressed and put to bed by Monique, the nurse with the rubbery clogs, or by Aunt Helen or by her only daughter. One was as good as the other to her mother now.

Or was it? Wasn't there that deeper connection, visceral—olfactory even—that still held fast, even after the upper reaches of memory had faded? The sense of smell was connected to the ancient part of the brain. Scent attracted woman to man, caused women to menstruate in synchrony, bonded mother to child. Her mother, even in her confused state, recognized her daughter, if only on that deep level, and was comforted. If that was so, and it seemed to be, she couldn't leave Ohio now. Shouldn't.

Thank heaven for that nurse, Monique. She'd set Adele straight about her mother in terms as blunt as one sister would use with another: "She's got dementia, honey. Short-term memory's failing. Oh, she'll have her good days, sure, but even her good days aren't going to be easy. You need to face that, okay?" The nurse had put her long fingers on Adele's back and rubbed round and round while she spoke, until she'd been able to stop crying and function rationally again. "You go have dinner with your mama," Monique had said. "Spend as much time with her as you can."

But that was the most shameful realization of all—she hadn't wanted to spend more time with her mother. No wonder she'd scheduled clients on Wednesday mornings, squeezing in short, superficial visits with her mother and then rushing back to the safety of her office, where she felt she had power. Power? Ha! She'd retreated to where she was comfortable. She'd gotten stagnant. Stuck. Old.

The sobbing started again, so hard that she had to pull over to the curb. She rested her head against the steering wheel and finally let out all the sadness and shame and frustration she'd been feeling, kept at bay by working too hard and denying that her mother was so far gone. A common situation. She'd seen it many times in her clients. But now the shoe was on the other foot and it felt horrible, like her too-tight Anne Kleins.

When all the tears were squeezed out of her, she took a deep breath and pictured an empty crater that gradually filled with rainwater that became a lake surrounded by willow trees.

She snuffled and reached for a tissue in her purse, blew her nose, took another breath.

Now she had to face Roger.

She put the car in gear and turned onto their street. Just as she was about to swing into the driveway, she noticed a middle-aged woman and a girl of maybe fifteen sauntering along the sidewalk, deep in conversation. The girl looked familiar, though the woman did not. She slowed the sedan to a crawl and then braked, lowering her chin to look through the distance portion of her lenses. It was the girl who lived a few doors down, the one who'd shot up so in the last year or two. Sometimes she walked to school with a much shorter girl. "Mutt and Jeff," Roger called them.

The girl was tanned and well-muscled. Did she ride? At her age, Adele had gone out to the farm whenever she could, preferring horses to boys, but this girl seemed more self-confident than she'd been, more at ease with people. Even now the girl was flipping her long, blondish hair over her shoulder and nodding slowly at the woman, as if she understood the effect her movements had on others. Maybe a young Aphrodite-type, focused on boys? If so, her parents would soon have their hands full—the girl was quite attractive, even in those baggy shorts and athletic shoes.

At that moment, the woman, who had her arm around the girl, pulled her close. Adele could see a resemblance—they both had the same tall, athletic build, though the older woman looked a little fleshier. Probably mother and daughter, out for a walk together.

A wave of sadness washed over her, not as strong as the previous wave, but strong enough to leave her feeling wistful as she watched the two. She wondered if there would come a time when this mother no longer recognized her daughter. If she and Roger had had a daughter, would she visit her mother at a nursing home, should it come to that? Or would their grown daughter, like so many of her clients' adult children, be too busy to bother? Is that what she had done, without realizing it? Maybe so. No, definitely so.

As soon as mother and daughter had rounded the curve of their street, Adele turned into the driveway. The lights were on in Roger's office, but he wasn't at his drawing board as she'd expected. One of the cats—Osiris, maybe—sat on the deep window sill in the dining room licking his paw. She reached up and touched the opener and the heavy garage door lifted slowly, each panel giving off a solemn *thunk* as it rose. She pulled her sedan into the garage beside Roger's station wagon and cut the engine.

While she was gathering up her things, he opened the door that connected the garage to the house. He stood silhouetted in the doorway, head cocked to the side. She nodded his way and opened the car door, shut it with a soft *whoosh* and stepped carefully around the front of her car, shoebox in one hand, briefcase in the other. She kept her eyes on the concrete floor of the garage, to prevent a fall. Last month she'd tripped over a rake handle and frightened Roger half to death. She'd frightened herself, in fact.

"Dell," Roger said.

She nodded and squeezed past him, into the hallway. He shut the door behind her and turned to face her.

"I was going to call you, but—" He shrugged.

"I didn't call you either," she said. "We both needed time to cool off. You in particular."

"About that—"

She held up her hand. "No need to apologize. We were both off base today."

"I shouldn't have walked out like that."

"And I should have been more aware." She kissed his cheek, which was slightly bristly but soft underneath, not unlike Roger himself. "I saw Mom today. She's not doing well. Not well at all."

"I'm so sorry." He hugged her, held her close. "The last few times we visited, I thought she was failing, but—"

"Don't," she said, pulling away from his arms. "Not now. We need to talk, but I need a moment to collect myself first."

"Why don't I fix you a drink? Or a cup of tea, maybe?"

"No thanks. I'd just like to sit down and gather my thoughts for a moment."

"Well, I could use a drink. Before we talk, I mean. Do you mind?"

"Go ahead," she said.

While he headed for the kitchen, she went into the adjoining great room. She set the shoebox and her briefcase on the floor, between the glass-topped cocktail table and the curving leather sofa, and kicked off her flats. After she'd tucked her feet up, she leaned back against the down-filled cushions. The leathery scent they released as they compressed reminded her of a saddle.

She thought of summer mornings riding at the farm with her cousins, winter mornings in the desert, galloping side by side with Roger. Idly she leaned over and lifted the lid of the shoebox. There were her Anne Kleins, unscuffed and shiny, with no conspicuous signs of wear. She'd taken better care of her shoes than her loved ones—or herself, for that matter. Sighing, she slid the lid back on.

In the adjoining kitchen, ice clinked. Most days after work she and Roger shared a drink, sitting here, looking out through the expanse of glass into their Zen garden, watching the sun set and the moon rise over their backyard. The sun had already gone down behind the tops of the trees, which were almost fully leafed out.

In a few weeks, lightning bugs would flash on and off to attract mates, their cool green lights signaling availability. Twenty-some years ago she and Roger had signaled to each other that they were available to pair up. Unlike the lightning bugs, they hadn't mated in the evolutionary sense. Now all they had was each other.

Roger brought out his usual drink, vodka with a twist of lemon in a low, cut-crystal tumbler. The ice clinked again as he stepped over the shoebox and her briefcase, as agile as a teenager, to sit beside her on the sofa. At moments like these, it seemed as if they had another three or four decades ahead of them. If only that were true.

He took a sip of his drink and then another. Finally he turned to her. "You okay now? You seemed pretty shook up when you first walked in."

How could she put this? She'd be as blunt as Monique. "Mom doesn't recognize me anymore."

He squeezed his eyes shut, as if in pain. "I can only imagine how that must feel. But I'm surprised you found time to visit her today. I thought you had clients."

"I cancelled," she said. "I didn't see how I could be of help to others when I couldn't help myself. Some therapist."

"Dell, you're too hard on yourself. Give yourself a break."

"I'd like to."

"Do less. Less is more."

"Always the architect, eh?"

He shrugged. "Maybe it wouldn't hurt to simplify."

"Stop taking new clients, you mean. Phase the rest out."

"I think so, but that's not up to me. I realized that after I left Pablito's. Only you can decide when you're ready to wind down."

"That's right," she said, "and I'm not willing to stop seeing clients. Not altogether. But I'll admit I've been too focused on my work, neglecting the people I love. Neglecting myself, for heaven's sake. And instead of tapering off, I'm working almost as many hours as I did five years ago. But I'm five years older. So are you. We won't be here forever. I need to keep that in mind."

"Those were my thoughts."

"As for my mother, she's obviously deteriorating. She doesn't seem to know me anymore, and it's worse in the evenings, from what the nurse says. From that perspective, I suppose it makes no logical sense to stay here in Ohio. Still—" She gave him a pained look.

"But you want to. You feel you have to."

She nodded. "But you had your heart set on moving."

"Not so much on moving as on getting the house built. I'd like to get it done before, well, while I'm still in good form."

"I understand. But do we have to move? Couldn't we commute for a while? Split our time?"

"With most of our time spent here?"

"Would that be so terrible?"

He downed the rest of his drink and set his glass on the cocktail table. "I know you, Dell. You say you're going to taper off, but I've heard that before. We'll end up spending two weeks there and fifty here."

She held up her right hand. "No new clients, I swear. And if anyone requires extensive treatment, I'll refer the client to someone else."

Roger interlaced his fingers behind his head and leaned back, staring out into the dusky backyard—his thinking-it-over posture. After several long minutes, his hands dropped to his thighs with a plop. He turned to her.

"I suppose we could try the snowbird thing. Live in Arizona for a few weeks in winter, and then add a few more, when you think you're ready."

She felt her face break into a smile. "Then I suppose we ought to start right away."

"Are you sure?"

"No," she said. "I'm terrified."

"Of what?"

She gave him a coy look. "There aren't any lightning bugs in Arizona."

He frowned, tilted his head, then shot her a lopsided smile. "Tell you what. We'll bring some along in a jar. Will that do it for you?"

She slid her arms around his sweet, saggy neck and brought her lips close to his ear. "It might."

"Might?"

"Um-hmm." She nuzzled his neck, taking in his clean,

soapy scent, then leaned back so she could see his face. She looked into his watery blue eyes, stroked his cheek. Unlike his still-dark hair, the stubble on his cheeks was mostly silver, like her hair. The badge of honor they both got for getting this far in life.

"That feels nice," he said. "Like the old days."

She smiled and traced her finger around the edge of his ear, ending at his wrinkled lobe. "Better than the old days," she said. The best she'd felt in years.

CHAPTER 37

Madeline

Madeline walked in the door through the garage with bags of take-out Chinese food in one arm and Jack's dry cleaning in the other. "I'm home!" she called to her family.

"Up here!" Jack's voice came from upstairs.

Madeline set the bags down on the kitchen counter, laid the suits across the couch in the great room, and walked down the hall, through the foyer, and up the stairs to their second floor. She followed the giggles and squeals to the master bathroom. Jack was standing at the sink in his boxers shaving—he always shaved at night before bed—and the kids were in the corner garden tub behind him splashing around. Shaving cream covered their faces.

"Hi, Mommy!" Olivia said.

"Mommy, look, I'm shaving like Daddy!" Noah said.

"I can see that," Madeline said. "How fun!" She walked up behind Jack as he studied his face in the mirror and put her arms around his waist, resting her cheek on his bare back. "I've got Chinese food downstairs. We can just eat in our pajamas."

"Don't forget, I'll be eating mine in front of the TV," he said.

Of course. It must be between innings right now. No doubt he'd planned the shaving and the bath accordingly. How could she be annoyed at his ingenuity? "Maybe we'll eat our food in front of the TV with you," she said, still hugging him.

"I call the egg drop soup," he said.

"I want fried rice!" Noah shouted from the tub.

"I want an egg woll!" Olivia squeaked. Whenever she tried to make her voice loud she ended up sounding like Minnie Mouse.

Madeline smiled. "I got enough of everything for everybody," she said. Noah and Olivia went back to fighting over a bath toy.

"Did you get a chance to finish the work you brought home?" she said, enjoying the feel of Jack's warm skin against her cheek.

"Actually, I did." He started on the other side of his face with the razor.

"I'm glad," she said. "I wish I could say the same. I still have hours' worth of grading to do for tomorrow's class."

"I'll make you a pot of coffee after the next inning."

"That'd be great." She stepped beside him and admired his reflection in the mirror.

Yes, she needed Jack. And that was okay. Like in the documentary March of the Penguins that she and Jack had taken the kids to, before they discovered it wasn't really a kids' movie. Still, the shocking portrait of a rigorous life in Antarctica—what those poor little penguins had to go through!—had provided the world with an exemplary model of team parenting. Penguins can't feed themselves and their young without the tag team effort of their mates to ensure the whole family's survival.

"I don't know how single parents do it, do you?" she said.

"No. But they manage. People do what they have to do."

"Well, I'm glad I don't have to."

Jack winked at her in the mirror.

"I'm going to get changed." She gave Jack a playful smack on the butt as she walked by him to go to her closet.

While she tried to decide which of her Victoria's Secret loungewear she wanted to pick, she thought about the phone conversation she'd had with Sharon outside of Kung Ho. Sharon had sounded so calm, so together. Maybe now she and Tessa would be able to have a long overdue heart-to-heart.

She took off her floral-fabric slingbacks and lovingly placed them on her shoe rack. After slipping into her matching black cotton pants and shirt with the letter V embroidered on it, she put on her pink fuzzy slipper socks, truly her favorite footwear. She would need to be comfortable for a rigorous night of cram-grading.

What a day it had been. It had started with Carol Wheaton criticizing her shoes. And now, according to Sharon, Carol Wheaton was wearing a pair of daring sandals. Was she trying on a new persona? It was true, new shoes could make you feel like a new person. Even kids knew that. Any time Noah or Olivia tried on a new pair of shoes at the store, they'd immediately take off running in them, as if the new shoes would somehow transform them into a superhero who could run faster, stop on a dime. In fact, that was the acid test—if they could run faster in the new pair, they knew they'd found the right one.

She hurried downstairs and opened up the take-out containers, sorting the food into separate dishes for each of them, white ceramic bowls for Jack and her, plastic character-themed bowls for the kids—Spiderman for Noah, Pocahontas for Olivia. She carried the food into the living room and set up the TV trays.

"Dinner's ready!" she hollered upstairs.

"Be right down!" all three of them answered.

She plopped down on the couch in front of the TV with her food in front of her and her stack of papers beside her. She wiggled her toes around in the soft slippers while she waited for Jack and the kids. The family she adored. She was definitely one of the lucky ones. And she'd hang on to what she had for as long as possible.

She thought about all of the women she knew, of various ages and at different stages in their lives. How many of them considered themselves lucky? She thought about all of the compromises and adjustments women make over a lifetime. Some prompted by circumstances beyond our control, like receiving orders from a judge. Or finding out about a pregnancy when the timing isn't right.

She reached over to the end table and picked up the Snoopy stationery Jack's mom had sent the kids. Evelyn couldn't stop herself from shopping for more stuff the kids didn't need. Noah could only write his name, and Olivia refused to pick up anything skinnier than a crayon.

She pulled a pen out of the end table drawer and propped a piece of the stationery up on her knees. Between Snoopy on the left and Woodstock on the right she wrote: *We women are constantly trying something new, sometimes even transforming ourselves in the process. And there is one thing that we all have in common and can choose for ourselves—shoes. Then we compare them, covet them, and cavort around them.*

She put the end of the pen in her mouth and laid her head back on the soft cushion. How many other mothers were in their fuzzy slipper socks tonight feeding their kids take-out food on TV trays while they finished work they had to bring home because they spent the day helping out a friend? How many women were slipping off designer shoes and under satin sheets, taking a chance on someone new? How many women were taking off a pair of sturdy shoes that had helped them make it through a demanding day?

She wrote: *Women's shoe choices mirror their stage of life. The shoes we choose vary over our lifetime. What once fit us well no longer suits us. So we shop for another pair. But we have to be comfortable in our own shoes before we can appreciate another woman's style.*

She looked up just as Jack rounded the corner with a giggling kid tucked under each arm. She smiled at her family. She'd finish writing her thoughts later, maybe even turn them into an article she could sell. Not to Sharon's magazine this time, but maybe another magazine. One that speaks to women of all ages.

Carol Wheaton had been onto something. Shoes tell the world who we are.

###

Dawn White grew up in McMinnville, Tennessee before moving to Michigan where she worked and raised her family in the Ann Arbor area. Dawn was a college-level writing instructor for sixteen years, and then transitioned to roles in business development, marketing, and copy writing for software companies.

These days Dawn can usually be found at her cottage on the Collins River near Rock Island State Park in Tennessee, where she spent much of her childhood. She now enjoys spending time in nature with her husband, Rob, her children, Emma and Jake, and her Boxers, LuLu and Belle.